A.T. Cullen is a barrister who instructed in numerous criminal trials before moving into court administration and then serving as a magistrate and coroner for over two decades. He was in charge of some of the busiest court complexes in Sydney before recently retiring to pursue his interest in writing.

THE ANCIENT CRAFT

A novel by A.T. Cullen

© 2019
alcul@bigpond.com
atcullen.com

First published by A.T. Cullen in 2019
This edition published in 2019 by A.T. Cullen

Copyright © A.T. Cullen 2019
atcullen.com
The moral right of the author has been asserted.

All rights reserved. This publication (or any part of it) may not be reproduced or transmitted, copied, stored, distributed or otherwise made available by any person or entity (including Google, Amazon or similar organisations), in any form (electronic, digital, optical, mechanical) or by any means (photocopying, recording, scanning or otherwise) without prior written permission from the publisher.

The Ancient Craft

EPUB: 9781925786514
POD: 9781925786521

Cover design by Red Tally Studios

Publishing services provided by Critical Mass
www.critmassconsulting.com

For Melissa, Angela and Amy

*I love the old way best, the simple way of poison,
where we too are strong as men.*

Euripides 480 – 406 BC

PROLOGUE

Life is precious – particularly when it is slipping away.

Dr Cornelius Vandermeer believed this with the passion of the converted as he struggled to gulp one last lungful of air. The muscles in his throat had constricted as he collapsed on the lush carpet of his surgery. His receptionist had left the surgery as it was the lunch hour, but even if she had been present, the realisation came to him that the epinephrine that should have been in the nearby medicine cabinet was not there. He had not bothered to replace it despite several reminders from his staff.

The doctor had always prided himself on his physical condition, his finely honed body being a source of pleasure that he often observed in the full-length mirror on the inside door of his surgery. As part of his strict diet, his personal health-drink concoction was carefully prepared each morning before leaving home. Always consumed during a relaxing lunch-break, between yoga and meditation, he had proudly proclaimed to one and all that this 'elixir of life' would see him fit and well to at least one hundred years of age. The liquid smelled foul and tasted worse, so he always downed the flask in one swallow. On this occasion, however, constriction soon followed the consumption of the elixir. His skin gradually took on a bluish hue as he spasmodically convulsed and slid into semi-consciousness. His hopes of a long and productive life, and his dreams of medical fame and financial wealth were receding all too quickly. A noise like loud static filled his ears, and a black fog filled his vision as his heart slowly ceased to pump blood.

His brain came to rest as his body twitched before becoming still. Then all was quiet.

Dr Cornelius Vandermeer, plastic surgeon to the stars, society darling of the newspapers and loving husband of Jessica lived no more.

Not everyone would grieve at the news of his demise. Some may even gain some pleasure from the fact that the very drink devised to extend his life had ended it.

Chapter One

Summer 1976

Matthew Jameson jogged slowly along the edge of the breaking waves, gazing occasionally at the sunset stretching across the western horizon.

The rural fire brigade had been backburning throughout the day in the Blue Mountains, and the western sky was ablaze with a brilliant orange glow. Having been raised in those mountains, the spectacle made Matthew feel a twinge of homesickness for his prior life.

Now a solicitor in his mid-thirties, he was reflecting on a murder trial he had acted in over ten years ago. He had chosen not to take advantage of the publicity the case generated by being admitted to the bar as a barrister. Instead he had opted for a quiet suburban life, where the home unit he was paying off afforded him access to a magnificent beach in the northern suburbs of Sydney. The life of a barrister might seem glamorous to outsiders, but the hidden cost of a broken marriage, an alcohol addiction or mental health issues which afflicted some of its members was something that Matthew was anxious to avoid.

Like many decisions made with the best of intentions, he was no longer sure he had made the correct choice, as he no longer found the humdrum work of a small solicitors' practice satisfying. Not that he cared much for money or status, but he felt that his skills were wasting away, together with his life.

He had hoped that by now he would be happily married, with two or three children and a thriving legal practice. Instead he was single, lonely and disillusioned.

At least he had Lena Wasilewski, his legal partner, to pull him into line when he started feeling sorry for himself. She was some ten years older than him, and their relationship, whilst purely platonic, was immensely valuable to him. Lena was a survivor of the Holocaust in Europe, and despite losing all of her family to the horrors of the concentration camps, she was always positive and supportive.

He knew now that it was time to move back to the city and challenge himself with life at the bar as a barrister.

What he did not know was how to tell Lena that he was deserting her.

Chapter Two

Autumn 1976

The officer investigating the death of Dr Vandermeer, Detective Sergeant Paul Brooks, who was attached to the homicide squad, made no public comment, nor any private one for that matter.

A middle-aged career officer, Brooks was regarded by his peers as a methodical and determined investigator who never left any clue unexplored. His drab clothes and thin physique often resulted in various suspects taking him for something of a fool, an impression that he carefully cultivated. This was something they would invariably regret. With no career ambitions, he was content to immerse himself in the cases assigned to him, leaving office politics and professional backstabbing to others.

From the instant that he entered the doctor's surgery, his instincts told him that something was wrong. There was no sign of physical violence nor any obvious poison when he examined the body, and he could see that Cornelius Vandermeer was in excellent physical shape.

He reported the death to the coroner, knowing that an autopsy would identify any toxic substance, and he planted that fact with a friendly journalist. Brooks hoped that the news would result in more information about the doctor's background emerging, and he was not disappointed with the results. No fewer than six women sidled up to one newspaper or another to whisper that the deceased had exhibited exceptional *after-hours care*, and it was not long before a name repeated itself several times as being his most persistent beneficiary.

Brooks smiled quietly to himself. He was reviewing the various patients' statements for the third time at his office desk. If Vandermeer was murdered, Brooks had to identify a motive. An affair with one of his patients could provide that. An imminent divorce and proposed subsequent marriage to that patient was even better. Revenge was of course one of the oldest and most powerful motives throughout history.

The pieces were falling into place.

Chapter Three

It was approaching midnight as Matthew Jameson and Angelo Cattani sat on the back porch of the modest fibro house that Angelo shared with his wife, Rose, his two young children and his aged Italian mother. The night had turned unexpectedly cool, but the ample supply of wine and beer had insulated the men, and they had been sharing legal gossip for over an hour since Angelo's wife had gone to bed citing an early morning alarm to get their children ready for school the next day.

Years ago, Angelo had played a critical part in Matthew's defence against a trumped-up assault charge, and they'd been close friends ever since. Without Angelo's assistance, Matthew knew that gaol and the destruction of his professional life would have ensued.

Angelo had emigrated from Italy when he was a child, and Matthew felt that his friend displayed the virtues of most arrivals from that country after the Second World War – honest, hard-working and loyal. He was of slim but powerful build, around six feet tall, and possessed dark good looks that many women found irresistible.

'I can't move,' Matthew groaned. 'Your wife's lasagne has done me in.'

'Well I did warn you about having two servings. Especially when it was only the first course,' Angelo answered with a chuckle.

Matthew gave a sheepish smile. 'How are things at the drug squad? I heard your promotion to Detective Sergeant resulted in a transfer from homicide. Out of the frying pan, into the fire.'

Angelo gave a shrug of his shoulders and swirled the wine slowly in his glass for a moment before replying. 'Drugs. They seem to destroy everyone they touch. The problem is that there's a small fortune to be made, even by small dealers. There's always cash available for bribes, and on our rate of pay it's all too easy for a young copper with a wife and kids and a mortgage to pretend that it's all right to take a cut of the profits, as it were. You just don't know who to trust.'

'And your bosses? What about them?'

Angelo did not reply but raised his eyebrows and shook his head.

'Surely there are some honest cops in the hierarchy?'

'Sure there are. But who's straight and who's crooked? I just keep my head down and let it be known that I'm not interested in taking bribes or doing favours or leaking information about forthcoming raids.'

'So you miss those days on the homicide squad where you just dealt with honest murderers?'

'Something like that,' Angelo replied with a grin. 'But one or two close calls got to me after a while. It's not as glamorous as it sounds.'

They both sat silently for several minutes before Matthew broke the silence. 'What was the worst?'

Angelo gave a loud sigh.

'About nine months ago. A bloke had bashed his wife unconscious and was on the hunt for her boyfriend, and he was full of drugs or grog or both. We received a tip-off that he might be hiding at an apartment in the inner city – a huge housing commission block that some genius of a social planner had thought would solve the problems of the disadvantaged. The problem was that we didn't know if the information was correct, so rather than call for reinforcements, the detective sergeant with me decided we'd have a look around first. If you call for a big raid with backup and nothing's found, then the bosses get very upset with you.'

'What happened?'

'We knocked, but there was no response. We had reasonable cause from the tip-off, so we forced the door. The power was cut off – probably the electricity bill wasn't paid. It was at that time that I told the sergeant we'd better call in the troops, but he was one of those old-fashioned coppers. You know – *I don't need anyone's help.*'

'This doesn't sound good.'

'It wasn't. There we were, groping around in dark rooms. I edged around a door jamb, and in one brief shining instant I was certain I was going to die.'

Matthew looked sharply at the detective, but said nothing. The glass of wine in Angelo's hand had started shaking almost imperceptibly.

'All I could see was the outline of a revolver pointing at my chest. I didn't see him at all initially, and then I heard the hammer fall as the trigger was pulled. Everything stood still, and then there was a loud explosion as the Sergeant fired at the bastard. The old Sergeant's shot went clean through his chest, and he jumped back as if pulled by a giant spring and was dead before he hit the floor.'

'His gun misfired?'

'That's what I thought at first, but when we checked the gun, it was fine.'

'What happened?'

'It was a six-shot revolver; a stolen police Smith and Wesson, in fact. A lot of coppers deliberately leave the chamber empty where the firing pin is resting. Some even leave the next chamber empty.'

'Why?'

'A safety precaution. In case the gun is dropped, or the trigger pulled by mistake. The hammer then falls on an empty chamber.'

Matthew shook his head slowly. 'And that was the difference between you living and dying?'

Angelo nodded. 'When I told Rosie, she went through the roof. She said that if I didn't leave the homicide squad, she'd divorce me.' He gave a wry grin. 'Not that she ever would. But I got the message. I'm not a cat with nine lives.'

'And drug dealers don't shoot?'

'Not usually. They're not often psychos – most have rat-cunning and they know an arrest doesn't necessarily mean gaol. In any event, low-level dealers don't get much. They're out in a year or so, and it's not worth going down for murder.'

'So Rose is happier now?'

Angelo glanced around to make sure that his wife had not gotten out of bed. 'I think blissfully unaware is more accurate. I'm about to give evidence in a big drug-bust committal next month and I have to say that I'm feeling a little apprehensive.'

Matthew picked up the empty wine bottle and shook it. 'Time for a refill then.'

After the new bottle had been produced, the cork carefully removed and their two glasses refilled, Matthew proposed a toast.

'Here's to success then.'

'Thanks.'

A silence fell over them until Matthew spoke quietly, as if to signify he was serious. 'Why apprehensive?'

'I've heard on the grapevine that the three crims from the drug bust, currently residing at Long Bay, are telling everyone that the trial's been fixed and that they'll soon be free.'

They both knew that Long Bay Gaol was the main remand centre for defendants who were bail refused, and that rumours flowed from there on a daily basis.

'They're probably just boasting,' Matthew replied.

'Perhaps, but I'm not too happy about my offsider. He and I are the only eyewitnesses to the drug deal, and he's been avoiding me lately. I can't put my finger on it, but I'm just not happy with his attitude.'

'You think someone's got at him?'

Angelo raised his eyebrows and shrugged his shoulders.

'The druggies know you're straight, so they won't try anything on with you, surely?' Matthew said.

'You know how it goes. If you can't attack the message, you go for the messenger. Don't forget, we're talking about crims facing ten years or more in gaol. These characters are not low-level street dealers.'

Matthew looked at him through narrowed eyes.

'You mean a contract?'

'It's not impossible.' He took a sip of his wine, seemingly lost in thought, then spoke again. 'But it's not likely. It's just another concern that comes with the job. I'll just have to live with it and see what happens.'

Matthew gave a shrug.

'I think I'll stop complaining about difficult clients. It certainly puts things into perspective when I hear your stories.'

After a few silent moments, talk eased into rugby league and the performances of their favoured teams. An hour or so slipped by in this fashion until Matthew held up his hands.

'Time to depart. I've got the VW outside, but I'd better call a taxi. I've had a few too many.'

'You can bunk on the lounge if you like?'

Matthew shook his head. 'No. Thanks just the same. I've got an early mention in the District Court and I can't be late.'

As they waited outside for the taxi that Angelo had called, the suburb was peacefully quiet, apart from the occasional distant screech of tyres and the roar of an engine under heavy acceleration.

'Rose must want you to ditch the coppers now that you've finished the exams?' Matthew asked.

Matthew had qualified as a solicitor after attending Sydney University Law School part-time, whilst Angelo had completed a similar law course but through the Barristers Admission Board of the same university. His admission as a barrister allowed him the right of appearance in any court once instructed by a solicitor.

'A sensitive issue you might say. There's plenty of room for promotion for someone with legal qualifications if they keep their nose clean, and I don't intend to end up a sergeant until I retire.'

Matthew appraised him with fresh eyes.

'Well, well. Commissioned officer material I see.'

'Could be. Let's just wait and see if I survive this drug trial. You never know, I might have to join you in the future if things go pear-shaped.'

Matthew smiled, but made no reply.

Chapter Four

Detective Brooks interviewed, amongst others, the quaintly named Angelina Smythe-Baker, and given the surgeon's reputation, it was no surprise that she declared her undying love for him, together with the news that they were shortly to announce their engagement. The fact that the doctor was living with his wife of twenty years seemed to have no bearing on her conscience.

Brooks would not have called the actress stupid – scatter-brained would be more apt. When he asked her about the doctor's widow, she breezily replied that the affair was not a secret, and that Jessica Vandermeer had already agreed to a divorce. Angelina was, he admitted to himself, very attractive, and Brooks knew she would have a strong allure to a mid-forties male like Vandermeer. He had recognised her immediately as a star in one of the teenage dramas on television. She was in fact twenty-two, but her long blonde hair and child-like face made her believable as a fifteen-year-old. Brooks had a wife and two teenage daughters who often demanded the latest episode be viewed during the evening meal, and, whilst he would have preferred the national news, the three-to-one vote was overwhelming.

It was during the initial investigation at the crime scene (as Brooks now referred to it) that he had seized one piece of evidence that he initially felt was inconsequential, but which might become a crucial piece of evidence in the subsequent trial. Looking through the doctor's briefcase, he had discovered an empty metal flask – empty apart from a residue of what appeared to be some type of foul-smelling liquid. His wife confirmed that each morning the deceased had concocted a health drink that he had proudly described to one and all as his 'elixir of life'.

Not much of an elixir, Brooks had thought to himself as he nodded sympathetically to the widow after her husband's body had been removed.

He had later spoken to the senior analyst at the government forensic laboratory, asking him to retain some of the residue in the container in the event that he was not able to come up with any positive result. After receiving negative results, Brooks had the exhibit taken to a highly specialised laboratory in one of the old sandstone universities with a specific request to search carefully for anything unusual.

It was ten days later that he received a phone call from the elderly professor that he had spoken to earlier. It was then that Brooks requested the senior analyst conduct further tests on the deceased's organs, to confirm the presence of a specific substance in his system.

Ironic how the smallest piece of evidence can be the cornerstone of the whole case, he mused to himself.

Chapter Five

An early morning doorbell was unnerving at the best of times, but when it rang just before dawn, a feeling of dread spread through Angelo Cattani.

He shook his head to clear the fog of sleep whilst trying to focus on the clock beside his bed. It was 6 am. Stumbling out of bed, he pulled on some old jeans and a tee-shirt, then made for his front door. He slid the top bolt, opened the deadlock and wrenched the door open. He stepped back in shock at what confronted him.

A grim-faced plain-clothes inspector whom Angelo recognised as Bill Etheridge from Internal Affairs held up an A4 piece of paper that Angelo could not read through his wire screen door. He had never worked with Etheridge, but Angelo viewed all Internal Affairs officers with caution.

'Angelo Cattani, I have a warrant to search these premises for illegal drugs,' came the strident voice, 'and you are required to co-operate fully with myself and my colleagues in that search.' The inspector jerked his head towards the two other plain-clothes detectives and three uniformed officers who stood behind him.

Angelo shook his head angrily. 'What the hell is going on?'

'In a few days you will be required to attend Internal Affairs where you will be directed to answer several questions regarding your recent behaviour,' the inspector said. 'Don't be stupid now. You know you've got no choice in the matter.'

Angelo knew that he was required to answer any questions put to him by Internal Affairs, without the right to silence. Failure to answer would lead to his dismissal from the force.

'At least let me wake up the wife and kids before you barge in like a herd of rhinos,' Angelo said.

'Sorry, we can't leave you alone for a second,' Etheridge replied. 'You know the drill.'

Angelo knew the drill only too well. The opportunity to dispose of any incriminating material was an issue, so he shrugged his shoulders in resignation.

'Can you at least be quiet? I don't want my kids to be terrified,' Angelo said. 'Someone's telling lies about me in a desperate attempt to destroy the drug case I'm about to give evidence in. Surely you haven't fallen for the thimble and pea trick? When you can't attack the evidence, the last resort is to attack the coppers. You must know that?'

The inspector shrugged his shoulders. 'I'm just doing my job. If you've nothing to hide, you've nothing to fear.'

'We both know that's bullshit,' Angelo replied angrily. 'Have you searched your so-called colleagues to make sure they don't have some white powder in their pockets to plant on me?'

Etheridge seemed taken aback by the suggestion, but after a few seconds, he reasserted his control.

'Just behave yourself, Angelo. I trust these blokes with my life. They're all straight.'

Angelo stood still momentarily before reluctantly opening the screen door to admit the group. He walked ahead to the main bedroom where his wife had pulled on a thick white dressing gown.

'What's going on, love?' she asked in a shaky voice.

'Someone's been telling lies to Internal Affairs and they're here with a search warrant. Don't worry, when they come up empty, it'll all blow over,' Angelo replied whilst wrapping a comforting arm around her shoulders.

Rose shook herself free from the embrace and angrily strode down the short hallway and into the main lounge room. 'He's given his life to the job, risking it over and over again, and this is all the thanks he gets, you bastards,' she yelled. 'You should all be ashamed of yourselves.'

After a stunned silence, their two children emerged from their bedroom followed shortly after by Angelo's mother.

'It's all right kids, it's just a big mistake,' Angelo said, attempting a reassuring tone. 'These men are here to look after us, not to harm anyone. Come on, we'll go to the kitchen and cook an early breakfast.'

'But why are they here?' Angelo's seven-year-old son asked. 'We're not bad people.'

'Don't worry, Sam,' Angelo replied as he ruffled his son's hair. 'They're just checking that we're all safe.'

Their daughter, Emily, who had just turned four, clung to her mother's leg with one arm and to her teddy bear with the other.

Angelo's mother, Maria, looked at the scene with narrowed eyes.

'Fascist,' she hissed as she passed Etheridge on her way to the kitchen. Clearly, memories of living with Mussolini's fascist police had come back to her.

After twenty minutes or so, Etheridge, who had been keeping an eagle eye on Angelo the whole time, spoke quietly to one of the plain clothes detectives. He then walked into the kitchen and motioned Angelo to move away from the children.

'The keys to the garage and your car,' he demanded in a quiet but insistent voice.

Angelo reached over to a nail beside the side door, grabbed a set of keys and tossed them to the inspector.

'Good luck,' he murmured.

'Luck is something we don't need,' Etheridge replied.

It was in that instant that Angelo knew the house search was merely a formality, and they were interested only in the family car. Internal Affairs were obviously acting on information that drugs would be found there. He knew how easy it would have been to plant something in the car when Rose was out shopping and the car was unattended in some car park. He had feared the drug conspirators might do something to abort the trial, and he realised that planting drugs on him was a simple solution to their problems.

'How many people have access to your car?' Etheridge asked.

Angelo looked at him silently.

'It's not a hard question. Do you want me to caution you?' he persisted.

'Some low-life scum has told you to look in the car, haven't they?' Angelo asked quietly.

'I'm not at liberty to divulge our sources, nor the content of any information. Just answer the question. Who would be able to open your car boot? Who would have access to the key?'

'Any one of a thousand crims wouldn't need a key, as you well know. A simple lock pick will open the door, and the boot release is on the floor.'

'I'm assuming that answer is no one but you and your wife.'

Angelo gave a cold stare but did not reply.

'If something, say drugs for example, were located in your car boot, can I assume that your wife has not placed them there?'

Angelo recognised that Etheridge was making a veiled threat against his wife, and by phrasing the question in that way he was after an admission of knowledge of drugs by Angelo.

'I'll not give you any assistance in falsely accusing and charging me or my wife with any criminal offence,' Angelo replied forcefully. 'Furthermore, I refuse to answer any further questions unless my solicitor is present.'

'Now, now, Angelo,' Etheridge persisted in a patronising tone, 'that attitude will only result in trouble for you. It's best to make a clean breast of everything right now and we'll keep your wife out of it.'

'You haven't found a thing yet. You must be convinced that this information about me is correct if you're talking about arresting my wife in front of our kids.'

'I'm only looking after your best interests, Angelo,' Etheridge replied with a smile.

An overwhelming urge to punch the smug-looking inspector in the face came over Angelo. As Sam ran over and grabbed his arm, he realised how stupid that would have been.

'Don't get cranky, Dad,' he called out. 'I'll look after you. We'll be all right.'

Angelo released the tension in his arm, and swept his son up into his arms. 'Sure, mate. We'll be good. Don't worry,' he murmured to the boy.

One of the uniformed officers came back into the lounge room and whispered something to Etheridge.

'Forensics will need to take the car for a thorough search. As soon as that is completed, you will be required to attend our offices for an interview. Until that time you are formally suspended,' Etheridge said in a formal tone. 'Warrant card and revolver please.'

The requested items were located, and Angelo thrust them towards the inspector. Etheridge took them, then nodded and left with the other police.

Rose came over and hugged her husband fiercely, and the children grabbed them both. They stood in the kitchen, encircled in silence.

Angelo's mother stood leaning against the bench top.

'At least with the Mafia back in the old country, you always knew they wanted to stab you in the back,' she muttered, almost to herself. 'Who do we turn to when the carabinieri are the crooks.'

Chapter Six

Detective Paul Brooks had no intention of rushing his investigation, and methodically set about building a watertight case against the person he instinctively knew was guilty. First, he called in for questioning every patient the doctor had treated in the recent past, occasionally deferring to a request to discreetly meet at a quiet location for those who had no wish to be involved in the publicity free-for-all. Vandermeer had established himself as the most in-demand plastic surgeon in Sydney, having operated on numerous actresses and society matrons, and his every appearance with Jessica at the latest glittering function was always highlighted in the society pages of the newspapers.

Brooks also obtained search warrants for the bank records of the deceased and his widow, and another search warrant for the marital home, a magnificent waterfront mansion on Sydney Harbour. He enlisted the aid of three experienced detectives to assist in the search, which took place some four months after the death, and which took the best part of a day. Brooks was often criticised amongst his fellow detectives for taking too long to conduct an investigation and make an arrest, but he always made sure that everything was in place before he sprang his trap. He usually pointed to his conviction record to justify this approach.

Upon his search of the Vandermeer mansion, Brooks could not believe his good fortune. Hidden in the garage wrapped in some old rags was a small bottle. A bottle that was to become the centrepiece of the prosecution case.

With everything in place, Brooks had composed at least thirty questions which, when answered after a formal caution, he was sure would not only result in a watertight case, but could even ensure a guilty plea to murder. It was thus with supreme confidence that he called in the deceased's widow, Jessica Vandermeer, for what he had called 'a little chat'.

His usual modus operandi would be to offer a selection of cakes and biscuits together with freshly brewed coffee and tea. He would then embark upon a sad litany of complaints about his senior officers, a nagging wife and his difficult children. The formal caution he usually apologised for as a legal technicality, something he had to get out of the way before his search for the actual culprit continued unabated.

It was a constant source of amazement to him how often this ruse was a success. Even clever, sometimes brilliant, individuals were only too eager to display their superior intellect to this drab detective whilst making damning admissions in the process.

At the requested time of 10 am, Jessica Vandermeer attended police headquarters, but to the dismay of Brooks, she was accompanied by a burly figure who smiled and held out his hand as he introduced himself.

'Matthew Jameson,' he announced. 'I'm the solicitor acting for Jessica Vandermeer, and I knew you'd be pleased that I'm here to look after her interests.'

Jameson was around mid-thirties with a thick mane of dark brown hair, hazel-green eyes and an easy smile. That name was familiar to Brooks, but he could not put it into any context. Still, if the lawyer was a little dim, perhaps the day would not be a complete waste of time.

Brooks effusively greeted Jessica Vandermeer, and indicated a chair for her before dragging another one from a far corner for the solicitor. Brooks had seen the woman in numerous photos in the society pages, and he could see how she could charm her way through a privileged lifestyle. Of slender build with jet-black hair and almond-shaped brown eyes, she radiated confidence and elegance.

'I know it's a bugger to have to call you down to the station for a chat, but I have to keep my bosses happy,' Brooks commenced with a smile. 'It's just a formality really.'

'So my client is not a suspect then?' Matthew asked.

Brooks gave a shrug. 'You know what they say – everyone is a suspect.'

'Including the Police Commissioner?'

'Hardly,' Brooks replied with some irritation. 'I'm just being thorough. I know you're as anxious to solve this matter as I am.'

'But my husband died of a heart attack,' Jessica Vandermeer said sharply. 'What is there to solve?'

Brooks was quite certain that the comment was part of her innocence act.

'Our investigation is ongoing,' he replied after a short pause.

'Perhaps you could tell Mrs Vandermeer the result of any toxicology examination on her husband. Was anything untoward discovered?'

The detective bit his lip unconsciously. He had not wished to disclose details of the chemical analysis just yet, but he felt that he could hardly lie. He reached to the side of his table, picked up a thick folder then leafed through it for several minutes.

'An examination has revealed the presence of a substance which we believe was the cause of your husband's death,' Brooks announced as he closed the folder, throwing it back onto a pile of papers. 'I'm not at liberty to give any further details at this time.'

'Are you saying that my husband was poisoned?' Jessica Vandermeer demanded in a shrill voice.

'Our investigation is ongoing,' Brooks repeated, any pretence of friendliness now absent.

'Well, what have you done about arresting the person responsible?' she answered in the same tone.

'That will come in due course,' he replied.

Matthew took his client's arm in his hand, partially to gain her attention but also to calm her down. 'Let me handle this, Jessica. You don't have to say anything further.' He glanced at the detective. 'I'm advising my client not to answer any questions. If there's nothing else you wish to tell us, we'll take our leave.'

Brooks shook his head slowly, his eyes never leaving Jessica Vandermeer's face.

'Good afternoon then, Sergeant,' Matthew said as he rose and half-lifted his client with him.

After the pair had made their exit from the interview room, Brooks grabbed a pencil that had been lying on his table and absent-mindedly snapped it in half. He then picked up his phone to speak to a colleague on another floor.

'What do you know about a bastard by the name of Matthew Jameson?' he growled.

Chapter Seven

As Matthew Jameson pushed open the main entrance door of the police headquarters building, cameras flashed incessantly, and questions were shouted in an explosion of noise from the assembled press.

'Has she been charged yet?'

'Will she plead guilty?'

'Did you poison your husband?'

Jameson stopped on the top step with one arm protectively around his client. He had been expecting this ambush.

'Mrs Vandermeer is devastated by the sudden and tragic death of her husband, and is here to assist the police in their investigations,' he announced loudly. 'She does not wish to make any further statement at this time.'

'Is she going to be charged with murder?' a voice roared from the back of the press scrum.

Matthew did not reply, but slowly forged a path through the reporters as he pulled his client's arm behind him.

'Bloody socialites, they think they can get away with anything,' another anonymous voice yelled.

Matthew had arranged for a taxi to wait for them at the kerb. He wrenched open the rear door, guided his client into the back seat, and then jumped in beside her. The taxi accelerated away as he sank back into the soft rear seat, then he fumbled with the seatbelt before fastening it correctly.

'That reception committee back there was organised by our friendly Sergeant Plod, of course. It's all part of his plan to keep you under pressure in the hope that you'll say something incriminating.' He glanced sideways at his client. 'We'll have a long talk about it at the office.' He inclined his head towards the driver, indicating that he did not want to be overheard.

Matthew had received a phone call at his suburban office just after he had arrived at 8 am that morning, and, as the young receptionist did not start until an hour later, he had picked up the phone. Jessica Vandermeer had told him in quick succession that she wanted to engage him as her lawyer, that Detective Brooks had called her to police headquarters, and that she thought it would be a good idea if he would accompany her.

Gossip is the main form of entertainment in legal circles, and although he had no interest in the society pages, Matthew's legal partner at the firm, Lena Wasilewski, had been keeping him updated. No doubt fueled by Detective Brooks, rumours of romantic involvement with several of Vandermeer's patients had been reported, followed by a suggestion that the doctor had not died of a heart attack as first thought, but had been poisoned.

Matthew instantly knew that the friendly chat with the detective was a trap, but sensed that if he went with his new client he may be able to gain some information as to the police case. He half-suspected that the intention was to arrest Jessica Vandermeer at the police station for the murder of her husband, but he felt that would be preferable to an ambush at some social function where she might blurt out something untoward without his presence. Her behaviour at police headquarters had certainly told him that she was no wilting lily, as she had stood up to Brooks without flinching. Whether or not she was a cold-blooded killer was too early for Matthew to hazard a guess, but at least this indicated that she would cope well with cross-examination if it came to a criminal trial.

Faint spots of rain appeared silently against the taxi's windows as it navigated the city streets before swinging onto an access road to the Sydney Harbour Bridge. The rain gradually became heavier and the driver flicked on the intermittent wiper. Huge steel pylons flashed past as the taxi climbed to the flat stretch of the bridge highway. Glimpses of the busy harbour and the Opera House flickered between the steel supports, until a hammering of rain on the car's roof replaced the gentle hum of the engine. The driver increased the wiper speed to maximum, but it was barely clearing the water before another deluge enveloped the windscreen.

Matthew leaned over to his client and yelled over the noise. 'We'll be there shortly. There's a great little café just down the road from the office and I'll grab a couple of coffees before we settle down with my legal partner. Her name is Lena Wasilewski, and she's a great listener. She's also much smarter than me as well.'

Jessica's eyes flashed in amusement.

'You can slow down if it's too heavy, mate,' Matthew said loudly to the driver. 'We're not in any hurry.'

The driver raised his left arm in acknowledgement. 'Should be all right. I'll just go carefully.'

It was as though they were isolated in an ocean storm, with visibility so limited that Matthew could not make out the streets, storefronts or vehicles around them, and only the roar of a passing lorry intruded on the noise of the storm. After another thirty minutes or so in stop-start traffic, the taxi pulled up outside Matthew's small suburban office block in the northern beaches area, about one hundred metres from the beachfront. Although the rain had eased marginally, it was persistent. Matthew asked his client to wait as he jumped out of the taxi and ran into his office, returning several minutes later with an old golf umbrella. He then shepherded her from the taxi to shelter under the footpath awning. After returning to the taxi and paying the driver, he guided Jessica into the building, walking down the corridor past a doctor's surgery, an accountant's office and some dentists' rooms before entering the modest office past a sign that read 'Wasilewski and Jameson Solicitors'.

After introducing the two women, he walked to the little café that he and Lena used each day for lunch, and then returned to the office with a cappuccino for each of them. He immediately noticed that Lena had put their client at ease, chatting animatedly to her about some celebrity that she had seen recently at an eastern suburbs function. Matthew often marveled at his colleague. Lena had been smuggled to England from Germany in 1938 as a young child, but her parents were unable to obtain more forged papers to join her. She had survived the war only to discover that internment, gassing and incineration at Auschwitz had been the fate of her parents and every other close relative. Despite this background, she was gentle and calm, without any trace of hatred or bitterness. How this was possible, Matthew could never fathom. He felt fortunate that she had agreed to leave her lucrative senior partner's position at a successful city law firm to start their own small legal business on the northern beaches with him. Lena was some ten years older than Matthew and their relationship was purely platonic, but they shared a rare common value system, and he trusted her implicitly.

The three of them spent the next hour discussing the circumstances of Dr Vandermeer's death before Matthew asked Jessica the question that had been troubling him.

'Why us? Why not some big city law firm? To be honest, we don't normally handle this type of case.'

'Your reputation, of course,' she replied. 'Tom MacGregor is the reason.'

Ten years prior, Matthew was involved in a murder trial, and the eventual acquittal of a government minister had attracted enormous public attention, as well as a certain legal notoriety.

'That case was unusual to say the least,' Matthew replied. 'We acted for a government minister who was charged with murdering his lover, and the barrister had a heart attack during the trial. The client wanted me to take over, so I did not have much of a choice. I could hardly leave him unrepresented. But that was a long time ago.' Matthew waved a hand dismissively. 'If the police do charge you, it would be unthinkable to ask a suburban solicitor to act by himself for you in a jury trial. A senior barrister would be essential.'

'But you also had a very experienced barrister in that trial – Oscar someone if I recall correctly. He had an Irish name.'

'Oscar O'Shannessy. He's getting on a bit these days,' Lena interrupted. 'Surely you'd want a Queen's Counsel, assisted by a junior barrister and instructed by a large city firm of solicitors.'

'It's a little disconcerting to say the least,' Jessica replied, 'when the lawyers you choose don't want to act for you.'

Matthew gave a small chuckle. 'That's not the case here. We're only too willing to act as your solicitors and instruct a barrister of your choice. I actually agree with you that it's not always the case that a Queen's Counsel is the best option, but certainly someone senior is critical. Lena and I are not only business partners but also a team, and I would need her to help me if we act for you.'

'I understand that and I agree.' Jessica raised her eyebrow. 'But Oscar is not your choice? What's happened to him? Is he senile? Has he had a stroke?'

'Oscar's fine. I have lunch with him every couple of weeks, and he's as sharp as ever.' He gave her a sideways glance. 'But I'm not sure that you did answer my question.'

'You and Oscar and Lena are my choice. I don't want some dispassionate Queen's Counsel whose main motivation is increasing his bank balance and enhancing his public profile. I want people who care. Reading reports in the papers about the trial and watching you on TV, I know you won't let me down.'

'Well, hopefully you'll never need any of us,' Matthew replied. 'It now seems that the cops believe he was poisoned, but the substance in his body could be some type of experimental drug that he was testing. Did he ever mention to you anything along those terms?'

'He was always trying out some new procedure or another and testing new drugs. He was at the cutting edge of plastic surgery, if you'll forgive the pun, and spent hours studying overseas medical literature on anything new.'

Matthew shrugged his shoulders.

'I know that some doctors like to think they're immortal. Perhaps he used himself as a guinea pig and made a fatal mistake. Anyway, that's something we'll have to look at closely.' He gave Jessica an inquiring glance. 'Any illegal drugs?'

'No,' she replied immediately. 'He hated cocaine and heroin and the rest of that crap. He often said that those drugs were for losers, and that he was a winner.'

'In any case,' Matthew replied, 'you did the right thing by calling me before you went for a little chat with Brooks. He has a reputation for obtaining critical admissions from suspects in murder cases. From now on, even if you're arrested, you only give your name and address to the police.'

'I know. On legal advice I decline to answer any further questions.'

'Call me immediately when you hear anything. Until then, all we can do is wait,' Matthew said.

'I'm sure it will all be fine,' Lena said, patting Jessica's arm in a consoling gesture. 'Just take it a day at a time.'

Chapter Eight

'What do you think?' Matthew asked.

Their client had departed in a taxi five minutes earlier, and both solicitors were now in Lena's office with the door closed and all veneer of formality gone. All entreaties to Matthew about smartening up his office had fallen on deaf ears, so their meetings were always held in Lena's small but perfectly tidy room. Matthew threw his coat over a spare chair, and leaned back in his chair with his feet on Lena's desk.

'Quite comfortable, are we?' Lena asked.

'Yes, thanks. Kind of you to ask.'

Lena gave a soft chuckle.

'I'm not sure what to say about our client. She is certainly as clever as she is beautiful, but her explanation about instructing us seems pretty thin.'

'You doubt that my fame has spread?'

'I do know that Brooks didn't call her in for tea and biscuits. She thinks that an arrest is imminent, and she's probably right. Her phone call to you wasn't a result of panic, but quite calculated. She chose us for a reason, but I can't put my finger on it just now. What about you?'

Matthew steepled his fingers in a reflective gesture.

'Not sure. For someone facing a sensational murder trial, she's very measured in her demeanour.'

'A cold fish you mean?'

'Or a *stonefish* perhaps.'

'Now, that's no way to speak of a valued client.' The crinkle of amusement shown in her face diluted Lena's admonishment.

'Poison is of course the weapon of choice for an unhappy wife.' Matthew replied poker-faced. 'And we've moved past the days of arsenic and rat-killer. There are so many exotic chemicals these days that they're spoilt for choice. A sterling example of women's liberation in action.'

'Matthew, Matthew,' Lena replied with a shake of her head. 'So cynical. Where's that romantic lad that I used to know?'

'My spirit has been broken. My love life is dead and buried.'

'What about that pretty young thing that you were telling me about? The one from that big city law firm.'

'Ah, well. I made a slight mistake there. A difference of taste you might say.'

'What happened?'

'You remember I told you I was taking her out to see a show?'

'Sounds good so far.'

'Turns out, Mozart was not to her taste. She said that she was hoping we were going to see some pop band. I hadn't forewarned her, and it turned out to be a big let-down.'

'She didn't like Wolfie?' Lena replied, shaking her head in amazement.

'Too many songs, she said. Also, too much talking, too many singers, and all in Italian.'

'She didn't follow the surtitles?'

'She didn't bring her glasses. Said she didn't know it was going to be some sort of reading test.'

'Ouch.'

'Not a happy night I'm afraid.'

'Sad. Very sad, Matthew. I'll have to see what I can arrange for you. Don't forget, there's plenty more fish in the sea.'

'Yeah. I'm just not sure I have the right tackle.'

Chapter Nine

Detective Sergeant Paul Brooks had scanned the society pages each day, searching for an upcoming event that would meet his requirements. The presence of a few politicians, the eastern suburbs glitterati, art patrons and various hangers-on would be ideal. It was three weeks before an announcement caught his eye, and he made his plans with the precision of an army campaign.

The evening was cool with intermittent showers. As the various taxis, hire-cars and limousines pulled up in the covered driveway of Sydney Opera House, attendees disembarked wearing warm coats and thick stoles over their expensive jewellery and designer gowns. The Queen had opened the iconic building in 1973, and since then it had been the premier location for society events in Sydney. Tonight was the opening performance of *Don Giovanni*, and the opera had attracted society darlings like moths to a flame. The article that had caught Brooks' attention had praised Jessica Vandermeer's fortitude following her husband's fatal heart attack, and mentioned that her first social outing since his death would be at this performance. Other newspapers had not been so fulsome in their appraisal of the widow.

Thus it was that Brooks and two detective constables had arrived early and positioned themselves in the first-floor foyer where the eager crowd assembled for food, tickets and the cloak room. Entry to the second-floor steps was gained by displaying the relevant ticket, whereupon the patrons climbed to a bar area where smartly dressed staff served an array of sparkling and still wines from a circular bar area. It would have been simple for Brooks to phone Jessica's lawyer and arrange for his client to attend police headquarters at a suitable time for everyone, where arrest, caution, charging and bail could proceed smoothly, but he was not interested in anyone's convenience. Who knew what a distressed widow might blurt out in the first flush of anger and embarrassment without her solicitor present? That was certainly Brooks' earnest wish, and a tip-off to his contact at a major Sydney tabloid newspaper ensured that both a photographer and a crime reporter were also on hand to report news of the arrest to the eager public.

Brooks waited patiently until the first-floor foyer was congested with patrons, and his target was about to climb the steps to the next level before he made his move.

'Jessica Vandermeer,' he announced in a commanding voice, 'I am placing you under arrest for the murder of your husband, Cornelius Vandermeer, and I have to formally caution you that you are not obliged to say anything, but that anything you do say will be taken down and may be used in evidence against you at your trial.'

A stunned silence swept through the crowd, followed immediately by several shrieks of unknown intent from various society matrons. The next day's paper reported that the accused woman never blinked, but gave a brief smile and shook her head slowly before being escorted down the entrance staircase and into a waiting police vehicle.

Within a few minutes of the arrest, Matthew received a phone call at his flat from a distressed woman who had been with Jessica at the Opera House. It was a measure of Jessica's astuteness that she had given his name and private phone number to the woman, realising that an arrest was a distinct possibility and that Brooks would not want Matthew around whilst he spun his web involving the good-cop, bad-cop routine. He arrived at police headquarters some thirty minutes or so after his client.

'My name is Matthew Jameson and I believe that my client, Jessica Vandermeer, has been arrested. I request that I be allowed to speak to her immediately.'

The grizzled station sergeant seemed somewhat taken aback by Matthew's arrival. He pointed to a wooden bench. 'Take a seat,' he grunted.

'That's not good enough, Sarge,' Matthew added with quiet determination. 'I want to see her now.' He glanced at his watch. 'The time is 7.15 pm. I'm taking a note of that time so that any unfortunate complaint which may need to be made to Internal Affairs is accurate.' He slid a business card across the desk. 'That's so that you are in no doubt as to my bona fides. I'm sure the arresting officer will remember me.'

The sergeant eyed him through narrowed eyelids, then slowly picked up a phone and spoke briefly into the handpiece before hanging up.

'Someone's coming out,' he said.

'Thanks, Sarge,' Matthew replied with a smile.

Almost immediately, Paul Brooks came bursting through a side door and walked over to confront Matthew.

'What's this bullshit about Internal Affairs?' he said loudly.

'I'm sure there's no need for that, Detective,' Matthew replied. 'Just let me have a quiet word with my client.'

'We're not finished processing her yet. She's been arrested and is in custody. Bail has not even been thought of yet.'

'Quite so, but if you refuse my very reasonable request for a few minutes with her, the matter will go further,' Matthew said. 'All the way to the top. More importantly, it'll be on the front pages of tomorrow's papers with all sorts of unpleasant allegations. We don't want that now, do we?'

Matthew could see that Brooks was torn between the opportunity to gain some damning admission versus a media storm if he stonewalled Matthew. Brooks may have had some contacts in the media, but his powers of influence only stretched so far, and he knew they'd turn against him in a heartbeat for a good story. After a moment of indecision, he grunted a reply.

'Two minutes, no more.'

'It's been a pleasure, detective.'

Brooks opened the door that he came through earlier, and then motioned for Matthew to follow him. If Matthew had feared that his client would be sobbing in a crumpled heap somewhere, the thought disappeared when he saw her. Jessica Vandermeer was sitting leisurely at an interview table, cigarette in one hand and a cup of coffee nestled in the other.

'That's what I call prompt service, Matthew,' she said brightly. 'I've been here for less than an hour. The sergeant has been a perfect gentleman, but apparently I'm to be refused bail unless I co-operate with a record of interview.'

Brooks had left them alone, apart from a uniformed single-striper standing guard, doing his best to impersonate a marble statue.

'That's not something Brooks will ever admit in court, but it's one of the oldest tricks in the book. Probably the bail sergeant will refuse you bail on some pretext, such as he fears you might be a suicide risk. But we've got a good chance of bail tomorrow in front of the stipendiary magistrate. If not, then we'll make a bail application to the Supreme Court, and as it's a purely circumstantial case, I'm confident we'll get you out. There may be a need for a surety, however. Any friends or relatives that you can rely on?'

She shrugged her shoulders. 'Depends on what we're talking about. What does a surety have to do?'

'Sometimes deposit cash, sometimes pledge property as a guarantee of your appearance, and make sure that you report to the police and stay on the straight and narrow.'

'How much cash?'

'Hard to say. Depends on whether the prosecution oppose bail, how strong their case is, and what the bench thinks of you. What we have in our favour is that you really aren't a suicide or flight risk and the chances of any serious offences must be miniscule. These are matters the magistrate must consider.'

'Can two persons go surety, half each?'

'Sure. No problem.'

She gave him a steady gaze.

'How strong is their case? What are my chances?'

'It's much too early to say. At court tomorrow, there'll be a brief fact sheet setting out the main points, but we won't get statements of witnesses for a few months. Only then can we know what we face.' Matthew gave a slight smile. 'At least there isn't a smoking gun for us to worry about.'

Jessica did not reply, but raised her eyebrows. Matthew had merely been referring to the obvious point that a gun did not shoot her husband dead, but his client's reaction unsettled him. The only thing that Matthew could be certain of was that representing Jessica Vandermeer would not be simple. The more he spoke to her, the more intriguing she appeared.

Chapter Ten

As Matthew predicted, the bail sergeant claimed that Jessica Vandermeer was a suicide risk so that he could justify refusing her bail overnight. The next morning, after a short submission by Matthew, the magistrate granted bail on condition that a surety promised to forfeit $10,000 if there was any breach of bail, together with a requirement that Jessica report weekly to the police.

After arranging for one of Jessica's distant relatives to provide surety, Matthew had a brief conference with his client in the cells beneath the court complex. 'Cool' and 'detached' were the words Matthew used to describe her demeanour to Lena later at their office. Whilst that was preferable to someone ranting incoherently, her behaviour certainly gave him pause. If he had been arrested and charged in full view of his friends and colleagues, he could not conceive – even with his legal training – how he could appear as controlled as Jessica Vandermeer. There seemed to be an undercurrent of planning behind her behaviour, and that did not correspond with an innocent widow, wrongly arrested and unfairly charged.

The police fact sheet handed to him in court was relatively brief, but the main thrust of the prosecution case fell into four parts. Firstly, it alleged that Cornelius Vandermeer had died of a seizure, caused by an unnamed substance.

Secondly, and most importantly, a young actress named as Angelina Smythe-Baker was to give evidence that she had been having an affair with Cornelius Vandermeer, and that Jessica Vandermeer had agreed to a divorce.

Thirdly, the fact sheet alleged that Jessica Vandermeer frequently assisted her husband by preparing his special health drink concoction, and that traces of the unnamed substance had been discovered in the metal flask he used on the day of his death.

Lastly, following the execution of a search warrant at the Vandermeer family home, Brooks had found a small bottle, wrapped in some old oily rags in a corner of the couples' garage. Obviously Brooks considered the bottle important, but Matthew could not see how it was relevant, unless perhaps it contained some toxic substance.

When Matthew arrived at his office an hour after the bail hearing, he waited until Lena finished speaking with an elderly couple about preparing new wills, and then poked his head around her door.

'Got a minute?' he asked.

'Sure,' she replied with her usual easy smile. 'How did the bail application go?'

Matthew outlined the bail conditions, and then commented on their client's behaviour.

'Is that going to be a problem?' Lena asked.

'More a puzzle than a problem. Our client is either the deadliest of our species, or a victim of a frame-up.'

'Which is it?'

Matthew gave a chuckle. 'I'm not sure. But if it's true that Dr Vandermeer was having an affair with that actress, it does provide the prosecution with a valid revenge motive against our client for murder.'

'So we now know for certain it was poison?'

'I'm not sure because they won't tell us what the substance in his body was. Why do you think they'd hold back on that?'

Lena paused in thought for a few moments before replying. 'Perhaps they're still trying to gain some evidence about her purchasing something that contains that exact ingredient. That would be fatal for her defence.'

'It certainly was for her husband.'

Lena tried to suppress a smile. 'This is serious, Matt. She'll get twenty years if she goes down.'

'Serious is my middle name. You know that, Lena.'

Matthew opened his briefcase and pulled out a folder. He flipped through the pages and extracted the fact sheet, then handed it to Lena. She skimmed the document, and then re-read it slowly.

'They also won't tell us what this small bottle contains,' Matthew said. 'It could be cough syrup, rat-killer or the elixir of life.'

'I think the ratkiller suggestion might be closest to the mark. Certainly they have to be searching for some type of poison.' Lena tapped the fact sheet that lay in front of her. 'I'll bet they're canvassing every outlet for this bottle to connect her to it, and they don't want us to interfere with their investigation.'

'You may be right. But we need to ask ourselves the critical question.'

'Which is?'

'Who would profit from his death? I overheard the police prosecutor at the bar table quietly asking Detective Brooks what was happening with the insurance policy. It wasn't part of the prosecution case in the fact sheet but I'm guessing that if there is a policy, our client may be the beneficiary.'

'That's not what I want to hear, Matthew.'

'Juries, as you know, love insurance policies. It usually kills any reasonable doubt lurking in the jury room. In any event, we'll get our client in and see what she says. But before that, I'll have to have a word with Oscar.'

'To discuss the case?'

'To see if he's up to another celebrity murder trial. Healthwise, I mean.'

'Is he up to it mentally?' Lena asked.

'I've no reason to doubt that, and our client seems adamant. This is a conundrum in itself. I still don't think that her explanation for instructing us seemed genuine.'

'Well, to be honest, it did seem a bit weird.'

Matthew placed his hands behind his head and arched his neck, accompanying his movement with a loud sigh. 'Why is nothing black and white?'

Lena's face crinkled into a grin. 'Don't complain. It makes life more interesting. Would you rather spend your time writing wills for old dears like the last couple?'

'You have a point.' Matthew fell silent for several moments before continuing. 'She reminds me of Rebecca, actually.'

He had come to the conclusion that Rebecca MacGregor had engaged he and Oscar to appear for her politician husband, believing their incompetence would result in a conviction. She assessed Matthew as being inexperienced and Oscar as being a has-been drunk. That was a woman that truly hated her husband.

'If Jessica's as devious as Rebecca MacGregor, then we have interesting times ahead.'

'That reminds me of the old Chinese saying, *May you live in interesting times*,' Matthew replied. 'Some say it's a curse and others say it's a blessing. We'll just have to wait and see which applies to us.'

Chapter Eleven

Angelo's formal interview with Inspector Bill Etheridge took place at police headquarters seven days after the execution of the search warrant. The proceedings were tape-recorded by a young clerical officer, and the atmosphere was as frigid as the bleak weather outside.

'You are formally required to answer my questions as a serving police officer, so let's not get involved with any legal nonsense about the right to silence,' Etheridge said in an attempted friendly tone. 'You be straight with me and I'll do everything I can to help you and Rose.'

Angelo instantly picked up the implied threat once again. 'Just get it over with,' he replied.

'There's no need to be hostile, Angelo. I'm just doing my job.'

'If I recall correctly, that's what the SS said after the war.'

'That attitude won't help, Angelo. You're in too much trouble to argue with me.'

Angelo gave an ironic smile. 'What did you find? No, let me guess. A stash of pot, or coke or smack. Just enough to be in the commercial quantity range, I'll bet.' He shook his head angrily. 'Surely you can't be that stupid? I'm the main witness in a drug trial involving crims that have unlimited funds, and access to any drug they want to plant. Can't you work out what's going on?'

'Then you admit that there were drugs in your car? You knew about them?'

'Don't put words into my mouth. I don't know what you found. When you tell me what was planted, we'll both know.'

'Very well.' Etheridge leafed through a folder that lay on the table in front of him. 'The analysis has just come back for the substance that we found in your car. It was heroin. Commercial quantity. You will be charged accordingly, and, of course, you remain suspended. This time without pay.'

A fog of frustration and despair flooded over Angelo. All of his adult life he had been completely honest and professional, refusing to cut corners or even consider the smallest bribe. He had even returned a case of beer he found in the patrol wagon one Christmas Eve to the publican who was thanking the force for their past help. Angelo lived with his young family in a modest fibro cottage and drove a ten-year-old rust bucket of a car, and now as a reward he faced disgrace and imprisonment.

Even his years studying law at night through the Barristers Admission Board of Sydney University had been a complete waste of time and effort. If convicted, he would be removed from the roll of barristers and any future job involving trust would also be ruled out. Rose had been correct all along. She had warned him that the crooks in the force would destroy him, and she had begged him over and over again to quit and use his legal qualifications. He now admitted to himself that his stubborn streak could destroy them.

Angelo's hatred of organised crime stemmed from his early childhood in Italy where the Mafia ruled by fear and extortion. It was this background that convinced him to join the police force, to make Australia a better place for his presence. What a joke his dreams had been, he now realised. He despaired of what would happen to his wife and young children when he was locked up for five, seven or ten years in a gaol where most of the inmates wanted him dead.

Etheridge formally closed the interview and motioned for the clerk to cease recording and leave the room. After she had departed, he dropped his formal tone.

'Look, Angelo, I know it could be a fit-up, but what can we do? We can't ignore the drugs or we'd be charged ourselves with misconduct. Off the record, I think you're straight, and anything I can do without getting myself into trouble, I'll do for you. Don't worry about Rose. I'd never involve her. That line was just for the recording.'

Angelo stared at him. 'Who spread the lies?'

'It was a low-level informant. No doubt he was just passing on a message from his bosses. You know we can't ID him. We don't want you putting a bullet in him now, do we?'

Angelo nodded. 'The message probably came through three or four crims before it got to you. Where did you find the drugs?'

'Someone went to a lot of trouble. We got info that they would be found inside the spare tyre in the boot. We had to take the wheel to a tyre-fitters to get the tyre off the rim, and there it was in the usual plastic bags.'

'No fingerprints, of course?'

'As I said, they went to a lot of trouble.' He held out his hand. 'It's nothing personal, but we have to formally arrest and charge you now.'

Angelo shook the proffered hand. 'Bail?'

'There'll be no trouble there. Unconditional bail with no surety or reporting conditions. That's about all I can do for you now.'

Angelo knew that Etheridge could have arranged for a walk-by in front of newspaper and TV reporters, or objected to granting any bail at all. He took some consolation from this small act of kindness.

Chapter Twelve

Oscar O'Shannessy had been contemplating retirement for several years, and the news that Matthew had conveyed to him made him realise that he would have to make a decision. Aged in his mid-seventies, with one heart attack and two minor strokes behind him, Oscar had to admit that he was not the barrister he would ever choose for himself if faced with serious criminal charges. His beloved wife had died more than a decade ago, but that did not stop him having a continuing conversation with her about everything that happened each day, and in his mind's eye he saw her smiling with that familiar response – a mixture of amusement and scepticism.

Matthew had spoken to him on the phone a few days earlier, outlining Jessica Vandermeer's instructions, and this placed him in an ethical quandary. Should he admit to his own misgivings, thus forfeiting a valuable brief, or simply trust in his experience and do the very best he could? Matthew certainly was entitled to hear his doubts, and he felt sure that he would give him the correct advice.

Although he and Matthew regularly had lunch together at Oscar's favourite pub, they had not worked together since the MacGregor trial, and he was thus part-apprehensive and part-grateful for the brief. If his health survived and they were successful, it would be the crowning glory of his career. Of course, he reflected that failure was also possible, and he gave an involuntary shiver as a flood of negative thoughts washed over him.

The buzzer on his phone interrupted his thoughts, and lifting the receiver he was pleased to hear that Matthew had arrived with a brief. Springing from his chair with energy that belied his years, he pulled open his door and called out for Matthew to join him.

'Well, this is both a pleasure and a surprise, Matt,' Oscar said as he shook Matthew's hand. 'A pleasure to see you and a surprise we were given the case.'

'Déjà vu, you might say. We've been here before.'

When they both sat down, Matthew slid the brief across Oscar's battered old desk. The file contained a police fact sheet and the instructions given by their client over two lengthy conferences. The prosecution witness statements would not be served on the defence for several weeks at least.

'She chose us because of the MacGregor trial?' Oscar asked as he slid the pink tape from the folded brief.

'So she said. I'll let you have a quick look at what we've got so far. Take your time.' Matthew leaned back in the chair, closed his eyes and clamped his hands behind his head.

After ten or fifteen minutes, Oscar tossed the brief back onto the desk.

'I'm not surprised they arrested her.' He grabbed hold of a tobacco-stained pipe, then commenced to chew on the stem. Ever since his second stroke, he no longer filled the pipe, but, like a security blanket from his childhood, he retained an attachment to the object. 'It's quite fascinating, actually. They won't specify the poison, but say this substance caused his death. I wonder what it is.'

'All will be revealed when we get the prosecution statements. Until then, you know as much as I do.'

Oscar stared at the brief with a wistful look. 'It reminds me of a similar trial I appeared in over two decades ago. Murder by poisoning. I did some research into the genre when I got the brief, and it's absolutely fascinating when you look at it over the centuries. Did you know, for example, that the famous Marie Lafarge case in 1840 in France was the first time that the presence of arsenic was proven during a trial to convict a wife of disposing of an inconvenient husband? Before that time, an unhappy wife was the most dangerous creature on earth, because there was no way to detect arsenic poisoning.'

Oscar was a history buff, who loved to give impromptu history lessons, something that Matthew had grown to appreciate.

'Long before that,' Matthew said. 'I seem to recall that ancient Rome was a hotbed of poisoners, the most ardent followers being the various empresses who decided who would become the next emperor by means of the 'ancient craft'. The poison was apparently tested on their slaves, so that the correct dose could be administered to the intended victim.'

'But even earlier,' Oscar replied, 'some fifty years before Christ, Lucretius famously said, *what is food to one man is bitter poison to others.*'

'Perhaps that is apposite to our case,' Matthew replied with a grin.

'Over time, anyone skillful in using the various poisons had a profession as a poisoner, and was greatly prized by the nobility,' Oscar continued. 'You of course know of the infamous Borgias, who poisoned their way to power in the fifteenth century?'

'Didn't the father end up as a Pope?'

'Pope Alexander VI. Unfortunately, when the son attempted to poison a difficult cardinal, the wrong bottle of wine was served by the butler, and both Cesare and Rodrigo Borgia were poisoned. The Pope subsequently died, and the son barely survived. I think you would call that poetic justice.'

'There's certainly a moral in there somewhere.'

'Then two hundred years later, another infamous family, the de Medici clan burst onto the scene. Catherine, who later became Queen of France, apparently poisoned everyone who crossed her, or stood in her way.'

'I take it that an invitation to dine at the Borgia or de Medici houses would have to be regarded with some trepidation.'

'Precisely. The fear that poisoning engendered was to result in some extraordinarily barbaric methods of execution on the practitioners, so that their terrible agony would dissuade further adherents of the craft. Water torture, boiling, burning and beheading were popular punishments, but you're much too young for me to give you any of the specific details.'

'And your client?'

'By my reckoning, she should be out on parole by now.'

'Another innocent crushed by the might of the state, Oscar?'

'Not really. Let's just say that I wouldn't turn my back on her, or let her make me a cup of coffee. As for the MacGregor trial, it's not really déjà vu. Rebecca MacGregor wanted her husband convicted, whereas Jessica Vandermeer surely cannot hope she is found guilty of murder?'

Matthew shrugged.

Oscar gave a crooked grin. 'What's she like?'

'One similarity with Rebecca is that she's very cool. As our old acquaintance used to say, she's a bit of an *ice maiden*. That could well apply to Jessica.'

The acquaintance was Fenella Montgomery, the instructing solicitor for the prosecution in the MacGregor case, with whom Matthew had a brief and passionate affair a decade ago.

'Ah, yes. Fenella,' Oscar replied. 'Sad tale that. Have you kept in touch with her?'

Matthew shook his head.

'She's married to a Supreme Court judge. You remember Horace Birmingham?'

'That's right. I remember now. But he's old enough to be ...'

'Quite.'

'Poor girl. That's the result of putting your career before your heart. I thought she was smarter than that.'

'A beautiful woman with a brilliant legal mind, but not one drop of commonsense. Life can be strange Oscar.'

'Which brings me to my own dilemma. I need your advice my boy, and I want it straight. No lies. Not between friends.'

'Sounds intriguing.'

Oscar paused for effect before continuing.

'When I first met you, I was rude enough to ask if you were up for the challenge in our murder trial. Now it's your turn to ask me the same question. But before you do, I have to say that I don't know.'

Matthew put his head slightly to one side in a questioning manner.

Oscar held his hands up. 'Two strokes have taken their toll, to be honest, and my short-term memory does tend to fade in and out. Always on some borderline insignificant detail, which annoys me no end. Someone's name, or the citation of some case I have quoted a thousand times before. Things like that.'

'I was reading an article about that issue recently, and a prominent American psychiatrist put it succinctly.'

Oscar raised his eyebrows apprehensively.

'He said that if you lose your keys, that's OK. But if you can't remember what function the keys serve, then you're in big trouble.'

Oscar gave a relieved chuckle. 'I'm all right then. What a relief.'

'In any event, I was also contemplating my future. Lena's a fantastic legal partner, but after ten years of conveyancing, probate, contracts and an occasional plea for a drunk driver or some drug induced assault, I think I've had enough.'

'You lust for the cut and thrust of the criminal court. I knew it, my boy.' Oscar's eyes shone with enthusiasm and he rubbed his hands together gleefully.

'I wouldn't exactly call it lust. More like I need a challenge. Something to test the grey cells and expand my universe.'

'I did wonder how long you'd last as a solicitor. I must say I never thought it'd be a decade.'

'Perhaps it was loyalty to Lena. Perhaps I was afraid I might not be successful. I do realise that if I stuff up, your client pays the penalty with ten or twenty years sometimes. No wonder so many barristers get divorced or hit the bottle. Or both.'

'There's no doubt you have to be mentally tough. To survive *the slings and arrows of outrageous fortune*, as the Bard put it. But don't forget that successful advocates earn a good income and can always take an appointment to the bench in their old age.'

'Or in their middle age sometimes. There's nothing like the security of a steady income and a judicial pension to attract someone with a few kids and a big mortgage.'

'One other aspect of life at the bar that I might mention is that I don't advise you to be a *staircase wit*.'

'A what?'

'The famous phrase – *L'esprit de l'escalier* – meaning *the wit of the staircase* – comes from the French philosopher Denis Diderot.'

Matthew held up his hands in exasperation. 'Clear as mud, Oscar.'

'In Diderot's essay, one of the diners at a statesman's home is left speechless by a remark, and can only think clearly when he reaches the bottom of the stairs.'

'So he thinks of the perfect reply, but it's too late?' Matthew said.

'Exactly. At the bar you have to think on your feet – it's no use thinking of the perfect riposte after you've left the courtroom.'

'Thanks for the advice,' Matthew replied with a grin, 'but that's easier said than done.'

'Anyway, back to the matter at hand,' Oscar said. 'What will you do with Jessica's brief?'

'I could be your backup. Effectively your junior. Lena could instruct us. What do you think?'

Oscar was lost in thought for a few minutes before replying by holding out his hand.

Matthew grabbed the offered handshake.

'Glad to meet you. Jameson is the name. New to the bar, but full of enthusiasm for the downtrodden and oppressed.'

'Don't forget the wealthy classes, Matthew. Legal aid is only a subsistence livelihood.'

Although Matthew had not raised the issue with Oscar, one doubt about joining the bar kept recurring. The 'cab rank' rule, named for the British tradition of Hackney Carriage Drivers at the head of a queue being obliged to take the first customer, required barristers to accept briefs if they were available. There were some exceptions to the rule, for example if the case was beyond the barrister's competence or he was briefed in another trial for that date. Otherwise, Matthew's next client could easily be an alleged child-murderer or paedophile, and he had severe reservations about using his skills and training to obtain an acquittal for someone who made his skin crawl at the very sight of them. Matthew knew that the rule was there to protect accused persons whom no lawyer wished to represent, ensuring that they had legal representation at trial. It also protected barristers from criticism for appearing for those unpopular clients. Regardless of the principle behind the rule, civil cases involving contract disputes, personal injury claims and workers compensation briefs would provide an alternative path to criminal cases.

He knew some barristers that he had spoken to about the rule had no such qualms, treating criminal trials as merely an intellectual challenge – a type of high stakes legal chess game. When questioned by Matthew about the morality of this, the answer was always the same – 'I don't decide guilt or innocence, that's up to the jury'. Matthew knew that he could not conduct his professional life based on this principle, and determined that he would avoid criminal briefs as far as professional ethics allowed.

Chapter Thirteen

It was a small item on page two of the *Sydney Morning Herald*, but the news hit Matthew like a physical blow. The paper reported that Detective Sergeant Angelo Cattani of the drug squad was granted bail on charges of both possession and supply of a commercial quantity of drugs that had been located in the locked boot of his car. The report was only a few lines in length, finishing with his suspension without pay, pending conclusion of the charges.

Matthew's arrest and charge on a trumped-up allegation a decade ago meant he knew the mental trauma that Angelo would now face. As he contemplated the best course of action, Lena's head appeared around the corner of his office door.

'What's up?' Lena asked. 'I heard a terrible groan and thought you'd suffered a heart attack.'

'Come in and have a look.' Matthew handed her the paper, waving a hand towards an empty chair. He watched her body stiffen and her eyes narrow into a frown as she read the item.

'That's terrible news,' she said softly. 'Surely it can't be true?'

'I'd stake my life on Angelo. Only a few weeks ago he was worried about being fitted up for something, and now this happens.'

'But why?'

'Because he's the main witness in a drug conspiracy trial. If he's convicted, how could the jury accept his evidence in the drug trial? Probably the Crown will file a 'no bill' and the conspiracy case will never come to trial. What a mess.'

'Poor Angelo. What I do know is that we have an obligation to do everything we can to help him. His family must be in despair.'

Matthew shook his head slowly.

'As you know, I probably owe him my current freedom, so I'm not going to waste any time.' Matthew glanced at his watch, which showed a time of 5.10 pm. 'I'm going over to his house, and if he won't let me in, I'll break down the door.'

'That's certainly a novel way to obtain instructions. Just don't end up in custody again.'

Chapter Fourteen

It was just after 6 pm when Matthew pulled up outside the fibro house. Armed with a bottle of expensive red wine, he bounded up the front steps, opened the unlocked screen door and then rapped on the front door. After a few minutes, the door opened and a bleary-eyed, unshaven Angelo came into view.

'Time for a chat,' Matthew announced.

Angelo shook his head. 'Not a good time, mate. I'll give you a ring.' With that, he attempted to close the door, but Matthew had already planted his foot between the door and the jamb. Pushing the door forcefully with his shoulder, Matthew was inside the house and closing the door behind himself before Angelo could protest further.

'Now is not the time for sulking,' Matthew said as he walked towards the only light showing in the house. 'Now's the time to plan our defence. Step by step, but small ones first.'

As he entered the small lounge room that was dimly lit by one coffee table lamp, he saw Rose sitting on a lounge chair, hunched-up like an elderly pensioner. She had obviously been crying, as evidenced by her puffy face and red eyes.

Matthew walked over to her, bent over and placed one arm around her shoulders. Holding up the bottle of wine with the other hand, he motioned to Angelo. He knew this was a time for being forceful, not diplomatic.

'Three glasses please. No arguments.'

Angelo started to object, but then turned and walked into the kitchen.

'It always looks bad at first,' Matthew said quietly to Rose, 'but we have an ace up our sleeve that is quite rare.'

She looked at him with widening eyes and a puzzled expression. 'What's that?'

'He's innocent. A true rarity in these drug cases, believe me.'

'That makes a difference? I don't see how,' she replied.

Angelo returned with the glasses and Matthew gestured for a corkscrew by twisting his free hand.

'You're forgetting your host duties, mate.'

'Sorry.'

'You're running on three cylinders at the moment. We need all eight.'

'It feels like one to be honest,' Angelo said before returning to the kitchen.

After Matthew had filled the glasses and passed them around, he held up his glass.

'A toast.'

Angelo and Rose replied with blank stares.

'It's finally my chance to repay a ten-year debt. Without your help, I'd be lucky to be out on parole. So, in a strange way, we've come full circle.'

'I know you're trying your best to cheer me up,' Angelo replied, 'but ignoring reality rarely helps in the long run. It only results in the probable clang of the cell door closing, as it were.'

'I'm not trying to cheer you up. I'm trying to make you stop feeling sorry for, and start defending, yourself.'

Angelo stiffened with irritation, but after glancing at his wife, he softened. 'I'm all ears. What's this magic advice you have?'

'We know who planted the drugs,' Matthew replied. 'We know why they did. We have to now trace backwards to discover who's involved. There's a chain of course, and we have to find the proverbial weak link in it.' He took a generous mouthful of the wine, and then paused for a few moments. 'Possibly there are one or more coppers behind it, in league with the drug syndicate.'

Angelo stared intently at Matthew.

'You've suspected that for weeks. Let's start with your so-called partner. What's his name?'

'Constable Phillip D'Ascenzio.'

'That's the one you said gave you a bad feeling last month, isn't he?'

Angelo nodded.

'He has to have played some part in it. Perhaps by taking a bundle of cash in return for your home address. Perhaps he helped even more than that, but he has to be bent if the principals were boasting in Long Bay Gaol that they would walk free.'

Angelo swirled the wine in his glass, not attempting to drink.

'Knowing it and proving it are two different beasts. D'Ascenzio is not likely to be making any admissions. He doesn't want to replace me in Long Bay Gaol.'

'I gather that Internal Affairs would not be likely to assist?'

'What do you think?'

Matthew paused for another sip of wine, and then gave an enquiring look. 'How are your finances?'

'Poor to terrible,' Angelo replied. 'I take it there's a reason for the question?'

'I think we might need a good private detective. You've got no financial worries with me or even Oscar if we need him, but I can't see a PI acting pro bono.'

'I know several,' Angelo replied, 'but most of them are ex-coppers and I'm not sure in whose interests they'd be working. I suspect that they'd sell to the highest bidder, and we know who's got cash to burn.'

'Lena has used several in her family law practice. You know, husbands that suddenly are on the bread line and destitute when the property settlements are argued. Lena is the type that engenders absolute loyalty, and she swears by a couple that own a small firm. If you're stretched, our firm will pay for them upfront.'

'We can't ask that, Matthew,' Rose interrupted. 'We're not a charity case.'

'It's not a problem. It'll all be repaid when you're awarded costs after the acquittal,' Matthew said. 'By the way, Angelo, your mother and the kids are quiet.'

'They're staying with Rose's parents in Queensland until the storm blows over. If it does, I mean.'

'*When* it does,' Rose said, rising from her chair and walking over to Angelo to place an arm around him. 'They don't need to be abused at school every day. Mum and Dad have a small farm in the country, so at least the kids will have a ball.'

Matthew drained his glass and stood up.

'You'll need to come over to the office to give formal instructions, and the sooner we get started the better. How about tomorrow?'

'I'm not sure,' Angelo replied.

'Tomorrow it is then,' Matthew said. 'Nine am sharp. No more excuses. Just remember your Catholic school mantra – *God helps those who help themselves.*'

Chapter Fifteen

Matthew admitted to himself that despite his enthusiastic talk to Angelo and his wife, he had the gravest misgivings about the charges. The oldest defence raised in almost every drug possession charge was a complete lack of knowledge. 'They were planted' was the call heard from every dock in every courtroom in the land. The larger the quantity however, the more difficult that defence became. Matthew could see the Crown prosecutor standing before the jury and, in a friendly, persuasive tone, asking how a small fortune in drugs could belong to someone else: 'Is there a drug Santa Claus that leaves presents of commercial quantities of heroin lying about? But it was not lying about. It was in the locked family car boot. What a clever Santa he was.'

It was just after 8 am the following day when Matthew arrived at their small legal practice. As expected, Lena was already hard at work.

'Got a minute?' Matthew asked.

'Come in, Matt. I'm just getting a few things ready for today. I'll grab you a coffee.' She reached behind her and grabbed a spare mug, then poured some coffee from the percolator she always kept plugged in on her side desk. 'How's Angelo and his wife?'

'Much as you'd expect: pretty low – depressed – angry – at their wits' end. He's due here at nine to give instructions.'

'Poor things.'

'I said we'd pay for a PI to do some background work. I hope that's OK.' As they were equal partners, Matthew felt obliged to mention the promise he had made to Angelo.

'Of course it is; you know that without asking.'

'Just making sure, partner.'

She eyed him with suspicion. 'What's that strange look for?'

Matthew shifted uncomfortably in his chair and made a fuss of sipping the scalding black coffee.

'Come on, out with it,' Lena persisted.

'I can't keep anything from you, can I?' Matthew replied, sheepishly. 'I've had a little talk with Oscar, actually.'

'Oh, yes.'

'He's trying to convince me to join him at the bar.'

'You lying devil, Matthew. I've been watching you for months, getting irritated and cranky over trivial incidents, and I've been wondering how long you'd last here,' Lena said with a smile.

'I'm not that obvious, surely.'

'I know what you're going to say before you've thought of it.'

'Mea culpa, mea culpa.' Matthew said with a shrug of his shoulders. 'You're correct, of course. I just feel guilty deserting you after I talked you into leaving our old firm and coming here.'

'Don't worry about me. I get an offer from one of the big city firms about once a month, and I must admit that I miss the hustle and bustle. There's also a slightly more attractive night life there rather than being hidden away in the suburbs, if you catch my drift.'

Matthew raised his eyebrows.

'Don't look at me like that. Everyone deserves a chance of a little shared happiness. Even a lawyer.'

Matthew held up his hands in surrender. 'If anyone deserves happiness, you come first in the line.'

Lena was eight when she was smuggled to England from Germany just before the outbreak of war in 1938, after her parents had paid for forged documents, telling her they would follow shortly thereafter. They never did, probably because they had run out of money, and her parents, grandparents, cousins and all of her close relatives shared a terrible fate at Auschwitz. Whilst she was always good-natured and patient, there was always a quiet sadness, and Matthew believed that she needed a partner who could empathise with her terrible experiences.

'That's settled then,' she announced. 'I'll speak to some of the other local firms and see if they want to take over our practice. Though I'll take our best clients with me to the city, of course.'

'Of course.'

'Including Angelo and Jessica. OK, Matthew, let's start making plans.'

Chapter Sixteen

The complete brief of the charges facing Jessica Vandermeer arrived by mail to Matthew's office a few weeks later. It was worse than he had anticipated.

The first civilian witness was Angelina Smythe-Baker. The twenty-two-year-old aspiring actress had breast implants inserted by Cornelius Vandermeer some twelve months prior to his demise, and her statement told of a passionate affair that had culminated in the promise of a future marriage as soon as a divorce could be arranged. More telling was her evidence that Matthew's client not only knew of the affair, but that she had also agreed to the divorce. When Matthew had raised the affair with Jessica Vandermeer at their initial conference, she had flatly denied any knowledge of it, claiming her deceased husband was always loving and faithful to her.

Herbert Rowbottom's statement was next, and it described a chartered accountant well versed in the Vandermeer family finances, having acted for them for many years. His statement laid bare the financial skeleton of the Vandermeer marriage, and a sorry tale it told. The lease on the waterfront mansion was about to expire; the matching pair of BMW sports cars were also leased; the relevant bank accounts were overdrawn; finally, Mr Rowbottom concluded that the extravagant lifestyle expenses were not matched by the doctor's income. Indeed, Matthew could imagine the Crown prosecutor describing the deceased to the jury as 'the plastic surgeon with the plastic lifestyle'.

The reason for the accountant's statement was clear to Matthew – there would be no generous divorce settlement for Jessica, and this in itself was a possible motive for murder. Cast off like an old lover without assets or income, and without children, Jessica would have to find some way to support herself. Under the provisions of the new Family Law Act, Matthew knew that Jessica could claim that she was no longer employable and would perhaps receive a modest amount of weekly maintenance from her soon-to-be ex-husband, but this was by no means certain. Whilst not a substantial motive by itself, when aligned with the oldest motive known to man or woman – pure revenge – it was a compelling argument.

There followed a number of statements by various technical witnesses who did not add to the weight of the prosecution case, but who completed the chain of possession for physical items, painting a more complete picture of the investigation for the laymen of the upcoming jury. Without their testimony, vital pieces of evidence such as the bottle found in Jessica's garage would not be admissible.

The statement that Matthew had been dreading came next – that of Professor Max Schultz. Matthew took a deep breath and straightened up in his chair. Having carefully tested the various samples of the deceased's vital organs, together with a small amount of the remaining health drink, the professor concluded that there was no evidence of poison as such. However, he had discovered the presence of a large amount of a shellfish protein. His belief was that anaphylactic shock was the cause of death – as the deceased had a severe shellfish allergy – triggered by the consumption of a shellfish compound that he found had been dissolved in the health drink.

A brief statement from one of the deceased's medical colleagues confirmed the chronic allergy. What Matthew now knew was that whoever had planned and executed the murder was not only cold-blooded but also extremely clever. The death had almost slipped through as a normal heart attack, and even the police forensic pathologist had found no obvious poison. It was only the dogged insistence by Detective Brooks referring the case to Professor Schultz that had uncovered the truth. Whilst Matthew held no feelings of warmth for the detective, he grudgingly admitted that it was intelligent police work. He recognised that Brooks fell into that small percentage of detectives who lived and breathed for the challenge of the hunt, and – like a bloodhound with a scent – he would never let go.

The last statement was from Detective Brooks himself, and it confirmed another damning piece of evidence foreshadowed by the earlier police fact sheet. During the execution of a search warrant at the accused's home, a small bottle was located hidden in some old rags in the garage. The nature of the substance in the bottle, confirmed by its label, was shrimp paste. The inference was that this bottle was the source of the shellfish in the health drink, and that the concealment of it in the garage could only have been by their client. One of the old rags was a women's tee-shirt, and no doubt Jessica could expect cross-examination as to the owner of the article. Withholding until now information that the bottle contained shrimp paste confirmed Matthew's suspicion that the police had been trying to link Jessica to the purchase of the bottle. Was this to be a killer piece of evidence during the trial? Only time would tell.

Surprisingly to Matthew, there was no mention of an insurance policy showing his client as a beneficiary, nor any further mention of Jessica preparing her husband's health drink at their house. No doubt, the prosecution was still busy at work, and more statements would follow.

Matthew slumped in his chair. Unless something dramatic emerged from the proverbial hat, the case appeared overwhelming. Certainly, Jessica's lavish lifestyle and high public profile would not endear her to the jury, neither would her cold and calculating manner. Matthew struggled to understand how he could mount a competent defence in the light of the evidence against her.

After sitting slumped in his chair for half an hour, he noticed the time was just after 5 pm. After gathering the documents together and locking them in the desk drawer, he waved to Lena as he passed her office. She was taking instructions from yet another distraught wife, deserted and desperate. He was glad that she was busy, as he felt that he needed some quiet time to collect his thoughts before he discussed the case with her.

He drove the short distance to the unit he had purchased some five years previously, in the Northern Beaches. It was not exactly a rundown block of flats, but at twenty-five years old, the first signs of concrete cancer were showing on the exterior brickwork. The small garden, the stairwell and the parking area (all part of the common property, and whose obligation to repair lay on the body corporate of the strata plan) showed only minimal signs of maintenance. There was also no lift, and the daily climb up and down three flights of stairs certainly did nothing to improve the unit's market value. There were two small bedrooms, one of which Matthew had converted into a study, and a combined living and dining area, together with a small kitchen and tiny bathroom.

The redeeming feature for Matthew was that the converted study overlooked the beach, and he never tired of sitting in a comfortable swivel chair, gazing at the ever-changing spectacle that nature provided. Some days displayed a crystal-clear blue sky combined with shimmering white sand and glittering blue sea, but the next day could be a raging storm with torrential rain, lightning and thunder. Rarely were two days the same, and even a short time in his favourite spot always renewed his spirits.

Having been raised in the Blue Mountains, more than one hundred kilometres from the coast, Matthew had never been a keen surfer, preferring to swim laps in the nearby Olympic pool rather than battle the rips and the waves of the surf. If he was truthful, he'd privately admit that whenever he did venture into the surf, he foolishly imagined there would be a great white or tiger shark waiting to greet him. As one of his ex-girlfriends had remarked dryly – 'you can take the boy out of the country but not the country out of the boy'.

He did however love to walk or jog slowly along the waterline at dusk, always barefooted, letting the end of the waves foam over his feet. In the past, he had tried to go for a fast run on the sand, but his knee kept giving way – a reminder of his football days. The knee had been reconstructed by a Macquarie Street orthopaedic surgeon some twelve years ago, a time that signalled the end of his football career and the start of a twelve-month rehabilitation period. He had played second row in both reserve and first grade rugby league, and considered himself a reliable but not brilliant participant. He still remembered the tackle that had ripped the anterior cruciate ligament from the bone, and the explosive pain that descended on him a split second later.

His car was a battered Volkswagen Beetle, some ten years old, but as Matthew had said when questioned about his choice, cars meant nothing to him, except to get him from point A to B. The fanatical obsession many, if not most, males of all ages held for cars amused and puzzled him. 'I must have a missing gene,' he always replied with a laugh when queried about his indifference. His one extravagance was a state-of-the-art Bang and Olufsen stereo system. Once he eventually overcame his shock at the ticket price, he found that the system had repaid him with hundreds of hours of pleasure. His taste in music was described by one of his football mates as 'living in the past'. It comprised of operas, chamber music, and show tunes from musicals of the forties and fifties – his choice of the day dictated by his prevailing mood. 'I'd rather live in the past with music that has survived for decades and sometimes centuries,' he had replied to his mate, 'than music that is forgotten as soon as it slips out of the charts.'

Matthew made a fresh pot of black tea, then pulled out a Vivaldi LP from his record stack and carefully placed it on the turntable, switching it on and turning up the sound. Pouring himself a generous mug of tea, he sank into his favoured swivel chair, then turned his head slowly one way then the other to ease the throbbing pain in his head. After a few minutes, the magic of *L'Estro Armonico* ebbed through his headache, dulling the ache and raising his spirits.

He gave up trying to make sense of the brief, and gradually strayed into a topic that occurred to him most days. It was Lena who had identified the problem, but it was not until he reflected on her comments that he had finally acknowledged how perceptive she was.

'I think she's set the bar too high,' Lena had commented during one of their Friday night pizza and wine evenings. 'You judge everyone by her, and they just don't make the grade'.

Matthew had instantly known to whom she was referring.

'You could be right,' he admitted.

They were speaking of Fenella Montgomery, a beguiling instructing solicitor, now an acting Crown prosecutor, with whom Matthew had a turbulent affair during the MacGregor trial. The affair had been a complete surprise to him, as was the intoxicating passion. Fenella was almost five-foot-eight tall, and slim whilst still exhibiting the lithe physique of a four-hundred metre runner. She possessed flaming red hair, and her perfectly symmetrical green eyes had dazzled Matthew from the first moment he met her. First class law honours and a brilliant mind completed the package. Furthermore, he ruefully admitted, she was a gold-medal lover.

Matthew smiled to himself as he recalled Lena's nickname for Fenella – 'Grace'. It had puzzled him for some time until Lena added 'as in Grace Kelly'. Ignoring the red hair, there was significant merit in the comparison.

The frustrating problem was that each time Matthew started a new relationship, it was not long before he began to notice that the voice did not have that sharp, private-school inflection; the skin was not as blemish-free; the eyes were not as luminous. If it was not one perceived shortfall, it was another. In his own heart, he admitted that the failing was always his. To waste his life fretting over a failed romance was the height of stupidity, particularly when the object of his obsession had a major flaw.

Ambition was Fenella's failing, particularly as she placed it above everything. When Matthew had been wrongly charged with a vicious assault on a woman shortly after the MacGregor trial had finished, Fenella had been instantly more concerned for her own reputation than anything else. She had immediately bypassed the concept of 'innocent until proven guilty', and was not only convinced of his guilt, but had decided that he would serve several years in prison for his behaviour. When Matthew thought rationally about her, he realised that any marriage would have been a disaster, and whilst he used to be contemptuous of drunks and gamblers and other assorted addicts, he was not any more. He had his own personal addiction and her name was Fenella. This year he'd be ten years clean. He knew it would be disastrous to relapse.

As the first side of the LP finished, he reached over and turned the record over. Using the break in concentration, he returned to the brief he had just received, and again he recalled the fact sheet and the statements, searching for some material that may be useful before a jury. He knew that revenge was the main motive for murder in thousands of novels and films, but in a modern world, would a jury today believe in that motive enough to convict? Certainly, the crime was cold-blooded, and the method typically was female, as Oscar had pronounced in his history lecture. But Matthew found it difficult to imagine the raging hatred that would be required to perform the act.

A jury always liked an alternative theory, Matthew believed, to justify a verdict of not guilty. But who else was there to benefit from the doctor's demise? Certainly not the budding actress who would no longer marry her lover. And who else but his client had access to both the shellfish paste and the health drink? Matthew's headache gradually increased in intensity. As he eased himself out of the chair, a long walk on the beach seemed the only likely respite.

Chapter Seventeen

The first court appearance for Angelo on the drug charges was short and clinical. The police prosecutor handed Matthew a copy of the fact sheet as soon as he sat down at the bar table, and, after nodding at Angelo, told Matthew that there was no objection to bail being continued.

The case was the first adjournment of the day. Outside the courtroom, Matthew spoke briefly to Angelo in the elegant, old-world foyer of Central Court of Petty Sessions, preparing him before they confronted the storm of reporters and photographers waiting for them on the steps of the building. He instructed Angelo to pause for the cameras so that the inevitable photos in tomorrow's papers did not show any sign of avoidance or anger.

'You're an innocent man, wrongly charged, so you've nothing to be ashamed about,' Matthew reminded him.

Matthew had earlier told Rose that there was no need for her to attend court. 'We'll leave that for the jury, if it ever comes to that,' he had advised. Her appearance when the case came before the jury in the District Court would be useful to show Angelo as a family man, but that was not required at the Local Court.

'Angelo needs support, and if I can't at least provide that, what does it say of me?' she had replied.

So it was that the three of them emerged from the main entrance doors, pausing briefly for the cameras before slowly making their way down the sandstone steps without answering or acknowledging the barrage of questions thrown their way. A white sedan with dark tinted windows pulled into the kerb as they crossed the footpath. Matthew opened the rear door and waved Angelo and Rose into the back seats. Slamming the door behind them, he jumped into the front seat and the vehicle accelerated away.

'Rose and Angelo, this is Rufus Tomlinson,' Matthew said, 'a man in whom we will be placing a great deal of trust and hope.'

'Morning, folks,' the driver replied, raising a hand but not taking his eyes off the busy traffic in Liverpool Street.

'Rufus is the best PI in the business, according to Lena,' Matthew added, 'and she is never wrong in her assessment of character. We'll go and grab a coffee and some cake for morning tea. Where do you suggest, Angelo?'

Angelo hesitated for a few moments before replying. 'I'm too well known in the city. Perhaps we'll take Parramatta Road and drive to Leichhardt. I know a great little café in Norton Street.'

Matthew was not surprised by his choice, as Leichhardt was the Italian heartland of Sydney. After following Angelo's directions, they soon entered a small family-run restaurant where the aroma of strongly brewed coffee and freshly baked pastries filled the room with an intoxicating aroma.

After they had made their selections, Matthew gave Tomlinson an enquiring glance.

'Lena tells me there will be a few of you on the case, but we'll only speak to you,' he asked.

'We always work as a team, but mostly in the shadows,' Tomlinson replied. 'You never know who's keeping watch at your firm's address or at Angelo's house, so I'll coordinate the work, but the operatives won't go near any of you.'

'That's good to hear. The criminals behind this have extensive resources, and you don't need to be reminded how dangerous they are,' Angelo said.

'So Lena told us,' Tomlinson remarked. 'What I now require is the background material so we can plan our scheme of operations. Let's get started.'

For the next two hours, the private detective fired rapid questions at Angelo, with an occasional query for Matthew. They consumed several courses of coffee and pastries before the elderly Italian nonna waddled out with a handwritten menu.

'Lunchtime. You all need to fatten up,' she announced.

They ordered, then leisurely devoured various pastas with assorted meats, together with two bottles of Italian wine.

'It's on me,' Matthew announced firmly when the bill arrived.

It was approaching 3 pm when they finally spilled out of the restaurant, and, after making his farewell, Matthew jumped onto a bus heading back into the city. Tomlinson drove Angelo and Rose to the nearby Stanmore railway station so they could catch a train back to the suburbs.

No one had noticed the dark panel van following them from the city, nor that it had parked some two hundred metres from the restaurant for the duration of their meeting. The vehicle contained two men, faces obscured by sunglasses and baseball caps, who sat motionless in the front seat. As Tomlinson's sedan had passed them on the way to the station, the driver pulled a notebook from his pocket and wrote briefly before replacing it. He then slowly pulled out into the line of traffic, allowing two other cars between himself and the private detective.

Chapter Eighteen

Matthew had arranged the conference with Jessica Vandermeer for 10 am the following day, and she arrived by taxi a few minutes early.

'Good to see you, Jessica,' Matthew said as he walked into the waiting room. 'Lena is waiting for us in her office. It's a little more organised than mine.'

After they had settled in, Matthew gave Jessica a copy of the prosecution brief.

'Take your time, there's no hurry,' Matthew said as she commenced reading. He had deliberately wanted to watch her as she took in the contents. But, from beginning to end, she displayed not a flicker of emotion.

'Much the same as we've been reading for weeks in the gossip columns and magazines,' Jessica said with a nonchalant shrug after she finished reading. 'Nothing new there.'

Matthew shuffled through the papers before extracting a photo.

'Brooks says he found this small bottle of shrimp paste hidden in the garage, wrapped in some old rags.' He handed the photo to his client.

'Never seen it before,' Jessica replied. 'Perhaps Corny put it there. Who knows?'

Matthew reflected on the abbreviation of her husband's name, said as though he was still alive. Perhaps there was some affection there after all.

'I take it "Corny" refers to your late husband,' Lena asked. 'We have to make sure we're talking about the same person.'

'Of course it does,' Jessica replied sharply.

'Does the company name on the label or the shrimp paste mentioned on it mean anything to you?' Matthew asked.

'Not a thing,' she replied, unblinking, looking at Matthew steadily.

'I take it you knew of his shellfish allergy?'

'Of course. That was something of which he was extremely careful. He well knew that shellfish could cause a severe allergic reaction.'

'Did you know that he had run out of his supply of epinephrine at his surgery?'

'He may have mentioned it. I'm not sure.'

Matthew deliberately held eye contact with her briefly, but she did not waver. He looked back at his notes.

'You've told us previously that you had no knowledge of your husband's affair with this young woman,' Matthew said. 'However, Angelina says that not only did you know, but you had also agreed to a divorce. Why would she say this, do you think?'

Jessica gave a harsh laugh then shook her head. 'Surely you have worked it out.'

'We need to hear it from you,' Lena responded.

'Spite,' she replied, 'or publicity for her so-called acting career. Perhaps even revenge, because she's got some harebrained notion that I poisoned him.' She paused for effect before continuing. 'Take your pick.'

'That may be so, Jessica,' Lena replied, 'but it's an issue that the jury will take on board, and we have to challenge it.'

'We don't bear the onus of proof,' Jessica replied immediately.

'That's true, of course,' Matthew said. 'However, we bear an evidential burden. That's not prescribed in any statute or regulation, but if the jury hears a sweet little thing sobbing her heart out for a lost lover, we have to attack her version of the story. Discredit her. Put doubt in the jury's mind about her honesty. You do see that, don't you?'

'I suppose so,' Jessica replied.

Matthew felt her tone was somewhat glib.

'In any event, that's for you to worry about. It's not my concern.'

Matthew sank back in his chair, inadvertently massaging his forehead, before Lena went through a series of questions clarifying the issues she wanted resolved.

'Anything else?' Lena asked after a few minutes, nodding towards Matthew.

'Not at present,' he replied.

Lena explained that Matthew would be admitted as a barrister before Jessica's trial, while she would be joining another firm. She then said there would be no real difference, as Lena would instruct both Matthew and Oscar to appear for Jessica at the trial.

'Excellent,' she replied. 'Two barristers instead of one. We can't lose now.'

After their client had departed, Matthew looked at Lena, shaking his head. 'If she comes over like that in front of the jury, we're dead.'

'It was certainly bizarre,' Lena answered. 'More like a scene from a Verdi opera. Perhaps that's where she picked up that attitude.'

'But surely she can't wish to be convicted and spend fifteen or twenty years in gaol.' Matthew raised his eyebrows in a quizzical gesture. 'You're the expert in assessing women, what's your opinion?'

Lena gently swung her swivel chair one way then the other, temporarily lost in thought.

'The world she inhabits,' Lena said after a few minutes, 'is such a false and pretentious place, that perhaps she can never conceive of anyone not believing her, or even blaming her. That is assuming, of course, that she is innocent and played no part in the murder.'

'Played no part?'

'Had someone else add the shellfish paste to the health drink.'

'I see,' Matthew replied with an ironic smile. 'So, despite clearly being intelligent, you think she lives in some type of fantasy world where nothing terrible could happen to her?'

'It could be. Many brilliant people in one field or another are children in the real world.'

Matthew took a few minutes to take in Lena's theory. 'In any event, it would be nice if we came up with an alternative suspect.'

Lena gave a knowing smile. 'Looks like you've got your work cut out, Matthew. Welcome to the bar.'

Chapter Nineteen

It was three weeks before Rufus Tomlinson gave his report verbally to Lena late one evening, and early the next day she called Matthew into her office. She closed the door and gave a huge sigh as she sat behind her desk.

'I've told Tomlinson that I don't want anything in writing,' Lena said, 'and not on the phone either. I've been meeting him at busy cafés at varying locations in the city where we stand less chance of being overheard or taped.'

Matthew appraised her thoughtfully. 'You sure that's necessary?'

'I've also had him get one of his experts to sweep our office for bugs, but he hasn't found anything as yet.'

'Bugs?'

She gave him a steady stare to emphasise her concern. 'It's bad news, Matthew,' she said quietly.

'What have you heard?'

Lena continued in a quiet voice, even though it was 8 am and the office was empty apart from the two solicitors.

'Tomlinson has a couple of experts who can follow almost anyone without being seen. As you know, we started with

Angelo's partner, Phillip D'Ascenzio, as he seems to be behaving strangely. After a week or so of non-stop surveillance, he was seen entering a nightclub in Kings Cross late last week.'

They both knew that the Kings Cross area was the red-light area of Sydney where both prostitution and drug dealing flourished with little or no interference by the police.

'Perhaps he was talking to one of his informants?'

Lena shook her head slowly. 'He was talking for half an hour to one of our old friends.'

Matthew caught his breath.

'Franz Mannheim,' Lena said.

'That bastard.'

'That bastard, indeed.'

Matthew stood up and paced the room for a few minutes. He felt a rising emotion of anger mixed with apprehension, and he tried to clear his head before replying.

Franz Mannheim was an extremely ruthless criminal who had framed Matthew for a violent crime as revenge for his part in the MacGregor trial all those years ago. When Matthew had avoided conviction and proved Mannheim's culpability, the tables were turned. Mannheim was convicted of conspiracy to pervert the course of justice and sentenced to gaol. But he was now free and bent on revenge once again.

'What's he doing now?' Matthew asked.

'According to Tomlinson, it's much the same as before – illegal casinos, prostitution rackets and SP bookies.'

'Starting price' or SP bookmaking was as old as the first horse racing events in Australia – completely illegal, but not frowned upon by authorities as it was considered a victimless crime. Police and politicians alike were paid to turn a blind eye to SP bookies, just as they did for casinos and prostitution premises.

The Ancient Craft

'Plus his new venture – drug importation and supply,' Lena continued.

'So he's probably behind the drug importation case that Angelo was supposed to give evidence in?'

'Possibly, but it's even more suspicious than that. Let's say that Mannheim wants to destroy Angelo because of the help he gave you in the assault case. He'd guess that Angelo would seek help from you and Oscar after being charged. What if it's all part of a scheme to gain revenge on all of us for his imprisonment?'

'You give him too much credit. He's not as clever as he thinks.'

Lena rolled her eyes.

'Even after all you've been through, you still don't understand the man. You don't comprehend that a ruthless killer of women and defenceless little children can also be highly intelligent.'

Matthew was lost in thought for a few moments before replying. 'Assuming that you're right, what should we do? It's the old story of knowing something to be true, but not being able to prove it.'

'Have a talk to Angelo. He's the detective. Perhaps he'll have a solution.'

'I'm not sure he's in any condition to think rationally. I don't want him to do something stupid.'

'As in?'

'As in take the law into his own hands. Leave it with me and I'll try a different strategy.'

'Which is?'

'When in trouble, go and ask a policeman for help, of course.'

Chapter Twenty

Inspector Mike Gordon was the head of Internal Affairs and Matthew had met him ten years ago when Franz Mannheim and Sergeant Harry Emerson were part of the conspiracy to send Matthew to gaol. Gordon had assisted in their conviction and Matthew believed that Gordon was both honest and intelligent; qualities he knew were not shared by all of the force.

Matthew had rung him to arrange a talk, but the inspector had refused to speak to him unless it was at police headquarters. Matthew duly arrived at the appointed time, but Gordon was wary of the solicitor and had adopted a formal tone.

'I'm speaking to you as the legal representative of Detective Sergeant Angelo Cattani, not on any personal basis,' Gordon said sharply. 'You will be aware that I cannot intervene in his criminal charges. It's now a matter for the courts.'

'Both you and I realise that this is a fit-up,' Matthew responded. 'It's nothing more than a tactic by the drug importers to avoid gaol. But, as you know, if a conviction is recorded against Angelo, it would destroy both he and his family.'

Gordon gave a sigh.

'You have a moral obligation to fight for your honest coppers, not to let them rot in prison whilst the drug kingpins laugh at us.'

'You could be right. I've known Angelo for nearly twenty years. Rose as well.' He paused, apparently selecting his words carefully. 'To be frank, I have the gravest doubt that Angelo is guilty of anything. I believe he's straight.'

'So, what are you going to do about it?'

Gordon held his hands up in surrender.

'My hands are tied. If we don't go by the book, then suspicion turns in our direction.'

'So you're going to leave him stranded?'

Matthew could see that his words were having an effect, as Gordon shifted uncomfortably in his seat and cleared his throat in a faintly nervous manner.

Before he could reply, Matthew raised his voice and banged his fist on the table between them.

'Are you on his side or not?'

'Only if I can help legally and by the book.'

'You mean that you'll just go through the motions but make sure to keep your hands clean at all times?'

Gordon stood up and moved towards the door. Matthew knew that the conversation was about to be terminated.

'I don't see that there's anything else I can do,' Gordon announced as he opened the office door, inclining his head for Matthew to leave.

'There's a crooked cop mixed up in the case.'

Gordon did not move for several seconds, but he then closed the door and sat back in his chair.

'You have proof of this, of course?'

'Proof in my eyes, at least.' Matthew briefly outlined what the private inquiry agent had reported to Lena about

Detective D'Ascenzio. 'But if you confront him, he'll just say that he was gaining information from an informer. We both know, however, that Mannheim is no informer.'

'Mannheim is a crook, but you're right, he's no slimy little informer.'

'What I'm asking you to do is bug D'Ascenzio's phone, both at home and at work. Legally – with the imprimatur of a search warrant. I guarantee he'll slip up sooner or later.'

Gordon raised an eyebrow in Matthew's direction. 'So that's why you've been softening me up.'

'But it has to be done, shall we say, discreetly.'

'You mean secretly?'

'What I mean is that if everyone in Internal Affairs knows about it, then D'Ascenzio will too.'

Gordon appraised him for a time before replying. 'I'll think about it.'

'Well, if nothing's done, I'll just have to wage our defence in the media. Papers and TV. We don't want this to end up in a royal commission, now do we?'

'First the carrot, now the stick.'

'No. Just doing my job to protect my client. You'd expect no less if I was acting for you on a similar charge, wouldn't you?'

'Nothing personal, but if I was charged with something like this, I'd be paying for the most expensive Queen's Counsel that money could buy.'

'But you know what they say, Inspector. Money won't buy you happiness.'

Chapter Twenty-one

Winter 1976

It never ceased to amaze Matthew how every year, on the first day of winter, a cold front would envelope the city to signal the change of season. He had caught the ferry from Manly, and a thick fog had shrouded the harbour for most of the journey. As he walked up from Circular Quay to the Central Court of Petty Sessions in Liverpool Street, his breath had frosted in the early morning air and he smiled to himself in satisfaction. Raised in the Blue Mountains at over three thousand feet above sea level, he was used to a colder climate than Sydney, and the brisk air invigorated him.

Matthew had explained to Jessica Vandermeer that the committal proceedings in her case were really a formality. The hearing was before a stipendiary magistrate, where the prosecution would call their witnesses to give evidence and they could be cross-examined by the defence. There was no obligation on the accused to give evidence or call witnesses, but occasionally it did occur if the defence felt there was a realistic chance that the court may dismiss the charges and discharge the accused. In cases where there was a chance of seriously damaging prosecution witnesses, these hearings could last days or even weeks at a time, but the danger in alerting the prosecution to any weakness in their case was its repair by the time a jury was hearing the evidence.

As there was not going to be any significant contest of the prosecution case at committal, Oscar introduced himself to their client for the first time in the court foyer. Arrangements were made to have a comprehensive conference with everyone present a few weeks later.

The task of the stipendiary magistrate, known colloquially as 'the beak', was to commit the accused for trial if he thought a reasonable jury would be likely to convict. As Matthew had anticipated, there was minimal cross-examination of the prosecution witnesses by Oscar.

When Jessica was asked to stand and the charge of murder was read to her by the magistrate, Matthew turned in his seat to watch her reaction. She showed no visible sign of distress, and no unsteadiness in her posture. When the magistrate asked her if she wished to give evidence or call any witnesses, her answer was clear and strong.

'No thank you, Your Worship.'

Jessica Vandermeer was committed for trial to the Supreme Court on one count of murder. Her bail was continued.

In the court foyer, Matthew outlined the necessity for several conferences with her and all three lawyers so that every detail could be gone over with a fine-tooth comb.

Jessica gave him one of her raised-eyebrow expressions, indicating her lack of interest. 'Is that really necessary, Matthew? I've told you everything I know. Perhaps one conference with Oscar if you insist.'

Once again, her behaviour was a mystery to Matthew, but Oscar expressed a different view after a friend in a waiting taxi had picked her up outside the court.

'Don't try to psychoanalyse our client, Matthew. No one knows what's going on in her head, and that's not something we need to worry about. When she's in front of the jury, that's the time to worry about her demeanour. Until then, she can behave as she wants.'

They were standing on the footpath outside the court, the taxi containing their client having departed in a cloud of black exhaust smoke and a screech of tyres. Both lawyers gave a fixed smile but declined to answer any of the shouted demands of the press, instead easing themselves through the throng of reporters, cameramen and curious onlookers, and walking steadily up Liverpool Street towards Hyde Park, in the direction of Oscar's chambers. About one block from the court, Matthew was not surprised to recognise a familiar figure appear from around a corner, as if by accident.

'You're always good value, Matthew,' she said as she stretched out her hand in greeting, 'but you've been a bit quiet since your two famous cases.'

Emma Saunders looked like a refugee from a local charity-clothing store, her large figure clothed in ill-fitting jeans, partially hidden by a dark woolen trench coat, which Matthew recognised as being favoured by the current crop of conforming university students. They apparently thought that it made them look like Che Guevara followers, or so Matthew had read in one of the weekend papers.

Matthew deliberately chose not to comment on her appearance, but instead greeted her warmly. He had guessed she would make an appearance when he was reported as acting for Jessica Vandermeer.

'Emma. Haven't seen you for years. Just a social call is it?'

Emma was the senior crime reporter for the *Sydney Morning Herald*, and their collaboration went back to the trials Matthew had been involved in a decade ago. She had stood by him when things were at their worst, and he had rewarded her with exclusive interviews at their conclusion. Matthew did not know exactly, but he guessed she was about his age. She was one of those very intelligent and competent women who seemed to frequently be embraced as 'one of the boys'. He valued her as not only an accomplished reporter, but also someone whose word could be trusted implicitly.

'Purely social of course,' Emma replied with a mischievous glint her eye. 'But, coincidently, I see that you are both involved in the two biggest criminal trials we've seen all year.'

'What a surprise then,' Matthew replied with a grin.

Oscar was less effusive. 'We meet again,' he said in a flat tone.

Matthew knew that Oscar was more conservative in his dealings with reporters. To be more precise, he had lectured Matthew at length on the topic, warning him to keep his distance. 'Tell the bastards nothing' was his common refrain. However, Matthew had learned from experience not only that favourable press could be invaluable at times, but also that an experienced reporter could be a wealth of information on a wide variety of topics. He had been hoping to speak privately to Emma for a while, and this meeting suited him admirably. It saved him from having to contact her at the newspaper offices. All that he now had to do was to extract Oscar from the conversation without hurting his feelings.

'By the way, Oscar,' Matthew said, 'weren't you going to speak to our witness in that case we have next week?'

'I can take a hint. See you later Emma.' He gave a half-hearted wave in her direction, and then loped off in his usual twisted gait.

'What about the old hotel on the corner over there?' Emma asked.

'Suits me. When it comes to hotels, the older the better, as far as I'm concerned.'

The ancient, sprawling hotel spoke of better days, but at least it had plenty of secluded areas where they could talk, confident of no one hearing them. Emma started with her usual schooner of beer, which she disposed of in three generous gulps.

'Ah. That hit the spot. Same again, love,' she called out in the direction of the bar whilst wiping froth from her upper lip.

'Slow down,' Matthew said. 'I've still got to go back to the office and get some work done.'

'Down to business then,' she replied with a grin. 'What's the inside info on our socialite darling?'

'Lawyer – client confidence, Emma.'

'But surely you can give me something. Surely you remember my motto – *quid pro quo*.'

'What's your *quid* for my *pro*?'

She took a long drink from her second schooner, which had just arrived, before replying with a knowing smile.

'Well, as you know, the good doctor was an expert in *post-operative care* for his patients.'

'Certainly the good-looking ones.'

'But this latest one,' Emma paused as she riffled through her large bag, then extracted a spiral notebook. She leafed through it. 'Here it is, Angelina Smythe-Baker. You've no doubt seen her on the telly. She's the *femme fatale* in the latest soapie.'

'I'm glued to it every night.'

'Now then, Matthew, sarcasm doesn't become you.'

'Sorry about that.'

'It seems,' she dropped her voice and leaned closer, breathing beer fumes into his face, 'that her sorrow might be ameliorated somewhat.'

Matthew's instincts sharpened and he subconsciously followed her example, leaning towards her until the fumes became overwhelming, causing him to retreat. She gulped another mouthful of beer, then smiled like a Cheshire cat.

'Come on, come on,' Matthew urged her. 'Out with it.'

'Word is that young Miss Angelina might soon be a wealthy young woman.'

'You mean she's won the lottery?' Matthew asked with feigned surprise.

'Sort of.'

'Where did you hear this?'

'As you know, I have a few contacts in the force.'

Matthew gave a chuckle and shook his head slowly in admiration.

'Are there any coppers that *don't* leak to you?'

She gave a smirk.

'Not many, only the stupid ones. Anyway, the cops investigating the murder were ecstatic when they rang around the insurance companies and found that one of them had a policy for our dear departed doctor.'

'I'd heard something about a possible policy. It provides a perfect motive for my client to add a little extra something to the homemade health drink.'

'Only if she's the beneficiary.'

Matthew put down his glass and leaned forward in a conspiratorial gesture. 'This sounds like very good news indeed.'

'The beneficiary was young Miss Angelina, and when the coppers found out, they were furious, so they've buried it. Told the insurance company to keep quiet.'

A smile spread over Matthew's face.

'Don't worry, we'll also keep quiet about it.'

'Don't bullshit me.'

'Until we need it, I mean. Revenge is a dish best served up in cross-examination. That's an old legal expression. There's probably a Latin maxim that covers it.'

'Forget the Latin maxims. Where's my quid or pro or whatever?'

'You know I can't give privileged information to you. But, as before, how about an exclusive interview after the trial. Win, lose or draw?'

Emma gave him a long stare. 'If that's all there is on offer, I guess it'll have to do. Now, what about Angelo's case?'

'I have no difficulty in saying that it's a fit-up,' Matthew replied sharply. 'You know of course that he's the main witness in a big drug conspiracy trial?'

'Of course.'

'It's obvious why the drugs were planted. But I need your help in poking around the drug scene. Anything that you hear might make a big difference.'

Emma held her hands up. 'I can't promise anything. The general rule is that the big fish keep their distance from the importers and the dealers. They provide the cash and the planning, but it's only the stupid ones that actually get their hands dirty.'

Matthew remained silent for a few moments before taking a drink, then replying in a somewhat dejected manner. 'It looks bad. I know Angelo's straight, but a jury can be very quick to accept the prosecution case against a copper, given half the chance. His committal is next week, and whilst I've got a few lines of investigation going on, nothing tangible has turned up.'

'Well, I'll do what I can,' Emma said as she banged down her second empty schooner glass. 'That's all for me, I've got to watch my figure you know.'

Emma gave a wave as she lumbered towards the hotel front door, leaving Matthew to digest the news regarding the insurance policy.

'Well, well,' Matthew murmured to himself as he sipped the last of his beer. 'A glimmer of hope at last.'

Chapter Twenty-two

Angelo Cattani imagined that he was on a glacier with a very gradual slope. He was struggling against the incline, his feet sinking into the powdery snow up to his knees – but each time he took his bearings, he realised that despite his furious efforts, he was always getting closer to the edge of the nearby precipice. He was not sure how tall the cliff face was, but his mind raced with terrifying images of a smashed and bloodied body at the bottom of the fall. The body was his. Then the bodies of his wife and children fell beside him, and he woke up with a violent start, usually at the same time each morning, just after 4 am.

He forced the nightmares from his mind during the day, but as night approached, he constantly thought of the terror-laden dreams that lay ahead. He knew that this all related to his upcoming trial, but keeping optimistic in the face of what appeared to be a cast-iron prosecution case was simply not possible. He appreciated the support of Matthew, Lena and Oscar, whom he knew were acting purely on loyalty, never asking one cent for their services. However, nothing had surfaced in the months following his arrest to justify any hope of an acquittal. Matthew had mentioned there was a line of enquiry regarding a detective speaking to some informant at a casino, but he refused to share any further details. Angelo had grabbed Matthew's shirt in frustration on one occasion, shouting that he deserved to know every detail of the investigation. Matthew had replied calmly that he did not want Angelo arrested and charged for the murder of a police officer, and that there were some details that he was not prepared to disclose.

When Angelo told his wife about his outburst, she had taken Matthew's side, saying her love for him was undiminished in all the years of their marriage, but that his explosive Italian temper could not always be trusted to act in their best interests.

Whilst he felt increasingly disappointed with the police hierarchy and the injustice of his current position, he had never for an instant contemplated suicide. But he had slowly slid down that incline of his dreams to a place where he admitted to himself that a conviction and a lengthy sentence of imprisonment were now almost certain.

Angelo never said as much to Rose, but over breakfast one morning after a particularly terrible dream, he told her that he wanted her to do him a favour. She gave him a concerned look.

'I want you to go to Queensland and stay with the children and your parents. I'll put the house up for sale. We won't clear much, but Matthew and Lena at least deserve something for their services. We're not a charity, and I've paid my way all my life. I'm not changing for those drug bastards, not now, not ever.'

Rose looked at him with tears welling up in her eyes. 'It's got nothing to do with paying legal fees, has it?'

Angelo did not raise his eyes from the table.

'Matthew will pull us through. You'll see. He'll never let us down.'

Angelo stirred his coffee slowly.

'I haven't shown you the prosecution statements. They were served on us last week.'

It was now Rose's turn to remain silent. He looked at her intently.

'They've got an informant. Some rat that's been given immunity to give Queen's evidence against me. He claims that I've been dealing drugs with him for twelve months.'

Rose immediately jumped up, grabbing Angelo by the shoulders and shaking him.

'We'll go and confront him. Make him tell the truth. I'll go with you.'

Angelo gave a shake of his head.

'Now you know why Matthew wouldn't give me that name. You just reacted as I did.'

She sank slowly back into her chair.

'The bastard's got a code name together with a new identity and a new life somewhere interstate. All for telling a pack of lies. It just makes you wonder if there's any hope at all in this life for us.'

They sat silently for a long time, both wanting to say some comforting words, but neither able to do so. Rose started to cry silently, her body shaking. Angelo stood up and moved to her, then knelt down and encircled her with a gentle bear hug.

'We'll be all right,' he said. 'We're not beaten yet.'

The words were hollow. Angelo had finally lost all hope.

Chapter Twenty-three

When Matthew first saw Angelo in the foyer of the Central Court of Petty Sessions for his committal proceedings, he was shocked by the detective's appearance. Angelo's eyes were sunken, his skin was a greyish tone, and his normally energetic manner had disappeared, replaced by a detached and vacant demeanour. It was as though he was on a strong tranquiliser or some illegal substance, but when questioned, Angelo shook his head.

'My only drug is reality,' Angelo had murmured, 'and it's a bastard.'

Matthew had to decide between his desire to let his friend know everything that he was doing, and his pragmatic side, which told him to say nothing.

'I've got a few lines of investigation going,' he said finally, 'and they're bound to come up with something. When that happens, I'll be the first to let you know, but until then …' his voice trailed off into silence.

'You don't have to patronise me, Matt – you're talking to a copper, remember,' Angelo replied, giving him a dark look.

Matthew gave an exasperated sigh. 'The last thing we want is for you to give up. We've got a fighting chance, but if the jury was to see you today, they'd stop listening. You bear no resemblance to an innocent man.'

'Thanks for the vote of confidence.'

'This is not some sort of game, Angelo, this is your future for God's sake.'

The detective held up his hands. 'Sorry.'

Matthew looked at him for several moments before making up his mind.

'You should know you've got friends. People who believe this is a fit-up. You're not on your own.'

'You and Lena can't give evidence. Friends are good, but they don't really help.'

'I'm not talking about Lena and myself.'

For the first time that day, Matthew saw a spark of interest in Angelo's eyes. 'Who then?'

They were standing in a crowded foyer, so Matthew nodded towards a quiet corner where they would not be overheard. He was pleased that Rose had heeded his request and stayed away from the committal.

'The PI is a friend of Lena's and he's getting some good information.'

'Juries don't believe PIs. They know they can be bought.'

'Mike Gordon.'

Angelo's head shot up and his mouth momentarily hung open. 'You're not having me on?'

'He's bent over backwards for you.'

'What do you mean?'

'He's organised a few phone taps.'

'Legally?'

'Search warrants and all. Don't ask me who. You know I won't tell you. Needless to say, not a word to anyone.'

Angelo gave him a lengthy stare. 'So you truly believe I'm in with a chance?'

'Of course.'

'Would you say that if you didn't think so?'

'Some questions are best not asked.'

Angelo gave a. smile. 'Why don't I know whether you're joking or not?'

'I'll be straight with you. We're onto a few good leads, but we've got to put the trial back for as long as we can. The longer the phone taps are on, the better the chance they'll slip up. I've got a little plan to cover that, provided I can get Oscar on side.'

'Here he comes now,' Angelo replied, nodding towards a blotchy, balding head weaving towards them through the crowd.

'I'm very worried about his health,' Matthew said with a straight face. 'In fact, he may have a turn for the worse just before the trial date. Hearts are such tricky things, don't you agree?'

The committal hearing commenced, with Oscar agreeing to keep questions to a minimum. The main interest lay with the witness who would convict Angelo unless they could discredit his evidence. Reginald Smithers was a sallow-faced runt of a man whose eyes darted nervously around the courtroom, as though he was a fox hunted by a pack of hounds.

'Any questions of this witness, Mr O'Shannessy?' enquired the magistrate.

'We've got a thousand or so questions for this particular individual,' Oscar replied, 'but we're going to save them for the trial when we will prove that his evidence is a total fiction, funded no doubt by the drug syndicate he is employed by.'

The police prosecutor jumped to his feet. 'I ask Your Worship that this scurrilous comment be struck from the record.'

'I'm not a jury, Sergeant,' the magistrate replied with a slight smile. 'Colourful outbursts might interest members of the press, but they have no impact on me. Let's just move onto something more productive.'

After Angelo had been committed for trial to Sydney District Court, Oscar and Matthew took him to their favourite hotel for an informal conference. Grabbing a quiet booth where they could speak privately, they waited for the drinks to be carried over by the young waitress before they discussed the day's hearing.

'Ever seen him before?' Matthew enquired.

'I've arrested him twice. We call him *Reggie the Rat*,' Angelo replied with a shake of his head. 'He's a typical low-life scumbag. Always arrested for minor drug dealing, and I think twelve months was the most he ever served.'

'Of course it's no coincidence that they selected someone that you've had dealings with,' Oscar said. 'I wouldn't be surprised if the weasel claims you skimmed drugs off his stash, and then later sold them back to him. The arrest records prove that you certainly would have had the opportunity.'

'There's no doubt he's a clever choice,' Matthew added. 'He wouldn't even cost the drug syndicate much for the lies. That's what he's done all his life anyway.'

'But there's a danger in relying on a fool to prove the prosecution case,' Oscar said before taking a long swig of his Guinness. 'A fool is likely to say or do something stupid, and if that happens, I'll be waiting to pounce.'

'I think it's a few years since you've pounced on anyone, Oscar,' Matthew suggested as he sipped his beer. 'Perhaps *trapped* might be the appropriate word for an elderly advocate.'

'Cheeky bugger,' Oscar replied with mock outrage, before turning to Angelo. 'He didn't know a thing when we first met. I've taught him all he knows. Not that that's much, in any event.'

Angelo gave a good-natured chuckle. 'Just so long as one of you destroys him. If the jury believes him, then I'm toast.'

'Don't worry,' Matthew replied, roughly slapping the detective on the arm. 'The only one being toasted will be a certain rat named Reggie.'

Chapter Twenty-four

Franz Mannheim paced the floor of his penthouse apartment, a cruel smile crinkling his face, something that many people had learned to fear instantly. His world consisted of numerous obedient acolytes, several beautiful mistresses, two bitter ex-wives and an assorted collection of criminal associates. Children had never been entertained in his plans – past, present or future. His own sense of self-belief was limitless, and although notions of friendship and loyalty were occasionally entertained, ruthlessness and revenge were his main pillars of faith.

Superbly fit, and of medium height, Mannheim possessed a wiry physique and sandy hair that in his mid-sixties was gradually turning to a light grey. In a previous life, he had been an SS officer – never a fanatical follower, because his own self-interest and survival was always paramount in his mind. He had been remembering those days just now, and he could not contain his smile. Apart from some glad-handing of senior officers, he had free rein to behave in any way he thought appropriate. 'Those were indeed the days' was his oft-quoted refrain.

'Can you imagine?' he had recently boasted to an associate, who was also one of the major drug importers into Australia. 'A time when you had the power of life and death over almost everyone you came across. Without any repercussions at all. No such thing as a rape or murder charge ever arose. There cannot have been many men like me in the history of the world. Hitler and Stalin of course, but leaders like Churchill and Roosevelt always had to justify their behaviour. I was as untouchable in my own small way as the great Caesars, or Attila the Hun, or Genghis Khan. We were truly the rulers of the world. Certainly the worlds we lived in.'

'Until D-day,' his associate had remarked drily, 'when things took a turn for the worse for you and your mates. In any event, that's what I do now, and no one touches me.'

Mannheim had let the insult pass without comment as he was planning a large drug importation and he needed a certain level of co-operation from the criminal beside him. He could have reminded him of several lengthy prison sentences handed down to two drug importers in the past few months as an indication that no one was untouchable, but felt that a degree of deference was important with the individual he was dealing with.

His thoughts strayed to that golden age of Hitler's supremacy, and a fleeting moment of remorse came to him as he recalled Franz Mannheim. The real Franz Mannheim that is – a true patriot who was willing to forfeit his life for the cause. He was also a rather simple-minded corporal of average height and a suitable age who bore a fleeting resemblance to the SS officer who was to take his identity. A bullet to the back of his head had resulted in very little blood staining the corporal's uniform, and a shallow grave covered with snow finished a few minutes' work that would set him up for life.

Heavy snow at that time meant that discovery of the body before spring was unlikely, as it was just one more discarded body amongst millions strewn over Europe.

He had toyed with the idea of having a coat of arms drawn up with a suitable motto proclaiming his brilliance to one and all, something like *victory to the ruthless,* but decided that any research into his adopted family background should be avoided.

He reflected that the only setback of any importance in the creation of his criminal empire had been some ten years prior when an unknown solicitor by the name of Matthew Jameson had turned his world upside down. Jameson had taken over a murder trial when the barrister had fallen ill. Mannheim had tried to influence the outcome by having Jameson attacked by two of his thugs, but the subsequent acquittal of one of his political enemies, Thomas MacGregor, had both infuriated and outraged him. In retrospect, he had underestimated Jameson, and his attempt to have him imprisoned for maiming a young woman had resulted in Mannheim himself serving a short sentence in prison. Mannheim's expensive legal team had ensured that the majority of the blame fell on the hapless co-accused, who received a lengthy gaol sentence. Jameson had been assisted in this by his law partner Lena Wasilewski, by the barrister he instructed, Oscar O'Shannessy, and – last but not least – by Angelo Cattani, without whose help Mannheim's plan would have succeeded.

Not that the gaol surroundings were overly unpleasant – they were merely restrictive to his activities. And when released on parole, he simply resumed his criminal activities involving drugs, prostitution and gambling. As his operations were aimed at the wealthy elements of society, the prostitution was always with high-class callgirls, never street hookers.

The gambling was mostly conducted in exclusive illegal casinos, with starting price bookies only a sideline. Finally, the drugs were always so-called 'soft' drugs – marijuana and cocaine. So-called because the gullible users fervently believed that they were both non-addictive and completely harmless. Mannheim never ceased to marvel at their stupidity, but was ecstatic, not only with the proceeds of the various arms of his business, but also with the power that his clients handed to him. Like most serious drug bosses, he never touched drugs himself, preferring Chivas Regal scotch and Cuban cigars for his legal drugs of choice. His power was built largely on the sexual preferences of several politicians, the gambling addictions of several bankers, and the drugs of choice for numerous lawyers and police. Not that each profession limited themselves to only one vice, but when he multiplied these examples with his entire clientele, only then was the extent of his reach into all levels of society understood. If he needed a favour, all he had to do was make a phone call, remind whoever was on the other end of the line about the intimate knowledge he had of them, and he'd secure a favourable outcome.

It was during his six-months incarceration in Long Bay Gaol that his mind had turned to a plan to extract revenge on those who had caused this misfortune. He believed that his success in life came from his two primary principles – planning and patience.

The first task was to wait until Cattani was involved with a major drug case, and then control a mid-level detective from the drug squad, who would act as directed by him. Whilst Cattani had been in the homicide squad, Mannheim simply had to be patient. Had Cattani not been transferred to the drug squad, then a phone call would have been made. As it turned out, the persuasion was not needed. It did not concern him that all of the pieces of his plan took a decade to assemble – his only concern was its ultimate success.

Although Phillip D'Ascenzio was originally in the licensing squad, it only took a quiet phone call to have him transferred into the drug squad and assigned as Angelo Cattani's partner. He had spotted D'Ascenzio at several of his casinos, always late at night, and to Mannheim's practiced eye his gambling addiction was clear. It was always the large desperate bets placed late at night after a night of losses, and the false bravado he exhibited when signing a slip for more credit. Credit that Mannheim knew he could not repay.

Mannheim had waited for over a year after the transfer before he made any further move, but this part of his plan was the most difficult. He had considered over a dozen candidates for the job before eventually selecting a low-level drug supplier who went by the nickname of *Reggie the Rat.*

Reggie had several advantages: he was single; Cattani had arrested him before, so that made his story seem more credible; and, finally, he was cheap. Reggie needed no luxury cars or overseas trips. Just a change of name, a new interstate address and a new life – all provided and paid for by the state. All it took for his complete co-operation was a car ride to a deserted warehouse where a well-known interstate hit man had explained the facts of life to a wide-eyed Reggie. The alternative to co-operation, he was told, would be a deserted shallow grave somewhere deep in the Blue Mountains.

Then all Mannheim had to do was wait until Cattani was involved in a drug bust, preferably a large importation. He didn't care how long he waited, but in fact news of a major arrest by Cattani and D'Ascenzio came only after a few months. He knew the defendants involved, and had frequently done business with them in the past, so if his plan was successful, it had the added bonus of placing them in his debt. His penultimate step was to have the drugs planted in Cattani's family car, and then arrange with a friendly senior police officer to introduce Reggie to Internal Affairs with his story.

He knew that Cattani was likely to ask for assistance from Matthew Jameson, his partner Lena Wasilewski, and the barrister Oscar O'Shannessy. If Cattani briefed other lawyers, then the destruction of his enemies would simply take longer and require an additional plan, but at least Cattani would be serving a lengthy sentence. A sentence where Mannheim could ensure that the detective would receive special treatment from more of his contacts.

The only disturbance to his plans had been the surveillance carried out by some private detectives. He was in no doubt that Jameson had put them on his trail, and that it would have to stop. Mannheim knew the perfect solution.

Chapter Twenty-five

Matthew felt that the pieces of Angelo's case had slowly been fitting together like a complex jigsaw, but he could not force those one or two final pieces into the remaining spaces. Knowing that Angelo was innocent was immaterial. Knowing that he had always been honest during his police career was irrelevant. Knowing that the parties in the drug conspiracy case had framed him was inadmissible in any trial without proof. Hard evidence was what he needed, and the date for trial must soon be upon them.

Matthew had kept in weekly contact with Inspector Mike Gordon, but after a few weeks of coded conversation between D'Ascenzio and Mannheim, all contact had abruptly stopped. Although Gordon had not spelt it out, it was obvious to Matthew that he suspected a leak in Internal Affairs. If that were so, the whole exercise in arranging and maintaining phone taps had been a complete waste of time.

Matthew never passed this information on to Angelo, but he was feeling more and more desperate as the weeks wore on. His remaining hope lay with the PI surveillance, even though

D'Ascenzio had made no further visits to any of Mannheim's establishments.

Matthew arrived at work just after 7 am, following another night's fitful sleep, when Lena surprised him by also arriving earlier than usual. She slumped into the chair opposite him in his office, her face drawn and pale. He knew that further bad news was imminent.

'Rufus Tomlinson was shot dead last night. A single large calibre bullet to the head. The police I spoke to are certain it was a professional hit.'

Matthew felt like a savage blow had crashed into his chest. He shook his head continuously but was unable to speak.

'He'd been tailing Mannheim for the past week,' Lena said quietly. 'He was led into a new housing development where no one was living yet. No other cars and no witnesses, you see.'

'That bastard.'

The two lawyers sat in silence, the destruction of the defence case now apparent.

'No trace of the killer?' Matthew finally asked.

'None. My guess is that Mannheim himself was the shooter. In a deserted housing estate, Rufus would have been an easy target for a cold-blooded assassin such as him.'

'What do you know about Tomlinson's family?'

'Married with three children.' Lena paused to compose herself. 'I spoke to his wife ... I mean his widow, on the phone.'

Matthew could see tears welling in her eyes.

'It's my fault,' Lena added quietly. 'I told him the job was easy. Just discreet surveillance, no danger involved.'

Matthew heard a muffled sobbing and he walked around his desk to embrace Lena with a fierce hug.

'I'm the one who asked you to get someone reliable that you knew personally. If anyone's to blame, it's me. But that's the end of it. I'm not risking his partner's life in the same way. I'll think of something else to help Angelo.'

'I agree,' Lena answered. 'I hate to admit that Mannheim has won, but he'd have no hesitation in killing anyone if he thought they were in his way and he could get away with it.'

'He might have won the battle, but he hasn't won the war.'

Matthew's boast had a hollow ring to it. The two lawyers remained silent, lost in their own private worlds, common only in their frustration and anger.

Chapter Twenty-six

The first conference at the barrister's chambers with Jessica Vandermeer took place a few days after Tomlinson's murder, and Matthew had not been able to shrug off the shock over his death, nor his despair over Angelo's defence. Willing himself to put these issues aside, he waited in the reception area of Oscar's chambers before greeting his client. When Oscar scurried out of his chambers, Matthew took the opportunity to re-introduce Jessica to him. Jessica Vandermeer looked to Matthew like she was out for a day's shopping at her favourite department store. Wearing an expensive looking powder-blue suit, together with matching pearl earrings and necklace, she appeared not to have a care in the world.

'This is once again a great pleasure,' Oscar said warmly as he escorted her into his chambers.

Jessica smiled and gave a brief nod, as if to placate an inferior being. Matthew observed that the chambers had not changed in the past decade, with papers strewn over Oscar's desk and the surrounding chairs, and almost everything displaying a fine sheen of dust. A musty smell of old books mingled with Oscar's crumpled clothes and wild hairstyle. Matthew knew that he had been a widower for well over a decade, and the lack of a woman's touch was clear for all to see.

Matthew removed several books and an old newspaper from one chair. He then dusted the seat with his handkerchief, and gestured for their client to sit down. He repeated the action for himself.

'I've been so looking forward to sorting out this mess with you, Oscar, if I may take the liberty of being familiar,' Jessica said.

'Of course, my dear,' Oscar replied, 'there's no formality here.'

'May I say,' she added, 'that I feel a little like a fraud asking you to appear for me.'

Oscar raised his eyes in Matthew's direction, and then raised his hands in an unspoken question.

'I mean, it's all so silly,' she replied with a smile. 'Who in their right mind would believe that I'd kill Corny? He was the love of my life. And to poison him with shrimp paste, no less. No jury would ever believe that. The case has to be thrown out in five minutes. I could appear for myself if it came to that.'

Oscar held up his hands to signify his alarm at the suggestion. 'That's not a course that I would ever recommend, my dear. As for the jury, I think you'll find that they can be extremely suspicious of beautiful women who've been dumped by their wealthy husbands for a younger version.'

'But that's just it,' she replied sharply. 'I had no inkling that he would ever leave me. Oh, I knew that he flirted with beautiful women. That's natural for a society plastic surgeon. But we're a team.' She exhaled sharply before continuing. 'We were a team, I mean.'

Matthew wondered if she had any acting experience. She seemed to be able to produce a variety of emotions to suit the occasion.

'This young woman,' Oscar said whilst riffling through his brief, 'Angelina Smythe-Baker, she says that …'

'That bitch,' Jessica said with a sour look on her face.

'Quite so,' Oscar replied with a faint smile. 'As you know, she says that you not only knew about her but that divorce had been raised between you and your late husband, and it was all settled.'

'She would say that,' Jessica replied. 'She doesn't want to go down as some bimbo that he was just playing with.'

Oscar gave a bemused frown, absent-mindedly scratching his balding head whilst searching for an appropriate response.

'Would it surprise you,' Matthew interrupted, 'if an insurance policy had surfaced?'

'What insurance policy?' she replied anxiously. 'Corny and I agreed that we were never to benefit from either's death. We were in love. Our marriage wasn't some type of business agreement.'

Oscar stared at Matthew apprehensively.

'It's all right, Oscar,' Matthew said. 'I know it's not in the brief, but our old friend Emma Saunders has been keeping her ears open. She has it on good information that the good doctor had recently insured his life for one hundred thousand dollars.'

'I don't believe it,' Jessica said. 'That's just nonsense.'

'She's never steered us wrong before, Jessica,' Matthew replied.

'That's a disaster,' Oscar said. 'It provides a perfect motive for the prosecution.'

Matthew looked closely at their client. She was maintaining her indignant face, and his impression was that either she was a much better actress than he had given her credit for, or she was telling the truth.

'It actually provides us with a glimmer of hope,' Matthew said with a smile. 'The beneficiary is Angelina Smythe-Baker. The question has always been why anyone would murder an eminent doctor in such a cold and calculating manner. There are now one hundred thousand reasons why. It provides an alternative suspect, if you like.'

'You mean ...?' Jessica asked.

'Exactly,' Oscar replied. 'A jury loves an escape clause. Something to justify an acquittal to friends and relatives. *I had to acquit her. It could have been the girlfriend. I just couldn't be sure*, you can hear them say. That's fantastic news, Matt.'

'Well it does us no harm,' Matthew replied. 'It's important, however, to clarify the issue that Oscar raised.' He glanced at Jessica but left the question unfinished.

'What do you mean?' she asked.

'It's your clear instructions,' Oscar asked, 'that you had no knowledge of Angelina Smythe-Baker, the marriage proposal or now this insurance policy?'

'Absolutely,' she replied. 'I don't tell lies. Not to anyone.'

'I'm not suggesting otherwise, my dear,' Oscar added in a soothing voice. 'I just have to know where we stand. If I put a line of questioning to prosecution witnesses, and then in the defence case a letter or something is produced in cross-examination that destroys that proposition, it can ruin our credibility in the jury's mind. If that happens, then a conviction is almost certain.'

'That won't happen, Oscar,' she replied. 'You can trust me implicitly.'

Matthew watched her closely. Perhaps she was telling the truth, he reflected. For the time being, he almost believed her.

They spent the next three hours going over every word in the prosecution brief. Jessica Vandermeer never wavered from her earlier position, which included complete ignorance of the bottle of shrimp paste, and when she eventually left Oscar's chambers, he slumped back in his chair.

'It never rains but it pours,' Oscar remarked with a shake of his head, 'or something like that. For years, I scrape along with odds and ends, cases of no great importance, and then suddenly we have two of the biggest cases of the year.'

'You don't fool me, Oscar, you love it. You can't wait for the cut and thrust of the courtroom. You look ten years younger when you're on your feet in your superman costume.'

'That's centuries of British legal tradition you're insulting my boy.'

Matthew had complained to Oscar repeatedly about the wigs and gowns worn by the barristers and judges in courtrooms. It was Matthew's opinion that barristers only dressed up in drag to intimidate witnesses and hide their own inadequacies. He had no complaint with the plain black gown worn by judges, but horsehair wigs and luridly coloured gowns simply made them look foolish in his opinion. Indeed, the preening behaviour he endured week after week in the superior courts reminded him of the children's fable, *The Emperor's New Clothes*.

'We've been over this before, Oscar. Your Irish heritage should cause you to despise British tradition. Or have you forgotten, for example, the Irish potato famine or the Black and Tan war? Both British atrocities.'

Oscar entwined his fingers around the back of his head in his lecturing pose. 'The British have civilised the far reaches of their old empire, but they destroyed many cultures in achieving that end. Somewhat like the great Roman Empire in many ways. If you bowed the head and obeyed the conquerors, you did just fine, but if you opposed them, they set out to destroy you. You could say my feelings are ambiguous regarding British tradition. In any case, back to Jessica. What do you think?'

'To be honest, Oscar, women are a mystery to me. Just think of Rebecca.'

'Ah, Rebecca. Probably the most beautiful woman I have ever met in my life. Certainly the most devious.'

Rebecca MacGregor had been a learning experience for both lawyers.

'Jessica could be telling the truth,' Matthew added. 'It is possible.'

Oscar gave one of his impish grins. 'Now, now Matt. If you're going to the bar, you always have to have trust in your client.'

'You mean professional trust but private scepticism?'

'All of my clients are innocent until the jury says otherwise,' Oscar replied.

'What about the clients with guilty pleas?'

'I would say that they have seen the error of their ways and are throwing themselves on the mercy of the court.'

Matthew gave a smile and stared pensively at the ceiling whilst Oscar methodically filled and then ignited his foul-smelling pipe. His resolution to cease smoking had not lasted very long. After a few minutes, Matthew held up his arms in a helpless gesture.

'There's just something in this case that makes me feel uneasy. Whoever poisoned the good doctor is truly an evil person.'

'You're taking the case too personally, my boy. Professional detachment, that's what you need. You'd never make a surgeon. Every slice of the scalpel has to be performed dispassionately. It's a good analogy to reflect upon.'

'Which brings us back to Angelo and that poor bastard who was murdered.'

'Yes,' Oscar replied thoughtfully, 'what was his name?'

'Rufus Tomlinson. We had a good talk after Angelo's first mention when we drove to a restaurant in Leichhardt. He was a very likeable bloke, and said that he was an expert in surveillance and that no one would ever detect him. He was so positive that I honestly forgot how dangerous and ruthless Mannheim really is.'

'Mannheim. Now there's a name to bring a chill to my bones.'

'Lena thinks he's the shooter. She's probably correct. She usually is.'

'So all surveillance is cancelled?'

'We had to. There's no second chances with Mannheim.' Matthew fell silent for a few moments before glancing back towards Oscar. 'When I think back on it, Mannheim could have had us followed from Central Court after the committal. If so, he could ID the investigator and his car, then trace the number plate with his police contacts. When you look at it in that light, he could have been onto us before surveillance even commenced.'

'Hindsight is a wonderful thing, Matt. No use looking back now. What about the phone taps? How are they going?'

'Another dead end, I'm afraid. Mike Gordon thinks that there's a leak in Internal Affairs.'

'There are leaks everywhere, it seems. Mannheim's behind the scene, pulling the strings, and we seem to be the puppets.' Oscar puffed vigorously on his pipe. 'Where do we go from here?'

'You tell me, Oscar. I just don't know.'

The mention of Jessica Vandermeer's case in the Supreme Court a few weeks later took only a few minutes. A duty judge confirmed the service of all the prosecution statements and a trial date was agreed upon. Matthew had appeared by himself and, with the consent of the prosecution, their client had been excused from attending. This did not stop a small group of reporters from shouting questions at him as he left the building and walked back down Macquarie Street towards Circular Quay to catch a ferry across the harbour. Matthew raised his eyebrows and gave a wide smile as he forced his way through the throng. Various insults as to his parentage floated back to him as he departed with a wave of his hand.

Chapter Twenty-seven

Lena Wasilewski raised one finger off her glass and the bartender moved effortlessly over to her. He silently filled the shot glass with another single malt scotch. After most working days, she stopped off at the same hotel, sat on the same bar stool, and drank two shots, varying the brand each day on a mental roster that she had perfected over many years. She would then drive to her beachside flat in the Eastern Suburbs where she had instant frozen meals waiting for her. Two drinks would keep her reasonably sober, as the last thing she could afford was being arrested for driving under the influence.

Only a Friday night pizza with Matthew and a shared bottle of red wine broke the sequence. Perhaps it was her personality that demanded an established order in her life, but deep down she recognised that these behavioural patterns were really an escape from her past. Each day had a plan so that there were no gaps during which her mind could wander. When the dark times occurred, she returned to pre-war Germany, where thoughts of her beautiful parents, grandparents, aunts and uncles, cousins and friends flooded over her. All gone now. All destroyed by a fanatical regime that perceived them as sub-human, not worthy of life. She asked herself the same questions over and over – how could this have ever occurred? How could an otherwise industrious and technically advanced people with an appreciation and love for the fine arts descend into depraved beasts of prey? Beasts that rounded up entire families, including helpless little children, then systematically destroyed them in their millions.

Of course, she realised that many ordinary German people, as well as vast numbers of other complicit nationalities, now feigned complete ignorance of these atrocities. The mantra was always the same – *It was all carried out by a handful of SS fanatics. Not us. We never knew.* How millions of Jewish people could have been rounded up all over Europe, transported thousands of miles to concentration camps and then gassed and incinerated by just a few SS zealots was still beyond belief to any sensible person, including Lena.

Lena's only way of coping was to organise her days so that she would be busy and not lapse into recollections of a past for which there were no credible answers or solutions. What she called her 'healing rituals'. However, those regimented days had several major drawbacks, not the least her failed attempts to find a lifelong partner. She had recognised many years ago that her occasional lovers, who had never faced any tragedy of their own, lacked empathy for her occasional black moods. They could never understand how she could be bright and cheerful one minute, then quiet and withdrawn the next. The conundrum was that, when she became involved with someone with a similar background, she often found that they were also reliving past terrors, drinking too heavily or living a life full of bitterness in the past.

Thus it was that in her mid-forties she was still single and childless, the latter being her greatest disappointment. Matthew had been her closest friend over the past ten years, and she had grown to love him in a platonic, younger-brother type of relationship. His droll sense of humour, honesty and complete loyalty always endeared him to her, but as she had recently admitted to him, she knew they were both ready for a change. He had become increasingly irritated with the minutiae of a suburban legal practice, and she could hear his lack of patience with some of the older or less intelligent clients that needed their lawyer to say the same thing five times before it registered with them.

She believed that Matthew was now ready for the bar, where barristers lived on their nerves, boosted by the deadline of trial dates and the adrenaline jolts of courtroom activity. She also recognised that she too was ready for a change, back to city life where the sharpest minds and biggest egos clashed daily in the big city law firms. Who knows, she reflected, perhaps she would meet someone to share her life with. After all, she always felt that her most valuable asset was her optimism. Provided she could keep busy. Provided the nightmares did not take over.

Chapter Twenty-eight

The District Court mention to list Angelo's trial date arrived soon after his committal had finished. Matthew knew that such a high-profile case alleging police corruption would encourage the prosecution to fast track the proceedings. There was also the pending drug trial where Angelo was still the main prosecution witness. The drug conspiracy trial could not commence until Angelo's charges had been finalised.

The usual melee of newspaper and television reporters surrounded Oscar, Matthew and Angelo as they tried to force their way into the foyer of the court. It was an overcast day with intermittent showers, a climate that Matthew felt was appropriate to their sombre mood.

Matthew pushed open the large wooden courtroom door and held it open for Oscar and Angelo to enter. As they approached the bar table, a figure dressed in barrister's robes and the usual legal wig swung around to glance at them. She gave a slight smile and a nod, then turned back to say something to her instructing solicitor. Matthew felt a wave of nostalgia as he took his seat beside Oscar at the bar table.

'Long time, no see,' Matthew murmured to her.

'Absence makes the heart grow fonder,' she replied.

The Crown prosecutor was Fenella Montgomery, his lover of a decade ago, and the addiction to whom he was trying to overcome.

Their case was the first called by the judge, and Oscar slowly rose to his feet to announce his appearance. Matthew had been lost in thought, taking in the surroundings, but mostly concentrating on the figure in the centre of the bench. He observed that the judge, Hugh Latimer, was in his mid-fifties, with slightly greying hair and a slim build. He displayed a thin smile and penetrating blue eyes. Matthew also knew that he took great pride in his proficiency as a marathon runner and in his history as an all-round sportsman in his earlier years. Not so flattering was his reputation as a ladies' man, to the extent that the Chief Justice had been forced to hire a male associate after a series of unfortunate resignations by his young female associates. Matthew cared little about this, but was more concerned with his background as one of the top defence barristers whilst he was at the bar. That was not in itself a problem, but, in Latimer's case, he seemed unable to shelve his role as an advocate, and was widely regarded as an interventionist.

Judges and magistrates were appointed by the Attorney-General on the recommendation of the bar council which represented barristers, the law society which covered solicitors. Senior judges also presented a multitude of varying opinions. The hidden group that made representations consisted of politicians, together with their aides and associates, who, for a variety of reasons, wanted their own nominations appointed.

In the past Matthew had had several friendly arguments with Oscar over the appointments to all three tiers of the state judiciary. He had argued that the only fair system of appointment was by an independent panel of experts, including heads of jurisdiction, members of the bar council and the law society, as well as members of the community. He believed that no politician should play any part in the selection process.

Oscar had been more traditional.

'The system has worked for hundreds of years. Why change it now?' he had said.

'What about purely political appointments? Not only to friends but perhaps someone who knows a secret about, say, the Premier? Or perhaps to someone that needs to be moved out of the way – out of politics that is?' Matthew had responded.

'I'm sure that would never happen, Matt.'

'Of course not. Just like the wrong person would never be appointed because he had the same surname as the intended recipient.'

'My lips are sealed,' Oscar replied with a broad smile.

'I rest my case,' Matthew had remarked, knowing that he had won the argument.

In his opinion, judges fell into a number of categories – there were the Easter Island judges, who sat silently like statues most of the time, rarely betraying any emotion; the Entertainers, who revelled in uttering supposedly witty ripostes to the captive lawyers at the bar table; and the Interventionists, who generally consisted of excellent, sometimes brilliant, trial lawyers who couldn't resist displaying their talents by frequently cross-examining witnesses and completely forgetting the principal of judicial impartiality.

There were many other categories – but the one most prized by both prosecution and defence was a mixture of the prior three, in moderation. A wry comment or a quiet admonition to the bar table was often all that was required.

Unfortunately, it was often said that Judge Latimer could never forget that he was once a barrister, who used his skills to try and manipulate the jury at his will. This landed him in the 'Interventionist' category – the most dangerous of all. Facial gestures of disbelief or heated questioning of a witness left no doubt in the jury's minds where the judge felt the truth lay. Not that every jury followed the judge's lead, and sometimes they actually rebelled against it. However, the intent by the judge was always there.

Matthew's attention was brought back to the present by Oscar's voice.

'O'Shannessy, appearing for Angelo Cattani, instructed by Wasilewski and Jameson solicitors, Your Honour,' Oscar announced in a croaky voice, swaying slightly on his feet.

'Are you feeling ill, Mr O'Shannessy?' the judge asked immediately.

'I'm fine, Your Honour,' Oscar replied.

'Montgomery, Your Honour. I appear for the Crown. Perhaps Mr O'Shannessy may need to have the case assigned to more healthy counsel.'

Although Matthew was a fierce opponent of barristers wearing wigs and gowns, he had to admit that Fenella looked quite stunning in her legal garb.

'My client,' Oscar replied in a voice that betrayed a shortage of breath, 'is adamant that both my instructing solicitor and myself represent him. It is true that my heart problems have re-occurred, but I am prepared to put my obligations before my health.'

The judge peered over his half-frame glasses.

'So you're ready to proceed next week, Mr O'Shannessy?' Latimer enquired.

'As soon as my cardiologist gives me the all clear, I'll be ready, Your Honour.'

Latimer gave a knowing smile. He felt that this 'illness' was a ruse to obtain a delay of the case, but he had no way to force the issue. 'And when might that be?'

'I'll advise the court each week or each month until I receive the all clear, Your Honour.'

Latimer glanced at the prosecutor with an enquiring look.

'The Crown is prepared to be reasonable, Your Honour,' the prosecutor replied. 'Within limits, of course.'

The judge pushed his wig to one side and scratched his scalp, grimacing briefly.

'Very well. I'll stand the matter over for two months, and then it will be from week to week. But you should be advised, Mr O'Shannessy, that we cannot delay indefinitely. Justice delayed is justice denied, you know.'

'Your Honour is too kind,' Oscar replied.

'Probably,' Latimer replied before fixing the next return date, continuing the same bail as before, and then excusing the parties.

After exiting the courtroom, Matthew, Oscar and Angelo were standing in a huddle in the foyer speaking quietly, when Fenella Montgomery approached them and tapped Matthew on the shoulder.

'My word, you seem to have improved, Oscar. You must be on the mend.' She handed Matthew a folded note, then added, 'Make sure you get well soon.'

Oscar held up his hands in a gesture of innocence. Angelo maintained a straight face. Everyone present knew that Oscar's 'illness' was merely a legal tactic.

As she walked off, Matthew gave his two companions a shrug of his shoulders, and then read the note.

See you at The Wig and Gown in ten minutes, it read.

'A royal command from the Crown,' Matthew said with a grin. 'Can't be all bad. She didn't threaten to destroy me this time.'

Chapter Twenty-nine

The Wig and Gown was a well-known legal haunt where Matthew had spent many pleasant hours some years ago, but on this occasion, he was both wary of the invitation and pessimistic of the outcome. The last time he had spoken to Fenella was a decade ago, when she had threatened him during a blazing argument, following Matthew's arrest after the MacGregor trial. She had severed all contact with him, believing a conviction was certain, until he sensationally proved his innocence at court. When he rejected her apology, she had transformed into the aggrieved party and had promised retaliation. Matthew now rarely ventured into the city whereas Fenella worked there exclusively and their paths had not crossed since.

When Matthew entered the café, Fenella was sitting at a window table, sipping a coffee. She waved him over, and then watched closely as he sat down opposite her.

'You're looking well,' she said.

'Thanks.' He hesitated before continuing. 'When I saw you today in your fancy dress, my heart missed a beat.'

She gave her usual questioning smile as Matthew ordered a pot of black tea from the waitress.

'Your star's on the rise. Crown prosecutor already. How's Horrie by the way?'

Horace Birmingham was an influential lawyer who had acted for Franz Mannheim when the property developer's perjury trial came to court. Shortly after Matthew had broken up with Fenella, Birmingham and Fenella were married, despite a thirty-year disparity in their ages. Soon after, Birmingham was appointed a Supreme Court judge.

'Horrie's just fine,' she replied, but in a flat, detached manner.

'Married life a little dull?'

'You're quick as ever.'

'Just an innocent observation.'

'There's nothing innocent about you, Matt. Still single by the way?'

'Alas.'

'No one appreciates your true worth, then?'

'Perhaps they do. Perhaps that's the trouble.'

She reached over and stroked the back of his hand with one finger. 'But you know that I've always appreciated your worth. Your physical worth in particular.'

Matthew pulled back his hand and raised both arms in surrender.

'You always could get under my skin, Ella. But you're also married.'

'So?'

'You forget I'm an old-fashioned Catholic and a country boy at heart.'

'That's a tired old line, Matt. You're a big city lawyer now and we're both consenting adults.' She gave Matthew an unsettling smile. 'How about we both do some consenting?'

'Why do I get this image of Horrie bursting in with a loaded shotgun?'

Fenella stirred her coffee absently, and then glanced around to make sure no one was within hearing range.

'I don't think that's likely. You could say we have an understanding. Horrie felt that his chances of judicial appointment would be improved immeasurably if he was seen to be a happily married man.'

Matthew screwed up his face. 'Seen to be?'

'His affections lie in other directions.'

'Then why didn't he marry her instead?'

Fenella shook her head, her face displaying a wry amusement. 'You're such an innocent, really Matthew.'

'Oh.'

'Oh, indeed.' Fenella gave him another of her familiar smiles – half-serious, half-mocking. 'So, you see, I'm quite free – Just think about it.'

The waiter arrived with Matthew's order, and he grabbed the opportunity to busy himself with the ritual of pouring the boiling tea into his cup from the teapot, blowing on the surface with a soft breath, then sipping carefully as he cradled the cup in both hands.

'Black with no sugar, just like always,' she said. 'You don't change, do you?'

'In some respects, I suppose I don't.'

Fenella took a sip of her coffee, all done with a practiced grace. 'Oscar's little pantomime didn't fool anyone, you know. Least of all Hugh,' she said, referring to the judge.

'Hugh. Would that be another consenting adult?'

'No comment. He is very fit though. Don't you think so?'

'To be honest, I don't think of him in those terms at all. And Oscar will have as many specialists' reports as Latimer may desire.'

'A sympathetic heart specialist comes in handy, doesn't he? An old university mate perhaps?'

'No comment.'

Fenella gazed at the crowd passing by outside the window. 'Things don't look too good for Angelo,' she said, changing the topic. 'The PI shot dead. Phone taps gone cold.'

'How the hell did you know about the phone taps?' Matthew replied in a voice louder than he had intended. Several other patrons glanced in their direction.

She gave a brief smile. 'Whispers. Rumours. Gossip.'

'Not from more consenting adults?'

'Let's just say that the Clerk of the Peace works closely with the investigating police. We share information for our mutual benefit.'

The Clerk of the Peace was the department whose solicitors instructed Crown prosecutors in criminal trials.

'So there *is* a bloody leak in Internal Affairs?'

'Where you have a bunch of coppers, you always get a leak of some sort.'

'Or a crooked cop who fits up a poor bastard like Angelo?'

'Not impossible. I won't be prosecuting at his trial, of course. I'm too junior, but I'll be assisting a QC, probably.'

Queen's Counsel was an appointment given supposedly to the cream of the bar, which entitled them to wear slightly different wigs and gowns, and charge treble the going rate of a top barrister.

'You know it's a fit-up?' Matthew asked.

'Once again, it's not impossible. However, it's your job to defend him. Ours is to present the facts and leave it to the jury.'

'Knowing that a conviction will ruin Angelo's life, and result in the drug kingpins getting off scot-free?' Matthew replied sharply.

'I don't make the rules. I just promise to be fair. If we discover anything of substance, we'll disclose it to the defence. I can't do more than that.'

Matthew sat in silence, trying to collect his thoughts before replying, when two voices drifted over from a nearby table.

'You can tell just by looking at her that she did it,' came the voice of a middle-aged woman.

'It's all sex and money. They're like rabbits. They can't get enough of it,' said the younger woman beside her.

'What – the sex or the money?'

'Both.'

Matthew and Fenella raised their eyebrows at one another across the table. Matthew glanced over and saw a newspaper clutched in the older woman's hand. It was obvious who they were talking about. He turned back to Fenella.

'Do you have anything to do with the doctor's wife?'

'His widow, you mean. No, not my baby. One big case at a time.'

'Angelo's case is a big one?'

'They don't come much bigger.' Fenella gazed out of the window again, seemingly lost in thought for a time before continuing. 'I like Angelo. But people can surprise you, Matt. Sometimes the last person you'd suspect will confess to doing something stupid. Or something criminal.'

'Not Angelo.'

'In this case, I hope you're right.'

'I know I am.'

Matthew was relieved when they parted on amicable terms. It was a strange thing, he reflected, that good relations between the prosecution and the defence could result in some small crumb of knowledge falling his way. Even a slight leeway given by the prosecutor in the questioning of various witnesses could be critical to the defence. Conversely, if the feelings between the two camps were acrimonious, no small concessions would flow in his direction. It was upon such insignificant matters that the jury sometimes finally decided criminal trials.

Chapter Thirty

Jessica Vandermeer's trial for the murder of her husband commenced in the same Supreme Court building where the earlier mention had taken place, some six weeks ago. It was austere and grey, with little architectural merit to commend it. Obviously, functionality had been foremost in the government architect's mind. *Bleak House* was the name Matthew appropriated from Dickens when he entered the tall, box-like concrete structure.

Despite his best intentions, Matthew had decided to delay his admission to the bar until after the trial. His overwhelming obsession had been Angelo's trial, and he realised that he could not do justice to Jessica Vandermeer's case as a barrister whilst in that frame of mind. He had therefore been dressed in his usual charcoal pinstriped suit, with white shirt and sombre dark grey tie when he arrived at court.

Whilst Oscar was looking his disheveled best in an old rumpled suit, Matthew knew it would not be long before he transformed himself into what would pass for a competent barrister, resplendent in his old black robe and discoloured wig. The faded colour of the wig signaled Oscar's decades of experience in the courtroom, and therefore commanded some respect.

The usual media circus and public obsession with a celebrity trial resulted in a large crowd, both on the footpath and inside the cavernous foyer. Matthew waited at the kerb for their client, and once the hire-car lurched to a halt, Jessica Vandermeer alighted and was greeted by a combination of camera flashes and television cameras, together with a barrage of shouted questions from reporters. Matthew had advised her to smile briefly but not to answer any questions, and she had taken the sensible course of following his directions.

Oscar and Lena were waiting outside the courtroom, having secured an interview room earlier that morning. As Jessica and Matthew stepped out of the lift, Oscar swept towards them, dressed in his barrister's robe, with one hand grasping his wig.

'Jessica, my dear, how are you holding up?' Oscar greeted her warmly.

'Holding on, Oscar, holding on,' she replied in a subdued voice.

They moved into the small interview room, where Oscar announced that by one of those strange quirks of fate, the judge was the same person who had presided at the MacGregor trial. Neither of them had altered their opinion of Anthony Benoit, QC, whom they regarded as scrupulously impartial and balanced, which were crucial traits, particularly when summing up to the jury. However, if a guilty verdict was announced by the foreman of the jury, Benoit was not regarded as a *dove* – that is, excessively lenient – and he usually gave a reasonably firm sentence. Whether that categorised him as a *hawk*, Oscar commented, was purely a matter of individual opinion.

'So I gather it's rather important to avoid being sentenced by him,' Jessica replied after Oscar had given her a thumbnail sketch of the judge's behavioural patterns.

'An acquittal would be preferable,' Matthew replied.

'An acquittal is essential,' Lena added with more emphasis.

'Then an acquittal it is,' Oscar announced. 'Into battle then. You know, on the first day of a big trial, I sometimes feel like a Christian being led into the Colosseum in Roman times; yet, by the end of the trial, I feel more like a victorious gladiator.'

'I think the Christians were worried more about the lions,' Lena said. 'The gladiators just slaughtered each other.'

'Let's hope that no one gets slaughtered then,' Matthew added.

Oscar glared at Matthew and took their client by the arm, leading her from the interview room towards the courtroom door. 'Ignore him, my dear; he's just a callow youth. Barristers only put up with instructing solicitors because they provide the briefs and collect the fees. In truth, they're the bane of our existence.'

'Don't worry, Oscar,' Jessica replied, giving Matthew a cool glance. 'We all have our crosses to bear.'

'I think my attempt to lighten the mood may have fallen flat,' Matthew said quietly to Lena as they trailed behind Oscar and their client.

'I think you could assume that,' Lena replied. 'You'd never be mistaken for a diplomat.'

Judge Benoit strode into the courtroom at precisely 10 am, and the barristers announced their appearance. The judge fixed Oscar with an appraising glance.

'I trust you've recovered from the health problems that one of my colleagues advised me is delaying his trial?' Benoit asked pointedly.

'Perfectly fit and well, Your Honour,' Oscar replied. It was obvious to him that Benoit knew his heart problem was a ruse, and Oscar felt a twinge of embarrassment over the deception.

'Excellent, I'll let Judge Latimer know the good news,' Benoit said. 'You're ready to proceed, Mr Del Assandro?'

'Absolutely, Your Honour,' the prosecutor replied, before leaning over towards Oscar.

'Ready to plead guilty are we?' he asked *sotto voce*.

'When hell freezes over,' Oscar replied in a similar vein.

The Crown prosecutor, Antonio Del Assandro, QC, was a bulky individual, whose ample girth and red, blotchy face indicated his love of the finer things of life. Tony, as he preferred his colleagues to call him, was both well liked and regarded as fair and reasonable. 'Admirable traits in a prosecutor,' Oscar had commented to Matthew, and their friendly banter at the bar table reinforced that opinion.

Matthew had explained to Jessica Vandermeer that swearing in the jury was a type of legal Russian roulette, as there was a prohibition against any enquiries as to the background or personal opinions of the prospective jurors. The Jury Act permitted unlimited challenges for cause if, for example, the accused knew the person called by the judge's associate. Challenges without cause, also known as 'peremptory challenges', were limited to twenty in a murder trial.

A good deal of discussion had occurred between Oscar, Matthew and Jessica as to the type of juror they would prefer, but – as Oscar was fond of repeating – jury selection was an art, not a science. In broad terms, he had suggested that both men and women of middle age and with some dress sense might be prudent. In Oscar's opinion, younger jurors may have little sympathy for a high-profile socialite, whereas older jurors, perhaps from a more austere background, may well disapprove of Jessica's lavish lifestyle.

'Why dress sense?' Jessica had enquired.

'It indicates a reasonable level of income, and perhaps a similar level of intelligence,' Oscar had replied. 'What we are after are well-educated jurors with an independent streak. Not likely to be swayed by the opinion of other jurors or a domineering foreman, and with a healthy distrust of authority.'

'Sounds sensible to me,' Jessica had added. Her comment ended the discussion.

Empanelment of the jury ensued with those parameters in place, and there were only six challenges that resulted in five somewhat scruffy looking young men in their early twenties and one severe-looking mid-sixties woman being excused.

With the jury in place and the lawyers poised to spring into action, the Crown prosecutor rose to give his opening address.

Chapter Thirty-one

The Crown prosecutor gave a low-key and succinct opening address to the jury. Matthew formed the opinion that obviously Del Assandro felt he should not overplay his hand in front of the jury, as the prosecution case was already overwhelming without any theatrics on his part. The prosecutor concluded by highlighting the main elements of the prosecution case, and then abruptly sat down. There were no surprises, and Matthew wrote on his foolscap legal notepad the issues the defence had to address.

The first and most important issue was the doctor's affair with Angelina Smythe-Baker, which the prosecutor claimed provided the real motive for the murder. The affair had caused Jessica Vandermeer to act out of revenge because a divorce was imminent, and her lavish lifestyle was at an end. There would be no generous property settlement as the pair lived an empty, plastic lifestyle.

Matthew smiled to himself when the prosecutor made the comment which he had predicted: 'the plastic surgeon with the plastic lifestyle'.

The prosecutor then turned to the proposed evidence of Professor Max Schultz, and said that the Crown would prove that the substance that triggered his death was the shellfish protein outlined in the professor's report. It had been discovered after extensive testing of the remains of the health drink the deceased had consumed that lunchtime, and was also present in the deceased's organs. With the deceased's severe shellfish allergy, the prosecutor said that the jury would be in no doubt that the consumption of the health drink and the resultant anaphylactic shock had caused his death.

Del Assandro then gave a theatrical pause whilst he pretended to search through his brief for further information. After fixing the members of the jury with a cold smile, he plucked one page from the bundle and held it high in the air, like a magician plucking a card out of the pack. In solemn terms, he advised the jury that the police officer in charge of the investigation, Detective Sergeant Paul Brooks, had executed a search warrant at the premises of the accused and had located a small bottle hidden in the garage wrapped in some old rags. That bottle, labelled *Shrimp Paste,* was the source of the shellfish protein found by Professor Schultz. A significant amount of the paste was missing from the bottle. A further search of the accused's kitchen had revealed the various ingredients that the deceased had used to make his daily health drink. Motive, means and opportunity were in place, Del Assandro concluded, and at the finish of the prosecution case, there would be no doubt in the jury's mind as to the guilt of the accused.

There was one piece of evidence that Matthew was hoping would cause the prosecution some difficulty – the insurance policy that Emma Saunders had uncovered for them. Whether that would be enough to plant the seed of doubt in the jurors' minds was problematic. The insurance policy and their client's denial of guilt was all they had, and Matthew could only hope that it would be sufficient.

Following the opening address by the Crown, Oscar had a right of reply, but it was his firm belief that it was better for the jury to swing slowly towards the defence case. Then his closing address would raise a reasonable doubt ... 'Keeping our powder dry' was his mantra.

The judge announced an early adjournment for lunch just before twelve noon, with a direction for the court to resume at one. The first witness would be the officer in charge of the police investigation.

Detective Sergeant Paul Brooks gave his evidence in a measured and calm manner, pausing at various moments to glance at the jury in order to reinforce a particular point. After he had finished a recitation of the material from his statement, Del Assandro sought to amplify some of the evidence.

'Whatever caused you to take a sample of the health drink to the university for special testing after your own police analysts found nothing amiss?' the prosecutor asked.

'Well, we might call that intuition, or perhaps old-fashioned experience,' Brooks replied with a smile. 'Most police would have taken it no further, but I pride myself on being diligent – as I have no doubt that you are – not just some paper shuffler looking for an easy result.'

'Very commendable, Sergeant, and let me say how that dogged investigation reflects admirably on you.'

Oscar jumped to his feet. 'This mutual admiration society is a little sickening, Your Honour. Perhaps my friend might reserve his praise until I have concluded my cross-examination. I think something may indeed reflect on this witness, but I doubt it will be admirable.'

The judge gave a fleeting grin. 'I think we'll let the members of the jury decide where to place their admiration, gentlemen. Let's just get on with the evidence in chief and then the cross-examination.'

Del Assandro affected an injured look at Oscar before turning back to Brooks. 'Whatever made you search in the garage of the accused's home?'

'As before, sir, just diligent police work.'

'No more than we would expect from you, Sergeant.'

Oscar raised his eyebrows incredulously in the direction of the jury, but made no objection this time.

'I think that, once the report from Professor Schultz was received,' the prosecutor continued, 'you requested that he conduct further tests to ascertain if that chemical substance was present in the deceased's organs. Is that correct, Sergeant?'

'That is so. I don't blame anyone for missing that evidence in the first analysis, but this case is quite unusual, as shellfish is not normally regarded as a substance which could result in death,' Brooks replied with a condescending glance towards the jury.

Oscar once again rose to his feet. 'I didn't realise that, apart from the sergeant's other talents, he is an expert forensic pathologist, Your Honour.'

Del Assandro raised his hands. 'I do not rely on the latter part of that answer, Your Honour. I will of course be calling Professor Schultz in relation to this issue. Nothing further from this witness.'

Judge Benoit gave the jury a direction to ignore the sergeant's opinion evidence, and Oscar rose to commence his cross-examination.

'I only have a few matters that I wish to clarify, Sergeant,' Oscar said. 'I take it that you have been both honest in your evidence and scrupulous in your obligation to present all of the facts to the court?'

'Of course. All of the relevant facts, that is,' Brooks replied.

'But who decides what is relevant?'

'I suppose that I do.'

'You don't seek the opinion of my friend at the bar table?' Oscar said, turning his head towards the prosecutor.

'I suppose that I might if I was in any doubt over an issue.'

Oscar paused momentarily as he stared at the ceiling, formulating the next question. He then returned his gaze to the sergeant.

'If something became known to you that provided a strong motive for murdering the deceased, you would immediately disclose this to my friend here, and also to the defence?'

'Absolutely.'

'Perhaps we have a different understanding of the word *motive*. Could that be the reason for this lapse?'

'What lapse?' The detective's eyes flicked between the prosecutor, the judge and finally Oscar.

He reminded Matthew of a small animal sensing imminent danger, but is not sure from which direction it will come.

'What is your knowledge of an insurance policy taken out over the life of the deceased?' Oscar continued.

Brooks stiffened his back as he sat up straight in his chair. He gave a small cough to clear his throat, but his words still came out in a slightly higher register. 'It was not relevant.'

Oscar gave his best impression of amazement as he glanced towards the jury, eyes opened wide and mouth ajar. 'Not relevant?'

'That's right.'

'Detective Brooks,' Oscar said in a deliberately slow manner, as if to explain a difficult subject to a child, 'do you think it's about time to tell the jury all about it?'

Judge Benoit cut in before the detective could answer. 'Mr Del Assandro, are you aware of an insurance policy that is relevant to these proceedings?'

'I know nothing about it at all, Your Honour,' the prosecutor said, holding his hands open in a gesture of innocence.

The judge stared at the witness with a pinched expression on his face. 'Do you have any knowledge of an insurance policy on the deceased's life, Sergeant? Yes or no?'

'Yes, Your Honour,' Brooks replied nervously.

'Perhaps then, Sergeant,' Benoit added coldly, 'you might inform us, belatedly though it may be, of the details of this policy?'

'Well – we believe – I mean, I believe that there is a serious doubt that the deceased ever signed the insurance proposal, and that is why I have not mentioned it.'

'Go on,' Benoit said.

'And the insurance company is refusing to pay on the policy.'

Oscar shot to his feet. 'I have no doubt that the good sergeant is a little embarrassed about a critical piece of evidence that he apparently has kept a secret from my friend and also the defence, Your Honour, but perhaps he could be directed to just give the court the facts, not supposition or rumour.'

'That would be a sensible course of action, Sergeant,' Benoit added.

'Yes, Your Honour. There is an insurance policy that was taken out on the deceased's life for one hundred thousand dollars, but as I have said, there are grave doubts about who signed the proposal,' Brooks replied, still trying to salvage the situation.

'Perhaps you might be so good as to tell us,' Oscar said, 'who is the beneficiary?'

Brooks stared at the edge of the bar table, avoiding eye contact with anyone.

'Angelina Smythe-Baker.'

A collective gasp came from the public gallery, and the jury, as one, stopped taking notes and stared intently at the witness.

Oscar let the answer hang in the air for several moments before continuing.

'Now, remind me, Sergeant, why was the insurance policy not relevant to this case?'

'As well as the doubt over who signed the proposal, Ms Smythe-Baker said she knew nothing about the policy when I raised it with her.'

'Very touching, Sergeant. Very considerate of you towards the beneficiary of the policy. And it's just a coincidence that it would not have assisted the prosecution case, is it?'

'I don't know what you mean.'

'Well then, I'll put it in simple terms for you,' Oscar said as he swiveled to face the jury. 'It provides a motive for Angelina Smythe-Baker to murder her lover. Is that not so?'

'I don't believe it.'

'But it's not a question of what you believe, Sergeant. That's for the jury to decide, not you. Your duty is to present all of the facts, not an edited version of them.'

Brooks remained silent and continued to stare at the edge of the bar table.

After a few moments, Oscar picked up the sergeant's written statement. 'You agree that in your statement when you say that you discovered this bottle in my client's attic, that she denied any knowledge of it?'

'That's what she said.'

'None of her fingerprints were found on the bottle?'

'No fingerprints at all were found on it.'

'So you don't know who put it there?'

'It was ...' Brooks began to answer, then checked himself. 'No, I suppose not.'

'Did you put it there, by any chance?'

Del Assandro immediately rose to his feet. 'I object in the strongest terms, Your Honour, to this outrageous suggestion.'

'It's an innocent question, Your Honour. Surely my friend wants to know the answer as much as I do?'

'Objection overruled,' Benoit announced sharply.

It was obvious to Matthew that the judge was annoyed about the insurance policy, and his face made a fleeting grimace towards the witness box.

'Of course not,' Brooks replied.

Oscar gave a brief smile as he resumed his seat. He leaned over towards Matthew and Lena and said in a voice that he knew would carry to Del Assandro, 'Nice to see the judge isn't happy with the witness. That's always half the battle.'

Del Assandro ignored the comment, but asked no questions of the detective in re-examination. As Brooks passed him at the bar table, the prosecutor turned his head away. It was obvious to Matthew that Del Assandro shared the judge's displeasure over the insurance policy. The first tiny crack had appeared in the prosecution case, and for the first time Matthew believed they had a fighting chance.

Chapter Thirty-two

Purely formal witnesses, totally boring to the members of the jury but essential for the prosecution to prove the necessary elements of the charge, took up the remainder of the day. They dealt mostly with corroboration of Detective Sergeant Brooks in relation to execution of the search warrant and the discovery of the bottle in the accused's garage.

The court finally adjourned shortly after 4 pm, and Oscar, Matthew, Lena and their client returned to the interview room.

'Looks like Matthew's information about the insurance policy has got the attention of the jury,' Oscar said, throwing his wig onto the small table before collapsing into a nearby chair.

'We'll have to shout Emma dinner at some posh restaurant,' Matthew replied. 'If we're successful, that is.'

'At least she prefers beer to French champagne,' Oscar said with a chuckle. 'Now, back to business. Tomorrow we hear from Angelina Smythe-Baker, and I believe it's going to be a very interesting day.'

'So you think it's possible she is the murderer?' Jessica Vandermeer asked quietly.

'A hundred thousand dollars is very tempting, my dear,' Oscar replied. 'Poison has been administered for a lot less to many unfortunate victims.'

'Whilst Oscar is correct as usual,' Matthew said, 'the real question is what the jury believes. Or, just as importantly, whether they ultimately accept that Angelina could benefit from the doctor's death to the tune of the insured sum.'

'Surely they know that already?' Jessica asked. 'The issue is beyond doubt.'

'Let's not get ahead of ourselves, Jessica,' Oscar said in a soothing voice. 'Del Assandro said to me after court adjourned that he may now be forced to call evidence regarding the insurance proposal.'

'But he can't do that,' Jessica replied. 'All of his witness statements have been served.'

Matthew sensed that their client was showing the smallest sign of panic. He wondered if it was because she had something to do with the signature on the insurance proposal.

'We raised the issue of the insurance policy,' Oscar said. 'The prosecution will no doubt be permitted to try and rebut that evidence with their expert.'

'You have to object,' Jessica replied immediately.

'If we object,' Matthew explained calmly, 'the jury will get the impression we are trying to hide something. On the question of procedural fairness, the judge has to allow the evidence. Best we sit quietly and smile frequently.'

'So you're going to sit there and do nothing?' Jessica demanded.

'I'm not quite sure why you're so upset about the signature on the policy,' Matthew asked quietly. 'Who do you think signed the proposal form if it was not your husband?'

'If it wasn't Corny, clearly it was her,' Jessica replied. 'It must have been part of her plan from the beginning. Probably months in the planning.'

'Who'd have thought,' Matthew replied with a bland face, 'such an innocent face hiding the soul of a murderer.' He paused a moment to allow his client to respond, but she merely gave him a cold stare. 'Still, it's not a disaster if the jury suspects that his signature was forged,' he continued. 'As I said before, all we need to do is raise a doubt in their mind, not prove anything.'

Oscar glanced at Matthew nervously, then changed the subject to arrangements for the next day's hearing. Lena elbowed Matthew sharply in the ribs as she escorted their client towards the lifts. He grunted involuntarily, but Jessica Vandermeer, whose back was towards them at the time, either did not hear the blow or chose to ignore it.

After Lena and their client had disappeared in the departing lift, Oscar and Matthew walked back to the interviewing room to collect their belongings.

'We don't need to question our client too closely, my boy,' Oscar remarked with a sharp glance towards Matthew.

'You don't think so?'

'Just remember, Matt, you're not prosecuting the case. Too much knowledge can be a dangerous thing.'

Chapter Thirty-three

Angelina Smythe-Baker was the centre of attention the following day as she paraded to the witness box. Her symmetrical doll-like features were accentuated by luxurious blonde hair and wide blue eyes, and she was dressed in a light pink designer suit which Matthew felt was intended to convey both vulnerability and trust. After giving her name and an address, care of her agent, she stated her occupation as 'television personality', probably at the suggestion of the same agent. Pretentious was the adjective that Matthew felt was most appropriate for that description.

The witness cried softly when asked to recall when she had been informed of the doctor's death, and then she recounted in some detail his outstanding attributes – a sense of duty, of humour, of loyalty and, of course, kindness. It sounded to Matthew like a script from her latest soap opera, but the jury seemed quite taken with her performance, smiling broadly towards her during the evidence in chief.

Oscar set the tone immediately as he rose to cross-examine. 'Did you poison Dr Vandermeer?'

'Of course not,' came the shrill reply.

'But you had a perfect motive. One hundred thousand motives in fact.'

'That is grossly unfair. I knew nothing of any policy until after his death.'

'The jury only has your word for that. Just as we only have your word that my client knew of your affair with her husband, and had agreed to a divorce.'

'My word is my bond.'

'So you are a completely honest person? You are never devious or underhand?'

'I'm always truthful and straightforward.'

'But what about in your acting career? Is your character always truthful and straightforward?'

'Of course not,' the witness replied with a dismissive shrug. 'That is role-playing, as you well know, sir.'

Oscar had done some research into her acting career, including the numerous roles she had played on stage and television, even to the extent of watching several episodes of her current soap opera. 'It was excruciating, my boy,' he had reported to Matthew. 'There should be a warning at the commencement of those programmes that extended viewing may cause loss of brain cells. If it's good enough to warn smokers about their simple pleasures, the same rules should apply to that rubbish.' The fact that she was currently playing a *femme fatale* seemed to interest Oscar, knowledge that he said may come in useful.

'Would you be in accord with me if I described you as a brilliant actress?'

'Well ... thank you. I am aware that many people hold me in high regard.'

'The adjective was pejorative.'

'What?'

'You are, in fact, an accomplished chameleon, aren't you?'

'A what?'

'A very clever lizard that can change its appearance to deceive predators. Sometimes applied to people who hide their real character, such as actresses.'

Del Assandro rose quickly to his feet.

'I take objection to the witness being called a lizard. That is an insulting suggestion, Your Honour.'

'It's merely an analogy, Your Honour,' Oscar replied with mock sincerity. 'No disrespect is implied.'

'Very well then, let's move on,' Benoit announced without raising his head from his notetaking.

'Let me put it this way,' Oscar continued, 'you could tell the jury lie after lie here today, and do so with a straight face and be completely convincing. After all, that's what acting is all about, is it not?'

Angelina Smythe-Baker turned to face the jury as she replied. 'There is one important difference, sir. I have sworn to tell the truth and that is what I am doing.'

'How does the jury know that? From such an accomplished actress, I mean?'

Del Assandro once again lumbered to his feet. 'I am always willing to be reasonable, Your Honour, but I do think this has gone on long enough. I do object to this line of questioning.'

'I won't press it,' Oscar said before the judge had time to make a ruling. 'I believe that we have made our point.' He glanced towards the jury and gave a conspiratorial smile. 'Have you by any chance put in a claim on the deceased's policy as yet?'

The witness blinked several times rapidly. 'It's ... in the hands of my solicitor. He's written to the insurance company, I believe.'

'But surely, my dear woman, you don't want to profit from your lover's death?'

'No, of course not. I don't want any money from the policy. That's a terrible thing to suggest.'

'Then perhaps you've asked the insurance company to pay the death benefit from the policy to a charity? To assist the homeless, or feed thousands of starving children in Africa?'

'I ... I'm not sure.'

'That's fine. We can subpoena a claims officer from the insurance company to let us know what is going on.'

'Do what you want,' she snapped back.

'Am I correct in assuming that the insurance company has not paid any monies to you as yet?'

'No.'

'Now, why would that be, I wonder?'

'I am forced to object once again, Your Honour,' Del Assandro said. 'This is nothing more than a smear campaign to attack the witness' credibility. It is not relevant what action the insurance company takes.'

'But it is relevant to ascertain what the witness thinks, Your Honour,' Oscar replied. 'If there is any doubt in my friend's mind, let me make it crystal clear – we are attacking her credibility. We do not accept that she is a witness of truth. In fact, she should be a suspect in the murder investigation.'

'You are entitled to challenge her credibility, Mr O'Shannessy,' the judge replied after a slight pause, 'but I cannot see how the actions of the insurance company are relevant.'

'Your Honour pleases,' Oscar said as he turned back to the witness box. 'You say in your evidence, madam, that you last saw the deceased on the morning of his death?'

'That is so.'

'A post-operative consultation perhaps?'

'We were in love, sir. You probably cannot understand that.'

'Oh, I understand love, all right,' Oscar replied. 'I understand greed as well.'

The witness stiffened her posture.

'You also said earlier that you normally called in to see the deceased every Monday morning. Perhaps you could tell the court what was the purpose of these early morning assignations?'

'Just to catch up ... to say hello ... to keep in touch.' The witness started to tremble then sobbed quietly.

'You didn't perhaps add a little something to his so-called "elixir of life" that morning, did you? Perhaps the very shrimp paste we have been hearing about?'

'Absolutely not.'

Oscar glanced at Matthew who briefly shook his head.

'Nothing further, Your Honour,' Oscar said as he resumed his seat.

Lena gave him a small pat on his arm, whilst Matthew gave him a brief nod of appreciation.

Del Assandro rose to re-examine. 'Did you play any part in the murder of Dr Vandermeer?'

'Of course not.'

'Did you at any time add anything to his health drink?'

'Never.'

'You maintain that prior to his death, you had no knowledge of any insurance policy?'

'I did not.'

'Nothing further, Your Honour.'

Matthew noted that, as the witness stood down, none of the jury was smiling at her. The seeds of doubt were starting to burst into life.

Chapter Thirty-four

The evidence of Herbert Rowbottom, chartered accountant to the stars, was exactly as the prosecutor had predicted in his opening address: it outlined in detail the financial reasons why the estate of Dr Cornelius Vandermeer would not proceed to probate. There was essentially nothing left, apart from some expensive clothes, an assortment of medical textbooks, and the jointly owned furniture of the marriage.

'The value of such things in a second-hand market would barely cover the costs of an auction sale,' Rowbottom announced. 'A garage sale might raise a few dollars, perhaps,' he concluded with an eyebrow raised in disdain.

'Everything was rented or hired then?' the prosecutor asked.

'Almost everything. Perhaps he had some surgical equipment at the private hospital where he operated, but the CEO tells me that the hospital provided all that was required for surgery.'

When Oscar rose to cross-examine, he adopted an almost paternal attitude to the witness. 'I take it that you are a well-educated man of the world, sir.'

'Some people may disagree, but I have no objection to the description.'

'You would agree with me, then, that my client had nothing to gain by her husband's death?'

'Not financially.'

'Indeed, she is far worse off now that her husband is deceased. She has no income at all to support herself, isn't that so?'

'As far as I am aware, that's correct.'

'She is in fact destitute?'

'That's one way to describe her.'

'So, as a man of the world, not as a narrow-minded lawyer,' Oscar said, glancing at Del Assandro with one eye, 'would you agree my client had a motive to keep her husband alive and well?'

'I suppose so,' the witness replied just as Del Assandro had half-risen to object, but was too late.

'Nothing further, Your Honour,' Oscar said.

Matthew suppressed a grin, turning it into a grimace lest the jury picked up on his reaction. The prosecution had introduced the witness to prove a financial motive – that Jessica Vandermeer's lavish lifestyle would collapse if her husband divorced her, as there would be no substantial property settlement – and that this had fuelled her act of revenge. What Oscar had cleverly done was turn the witness inside out, by showing Jessica had more of a financial motive to keep her husband alive. As Oscar frequently commented to Matthew, 'There's more than one way to skin a cat, my boy.'

Matthew glanced over to the jury box, and was quietly pleased to see several of the jurors scratching their heads, their faces creased in puzzlement.

Matthew, Oscar, Lena and Jessica Vandermeer dined on sandwiches and coffee during the adjournment. Lena had left the courtroom ten minutes early to collect lunch, thereby avoiding the luncheon crowd at the café a few floors up from the courtroom.

Matthew noticed that their client was only nibbling on the bread, occasionally sipping her coffee. She was still a mystery to him, and the more the trial continued, the more confused he was by her. Surely she could not be so crazy as to want a conviction for murder, yet her casual attitude regarding the trial left him bewildered. He did not believe her to be a stupid woman. Indeed, he was coming around to the opposite view, and in the back of his mind he suspected there must be a plan, which would slowly reveal itself as the trial wore on. The next witness was about to deliver what he feared would be a fatal blow, yet all Jessica had told them was that she knew nothing about the bottle of shrimp paste found hidden in her garage. Matthew was of the opinion that the jury would never believe that, and he would not blame them.

Oscar was the first person to break the silence. 'Does anyone have any suggestions as to what questions I can put to Professor Schultz?'

After a short pause, Matthew tapped the folder that lay before him. 'I think we should attack the premise that he died of an anaphylactic shock as opposed to a normal heart attack. Looking up various medical publications, the occurrence of sudden death by unexplained heart attack in healthy adult males is not that rare. It happens unexpectedly, and no one can pinpoint the cause. I recall that when I worked in the court system there were several reports to the coroner of that exact occurrence.'

'But what about the presence of the shellfish protein?' Oscar queried.

'If the jury believes there is a reasonable chance that an unexplained heart attack caused the death, that can raise a reasonable doubt,' Matthew replied. 'We don't have to *prove* that it was the actual cause of death.'

'If the jury is to believe that I caused his death by putting shrimp paste into his drink,' Jessica replied quietly, 'they would have to believe that I am a complete fool for keeping the bottle and not disposing of it.'

Oscar gave a slight smile. 'But you had no way of knowing that a search warrant was to be executed at your house. At least that is what the prosecutor will say to the jury in his summing up. Gaols are full of otherwise clever people who make a simple mistake whilst carrying out their crimes.'

'The use of shrimp paste to kill someone with a severe shellfish allergy is actually quite brilliant,' Matthew added. 'Whoever did this almost got away with it. They just didn't count on Sergeant Plod using his brain cells. You don't have to look any further than the example of rat poison. Anyone can stroll into a supermarket and grab a packet. Its sale is not restricted at all. Indeed, as Oscar will attest, it was the suburban housewife's poison of choice for an unwanted partner. Apparently knocking off a few husbands is worthwhile, provided we keep the rodent population in check.'

'Subtle, as usual, Matthew,' Oscar said, shaking his head.

'The thing about rat poison, however,' Matthew continued, 'is that it's easily traced in the body of the victim. Shrimp paste, on the other hand, is quite innocent. Unless you know of the allergy.'

'You're not trying to rattle me, are you Matthew?' Jessica asked.

'What I'm trying to do,' Matthew replied in a deliberately even tone, 'is to engender some passion. We're in the middle of a murder trial, and unless we can attack the professor's evidence, things look terrible.'

Jessica gave a brief smile, as if to placate a fussy child. 'So passion will solve our problems, will it, Matthew?'

Matthew shook his head. 'Not by itself. I just can't sit in the courtroom, smile at everyone and wait for the guilty verdict. I want to give Oscar something to fight with. To challenge the witness, to put doubt in the minds of the jury. In other words, to do my job, not just go through the motions.'

An uneasy silence settled on the group, until Oscar leaned over and patted Jessica on the shoulder in a fatherly gesture.

'We're only trying to do our best for you, Jessica. Is there anything about this bottle and its contents that you can tell us? I think you've hinted to us before that perhaps your husband put it there for some reason. Is that a reasonable line of questioning that I can put to the professor?'

'I only know that I didn't put it there. If the police or someone else didn't plant it, then Corny is the only one it could have been. Perhaps he used it in small doses to overcome his sensitivity to it? I've heard of that being tried to help people with various food allergies. He could have then hidden the bottle so I wouldn't find out. To prevent an argument, you see.'

Oscar scratched his scalp through his thinning hair before he replied in a somewhat sceptical tone.

'I doubt that the jury would look favourably on a suggestion that your late husband deliberately poisoned himself.' He paused for a few moments before continuing. 'You didn't by any chance hear Cornelius talk of using the paste in his professional work?'

'Sorry.'

'My advice then is to run with Matthew's suggestion of sudden unexplained heart attack. It's something the prosecution cannot refute absolutely, so it comes down to whether it leaves a reasonable doubt.'

'I agree,' Jessica responded to end the discussion.

No further suggestions were forthcoming, and the conversation drifted on to the prediction of when Jessica would commence her evidence. Oscar highlighted the matters that he would ask her in evidence in chief, warning her not to lose her composure and involve herself in an argument with the prosecutor during cross-examination.

Their client responded with a knowing smile. 'That's something you don't need to worry about, Oscar. The rules of the contest are clear, as are the pitfalls.'

Chapter Thirty-five

Professor Max Schultz commenced his evidence after the luncheon break. He was a dapper, bright-eyed sparrow of a man, with a clear and commanding voice, a receding hairline and a bright blue polka-dotted bow tie protruding from his brown suede coat. He seemed oblivious that the tie clashed with his pink shirt and brown coat, and he reminded Matthew of the archetypal university professor – very intelligent but somehow a little strange.

'Perhaps, Professor,' Del Assandro asked after the witness had given the bulk of his evidence, 'you could tell the court in layman's terms just what anaphylactic shock is, and how it causes death?'

'It's quite fascinating, really,' Schultz replied eagerly. 'When a subject has sensitivity to insect stings, or grass pollens, or chemicals such as penicillin – or in this case a food allergy to shellfish – it is called a Type 1 reaction. An antigen that results in an allergic reaction is an allergen. Food allergens are proteins within the shellfish that enter the bloodstream. When exposed to the allergens, the immune system produces antibody immunoglobulin E, or IgE antibodies for short. They attach to mast cells or basophils, causing them to degranulate – that is, to release chemical mediators, such as histamines. This causes blood vessels to dilate and leak fluid into the surrounding tissues, resulting in the smooth muscles in the airways contracting.'

'I'm grateful that my friend did not ask for a technical explanation,' Oscar interrupted with a grin.

Matthew noted that most of the jury smiled at the barrister's little joke.

'Perhaps, Professor Schultz,' the judge said with a smile, 'for the benefit of we ordinary laypersons, could you please simplify your last answer?'

'If it is required,' Schultz replied with a puzzled frown. 'Well, firstly it is necessary for there to be a prior exposure to the food which the person is allergic to, causing the IgE antibodies to attach to the surface of the mast cells. An initial exposure will not trigger a response.'

'But what is the eventual response?' Del Assandro persisted.

'Well, blood pressure may drop sharply, there may be convulsions, or shock, or unconsciousness, but most of the anaphylactic deaths are occasioned because of vasodilation and constriction of smooth muscles, including those of the bronchus.' The witness sat back in his chair, satisfied with his explanation.

'But what happens then?' the prosecutor asked plaintively.

'The subject can't breathe,' the professor replied slowly and deliberately, as if tutoring a young student. 'Without oxygen, we cannot exist, Mr Del Assandro.'

The prosecutor looked to the ceiling briefly whilst he composed his next question. 'This fatal reaction, would it take hours or days?'

'Oh, it can be almost immediate. Within a minute or two in a particularly sensitive subject.'

Del Assandro sank back into his chair with a barely suppressed sigh, and then Oscar commenced his cross-examination.

'I do accept that you may be brilliant in your field, Professor, but you cannot be sure that the deceased died from anaphylactic shock, can you?'

'I certainly can.'

'Well, let me put this situation to you. Surely you have heard of supremely fit young adult athletes dropping dead on the sporting field, and subsequent investigations finding no cause?'

'I have heard of that,' the professor replied with a shrug of his shoulders.

'Clearly, that could have happened to Dr Vandermeer, could it not?'

'You mean, if we totally ignore the substantial presence of shellfish protein in his vital organs.' The witness glanced at the jury box with raised eyebrows to signify his disbelief. 'Particularly when he had a severe shellfish allergy.'

'Putting the shellfish protein to one side for a moment, I put to you that a sudden unexplained heart attack could have been the cause of death.'

'Surely that would be like saying that apart from his vital organs having been removed for pathology, he was perfectly healthy. The only person I can think of that would say that would be a lawyer.'

'A heartless lawyer, perhaps?' Del Assandro quipped with a grin.

'Or a brainless one,' the professor added pointedly.

A wave of laughter rolled around the courtroom.

Oscar tried to rescue his point. 'I put to you that I could drop dead right now, and it would be possible that no cause could be found.'

The witness shook his head. 'I'm afraid that you're neither young nor healthy. I can tell from just a glance at your face that you have obvious medical problems.'

Oscar held up his hands in surrender. 'You may have a point there, Professor.' He stared at the ceiling for a moment before altering his line of attack. 'Perhaps I can put this to you. The shellfish protein could have caused a heart attack because of some genetic problem that had never been diagnosed previously.'

Del Assandro jumped to his feet. 'That would not assist the defence, Your Honour. You have to take the victim as you find him, imperfections and all.'

'Eggshell skull cases, Mr O'Shannessy,' Judge Benoit said. Turning to the jury, he continued, 'Perhaps I should explain the issue so there is no confusion. If there is an assault on a person who has, for example, a very thin skull, and the subsequent skull fracture is fatal, the accused would still be responsible for the death. Those cases are commonly called *eggshell skull* cases. In the case here today, if the shellfish protein triggered an unknown health factor, the accused could not raise this as a defence. I must make it clear, however, that the prosecution must prove beyond a reasonable doubt that the accused by her actions, either directly or indirectly, caused the deceased to ingest the allergic substance.'

'Your Honour is too kind,' Oscar replied. 'The question is withdrawn.'

Oscar continued questioning the witness on the connection between the shrimp paste and the death for over an hour, but Matthew's assessment was that the longer the cross-examination continued, the stronger the prosecution case became. As Oscar resumed his seat, he leaned over towards Matthew and murmured out of the corner of his mouth.

'That went well. You don't have a gun handy, do you?'

'Chin up, Oscar,' Matthew replied quietly. 'Remember what you always say – keep smiling for the jury.'

'And, of course, for our client,' Lena added.

Matthew glanced back at Jessica Vandermeer. She looked to him as though she was enjoying the theatre of the trial.

Chapter Thirty-six

Dr Alex Phillips was the next witness, and he gave evidence of being phoned by Jessica Vandermeer, who in a state of extreme distress had asked for him to attend her husband's surgery as Cornelius had been found dead.

'When you attended the surgery, what did you find?' Del Assandro asked.

'I checked Cornelius for a pulse, but found none. His face was a bluish colour and rigor mortis had begun to set in.'

'Was Jessica Vandermeer at her husband's surgery when you arrived?'

'No, she arrived a few minutes after me.'

'What did she say to you?'

The witness paused for a few seconds to compose his answer. 'She was very upset and not at all coherent.'

'Did she ask you to sign a medical certificate of cause of death?'

'I ... ah ... don't recall. In any event it was clearly not a case where I would do that.'

'Why not?'

'I had not been treating the deceased for any illness, and I could not tell just by looking at the body what had caused his death. Clearly an autopsy would be required.'

The prosecutor pursed his lips momentarily. He did not believe that the doctor was being truthful about Jessica's conversation, but as he had called the witness, he did not have the right of cross-examination.

'Perhaps then you could tell the court if you have any knowledge that the deceased had any allergies?'

'I certainly can. I know from conversations with the deceased that he had a life-long allergy to shellfish. On one occasion I observed him peeling some prawns for his wife at a barbeque at my house, and the allergy was so severe that his hands swelled to such an extent that he could not even make a fist.'

'How would you categorise the allergy?'

'Extremely acute.'

'Nothing further, Your Honour.'

Oscar did not ask any questions and the witness stood down.

Matthew gave Lena a knowing glance, and she nodded briefly in silent agreement that they had dodged a bullet. Had Dr Phillips disclosed that Jessica had asked him to sign the medical certificate in order to avoid a police investigation, it would have proved detrimental to their defence. Matthew shared the prosecutor's obvious scepticism about the doctor's memory.

Chapter Thirty-seven

The final prosecution witness was an insurance broker by the name of Hans Schrieber, called by the prosecution to clarify the mystery surrounding the insurance policy. Although Matthew received his statement only that morning, Oscar counseled their client that it would be in their best interests to allow the witness to give evidence, as cross-examination might prove to be fruitful.

Schrieber was immaculately dressed in an expensive-looking bespoke dark suit, complete with a cream shirt, a maroon tie and a matching handkerchief, which poked from his suit pocket. Jet-black hair and a face that boasted some type of fake tan gave the overall impression of a new car salesman, one notch up from his used-car colleagues. The type, Matthew felt, that would leave you checking for your wallet after shaking their hand.

'You never met the person who signed this insurance proposal?' Del Assandro asked after the existence of the policy was established and the proposal form admitted as an exhibit.

'No, it's quite common for proposals to be sent to me through the mail,' Schrieber answered. 'Some clients are overseas, some in distant parts of the country, and others are simply too busy to attend in person.'

'But this client lived in Sydney. Why didn't you attend his surgery to make sure that everything was above board?'

'We take people at face value. The first year's premium was attached in the form of a bank cheque, and there was nothing to suggest anything untoward.'

'Now, I believe that subsequent to the insured's death, some questions have arisen as to the validity of the proposal?'

Schrieber picked up the document in front of him.

'That is so. Our investigators have compared the signature on this form with samples of the deceased doctor's signature, and it is clear even to a layman that the signatures do not match.'

'Do you personally have any knowledge of who may have signed the proposal form?'

'None whatsoever.'

The prosecutor resumed his seat.

'It is exceedingly generous that your company makes no enquiry whatsoever regarding the bona fides of any proposed insurance policy, don't you agree?' Oscar asked.

'I'm not sure what you're referring to.'

'Let me put it this way, then. The company welcomes new clients with open arms and a beaming smile, until a claim arises. Then it commences the most rigorous investigation of every aspect of the policy before the matter of payment is even considered?'

'That's not how I would phrase it.'

'So how would you phrase it, in insurance speak?'

'We follow normal commercial practice.'

'I see,' Oscar replied, raising his eyebrows in the direction of the jury. 'Is it fair to say, then, that your company is not prepared to honour the policy as it suspects that the proposal was signed by the beneficiary?'

'I object most strongly, Your Honour,' Del Assandro said as he rose to his feet. 'This is an outrageous slur on the character of a prosecution witness without any proof of any wrongdoing.'

'My friend called the witness, Your Honour,' Oscar replied with a barely suppressed smile. 'I didn't say that Miss Smythe-Baker signed the proposal, I merely asked about the suspicions of the insurance company.'

'Well then, the suspicions of that company are not relevant, Your Honour,' Del Assandro replied. 'The question must be disallowed.'

'I am inclined to agree with the prosecution,' Benoit replied. 'Suspicions do not amount to evidence, and do not serve any evidential purpose. I disallow the question, and the jury is to ignore it.'

'Your Honour pleases,' Oscar said with a faint smile as he resumed his seat.

It was clear to Matthew that Oscar's question had planted another seed of doubt in the minds of the jury as to who arranged the insurance policy. The direction of the judge to ignore the question did not mean that they would forget the issue when it came time to consider their verdict. Matthew looked at the jury box and observed that two of the members were shaking their heads, several were writing industriously on their notepaper, and the balance were staring at the insurance salesman. Oscar's veiled allegation was having the desired effect.

Chapter Thirty-eight

The judge ordered an early adjournment so that the defence could have some breathing space before commencing evidence the next day. Oscar once again waived the right to make an address to the jury, this time at the close of the prosecution case, for the same reasons he had outlined earlier to their client.

'Best to leave the theatrics for the final address,' Oscar remarked. 'We don't want to show our cards too early.'

Oscar then assumed his lecturer's face to make it clear that he was now completely serious. 'Although we've talked about it several times before, Jessica,' he continued, 'we are still able to change course. You are not obliged to give evidence. You do not bear the onus of proof, and, as the case stands, I am reasonably confident that the jury could acquit.'

Their client gave a fleeting smile.

'*Reasonably confident – could acquit.* That's not an overly optimistic opinion that I'm listening to, is it?'

'Juries are a little like the wind. They blow this way and that. Unpredictable would be a fair comment.'

'You are talking about the infamous *dock statement*, I take it?' Jessica asked. 'I believe they call it *the coward's castle*.' She nodded towards Lena. 'We briefly spoke about it during an early conference.'

The lawyers well knew that dock statements were another hangover from the system of British justice, imported into Australia together with convicts, a few upper-class refugees and the Rum Corps military that formed the European settlement. Several hundred years ago, persons charged with a serious criminal offence in England were not only disallowed legal representation but were also not allowed even to give evidence. The law permitted an unsworn dock statement, and the prosecution could not cross-examine the accused or comment on the failure to give evidence. Why it still existed in Australia in the present day was a complete mystery to Matthew. It had been said many times that it was a safeguard for illiterate or poorly educated people, who by making the dock statement could avoid cross-examination by a skillful Crown prosecutor. The reason for its nickname, *the coward's castle*, was that it was often used as a device to make outrageous claims that the Crown could not rebut, except in rare and unusual circumstances.

'I have heard it called that,' Oscar replied. 'But, as Matthew and I are only too aware, some accused think that they are in a battle of wits with the prosecutor … that it's all some sort of a game. They can't wait to go into the witness box to show everyone how clever they are.'

'Invariably, that's exactly what they do,' Matthew added dryly.

'So I would describe the dock statement as a prudent course of action,' Oscar added. 'If we were in a desperate situation, the witness box might be forced on us, but in my assessment this is not the case.'

'Surely if I don't give evidence,' Jessica replied, 'the community at large, my friends and associates, my family members even, would be saying privately, *she was afraid to give evidence – she must be hiding something*. I may be legally acquitted but still considered guilty in the court of public opinion.'

'I'm just a simple barrister doing his best to have you acquitted. I can't predict what other people may think.'

'You're worried about your place in society?' Matthew asked. 'To be shunned by your former friends and associates? Is that what we're talking about?'

Jessica gave a cold smile. 'You may well think that I lead a frivolous and empty lifestyle, Matthew. Nevertheless, it's my life and my friends. I believe that you used to be a footballer of some note, didn't you?'

'Depends whom you ask,' Matthew replied.

'Well, what would all your old football mates say if you were accused of being a child molester, for example? You'd be ostracised by all your former teammates, who would now regard you with disgust. They would never associate with you again. Are you saying that wouldn't affect you?'

'I think they'd probably give me a bashing as well. Take the law into their hands, as it were,' Matthew replied.

'To put it simply, I don't want to be given the benefit of a grave doubt,' Jessica said. 'I want my name cleared so that I can resume my life as before. I will be giving evidence.'

Oscar gave a small sigh. 'If that's your decision, my dear, then I will support you. However, let me make this crystal clear – under no circumstances enter into any type of debate with Del Assandro. His cheerful and friendly facade can change in an instant – usually resulting in a deliberately personal attack. Never forget that he is saying to the jury that you are a cold-blooded murderer.'

'How should I reply?'

'Calmly and forcefully,' Oscar replied. 'I'm not suggesting that you should be a meek lamb – the jury would of course expect you to react with some spirit. But no speeches and no hysterics. Not that I would ever envisage that of you. I merely say that for my own benefit as much as anything.'

'No doubt you deal with clients who are terrified or neurotic or who go to pieces in the witness box,' Jessica replied in a measured tone, 'but that does not apply to me. You have never met anyone like me, Oscar. I am truly unique.'

Chapter Thirty-nine

When court resumed the following day, Oscar carefully led their client through her evidence in chief. Jessica denied any knowledge of the marriage proposal or how the bottle of shrimp paste could have been located in her garage, which was always kept securely locked. When asked if she had caused her husband's death, she was the perfect grief-stricken widow, with just the correct mixture of sadness at his demise and outrage over the charge of murder. The measured coldness that Matthew had observed earlier in the interview room had vanished, and a polished performer was now on display.

During Oscar's gentle questioning, Del Assandro smiled like a benevolent friend and raised no objections, but Matthew could feel the undercurrent of tension building as cross-examination drew closer. He knew that the smile would not last long.

The prosecutor rose as Oscar resumed his seat. He commenced in a quiet, almost consoling tone as he leisurely covered the material given in chief. After a brief pause, the tone of his voice rose an octave or two.

'When you first heard about your husband's death from his secretary, what did you do?'

'I rang for medical assistance of course.'

'But rather than ring for an ambulance, is it true that you rang an old family friend, Dr Alex Phillips to go to your late husband's surgery?'

'That's correct. His secretary found him after she came back from lunch, and she immediately rang me. She is a registered nurse and after checking his pulse she knew it was too late for an ambulance.'

'It wouldn't be, would it, that you wanted Dr Phillips to sign a medical certificate of cause of death so that there would be no inquest and no post-mortem?'

'Absolutely not. I just wanted a friend of my husband to care for him, not some stranger.'

'A stranger who might inconveniently call the police?'

'This is all some prosecution fantasy. It bears no resemblance to reality.'

The prosecutor gave a cold smile as he turned over a page on the brief that lay before him. 'How was your relationship with your husband just before his death?'

'Normal.'

'That's a strange word to describe a marriage.'

'Perhaps you're talking about your marriage, not mine.'

The prosecutor gave a chuckle. 'I would describe my marriage as loving and caring. What about yours?'

'We were married for over fifteen years; we weren't love-struck teenagers. We had the normal relations that mature adults share.'

'More a business relationship, perhaps?'

'Of course not. If you want me to spell it out, we were in love.'

'No talk of divorce?'

'I just said we were in love. Why would we divorce?'

'Why indeed? Are you saying that you knew nothing about the passionate affair your husband was having with a glamorous young actress?'

'I did not.' Jessica glanced towards the public gallery where the previous witnesses were sitting. 'Glamorous is such a subjective term, don't you think?' she added sarcastically.

The prosecutor swung around to glance at the gallery. 'How would you describe Miss Smythe-Baker, then?'

'I would describe her as the chief suspect in my husband's death.'

Matthew glanced at the jury and saw several of the members smiling although it was clear to him that the answer was never intended to be humorous. His opinion of his client as a witness was improving by the minute.

'Touché,' Del Assandro replied with a rueful smile. 'Perhaps we can move on to the subject of the shrimp paste. You were of course aware of your husband's severe shellfish allergy?'

'I was.'

'You knew that if he consumed shrimp paste, for example, that it could prove fatal?'

'I never considered it. I have never seen that bottle of shrimp paste before.'

'Never seen any similar bottle?'

'Perhaps in the supermarket shelves. But it's not something we have ever purchased, so it wouldn't register with me.'

'Now, that's a very interesting answer. Are you sure that you're telling the truth?'

The witness gave a quizzical look. 'I am.'

The prosecutor studied his brief of evidence before addressing the judge.

'Could the witness be shown exhibit twenty-seven, Your Honour?'

The judge nodded towards the Sheriff's Officer, and the exhibit was delivered to the witness box.

'Would you please inspect that tee-shirt?'

Jessica glanced briefly at the crumpled item.

'Is that your tee-shirt?' the prosecutor asked.

'I can't be sure. It could be.'

'Can you tell us what sized tee-shirt you wear, Mrs Vandermeer?'

'A size six or eight, depending on the brand.'

'Does that tee-shirt have a size printed on the label?'

Jessica looked at the tee-shirt briefly before replying, 'It has an eight printed on it.'

'And the brand?'

'Bonds.'

'Is that a brand that you wear?'

'Yes. Along with millions of other women.'

The prosecutor gave a theatrical pause and glanced towards the jury box. 'I see. Could you tell the court where you used to work?'

'I worked for dozens of different companies. Not only when I was single, but I also worked occasionally until a few years ago. It's always handy for a girl to have a little spending money without relying on her partner.'

Matthew observed that this attempt at humour had no discernable effect on the jury. It was one thing for the barrister to share the occasional *bon mot* with them, but not someone facing a charge of murdering her husband.

'What type of work did you do?' the prosecutor asked.

'Analysing various products.'

'What type of products?'

Oscar jumped to his feet. 'I am loath to interrupt my friend, but this is clearly not relevant to these proceedings, Your Honour. Nor is my client's tee-shirt size. It is a form of badgering the witness and should be disallowed.'

'My friend will grasp the relevance very shortly, Your Honour,' Del Assandro replied. 'It is critical to this case.'

The judge gave the prosecutor an enquiring glance before nodding his head and replying. 'I will allow some leeway.'

'To cut to the chase, madam,' the prosecutor continued in a smooth voice that almost purred with enjoyment, 'is it correct that you have a bachelor's degree in chemistry from Sydney University, majoring in food technology?'

The witness gave the briefest of smiles, as if to acknowledge a point well made before replying calmly. 'It is.'

Occasionally during the course of a criminal trial, something critical arises which is not only a complete surprise, but which can result in a suggestion of professional incompetence. Matthew had this reaction instantly, as he realised that he had not canvassed his client's professional qualifications. Perhaps it was mental laziness, or some hidden prejudice against someone that he regarded merely as a society wife who, once she had hooked her spouse, then milked him for as much as she could. Had their client been a businessman, Matthew would have gone over his schooling and tertiary years in some detail, but he now recognised that he had a blind spot in his appraisal of this woman. Regardless of how he qualified the error, it was clearly incompetence, and Matthew felt a rush of embarrassment sweep over him.

'Would you be surprised, madam,' the prosecutor continued, 'to learn that Detective Brooks has made enquiries with a certain company and their records of employees stretching over the past five years?'

'No. I regard the officer as competent. Even dogged, you might say.'

'Do you know the company I am referring to?'

'As I have already said, I have worked for dozens of companies.'

Del Assandro waved a sheaf of papers in the air as he glanced at the jury. 'Does the name, Orian Foods Pty Ltd ring a bell at all?'

Matthew's embarrassment vanished and a feeling of despair emerged. His incompetence was rapidly expanding into professional negligence.

'Not offhand,' the witness replied.

'Now, that is a surprise,' Del Assandro continued. 'Detective Brooks' enquiry has revealed that for a period of three months some two years ago you worked as a food technologist with this company. Testing various food products, including shrimp paste.'

'If you say so. I don't recall the exact details.'

'Perhaps the witness can be shown the bottle containing the shrimp paste, exhibit twenty-five, which was found wrapped in exhibit twenty-seven, the tee-shirt.' The prosecutor waited patiently as the elderly Sheriff's Officer hobbled over to the witness box with the exhibit. 'Could you look at the bottle, and read the name of the company which is written on the label please?'

'Orian Foods,' the witness replied after glancing at the bottle.

Matthew closed his eyes and his head sank towards his chest. Oscar sat beside him, goggle-eyed.

'Do you deny, madam,' Del Assandro queried in a booming voice, 'that you have tested the paste which caused your husband's death, and knew exactly what it contained?'

'I may have, I don't recall,' she replied quietly whilst remaining composed.

'Is that the best answer that you can give to the jury?'

'I have tested thousands of products over the years. I certainly don't keep records about the various items.'

Del Assandro glared at the witness for several moments before continuing to attack her evidence concerning her qualifications and prior employment. Remarkably, in Matthew's opinion, Jessica remained calm, despite an intense cross-examination that continued throughout the day. The clock showed just after 4 pm when Del Assandro indicated that he had no more questions of the witness and Judge Benoit mercifully announced the day's adjournment.

Chapter Forty

During the luncheon adjournment, as their client was still being cross-examined, Matthew and Oscar could not discuss with her the evidence she had given. When everyone settled in the interviewing room after she had finished her evidence, Oscar eventually broke the silence in his usual diplomatic tone.

'Do you recall, my dear, at an earlier conference we asked whether you had ever seen the bottle of shrimp paste or knew anything about it, you replied in negative terms? In cross-examination, you admit that you probably analysed it when employed with the firm that manufactured it. I have to say that I am completely dumbfounded. If I knew about your qualifications and prior employment, I could have raised it in chief and lessened the impact it had on the jury. Would you mind explaining what is going on?'

'It's quite simple really,' Jessica replied, calmly. 'As to my qualifications and prior work experience, you never asked. As to the actual bottle of shrimp paste, there is no way I would ever remember analysing something so insignificant.'

'Insignificant is not the expression that I'd use,' Matthew said tersely. 'I have to apologise for not discussing employment and qualifications with you, but you knew from when you first read the prosecution statements just how important this bottle is. Why did you not tell us about this company? Are you saying that you completely forgot that you worked there for three months?'

'It simply didn't register that the company was the manufacturer of the shrimp paste. I only glanced at the photograph in the prosecution brief, and the first time that I held the bottle in my hand was in the witness box today.'

Lena had been sitting quietly as she examined her client's face intently for some clue as to her motivation.

'Why didn't you tell us about your expertise in this area?' Lena asked. 'Surely you knew the prosecution would raise it?'

'As I said earlier, you did not ask.'

'Isn't that a little like forgetting to tell us that a prior husband had also died of anaphylactic shock?' Lena persisted. 'Whilst we may not have asked the exact question, surely you knew how important it was to tell us?'

'Not at all. The fact that I worked for Orian Foods was not pertinent to this case, as I never examined the photograph of the bottle closely and never connected the company with the product.'

'The difficulty that I have with that answer,' Matthew said, 'is that when we had a conference with Lena at our office, I showed you the photo and specifically asked you if you knew anything about the shrimp paste or the company which was named on the label.'

'Did you?' Jessica replied with an innocent face. 'I only glanced at the photo, so I guess that was my mistake, not yours. Sorry about that.'

'I have to say, my dear,' Oscar said after a long silence, 'that things don't look too favourable for us at the present. The jury may form the opinion that you are being deceptive about your work experience, your employment with this company, and your precise knowledge of the chemical makeup of the shrimp paste.'

'You mean you think I'll be convicted, Oscar?'

'That is now a distinct probability, my dear.'

Their client began to look faint. She pulled a handkerchief from her purse and held it to her face.

'I'm sorry,' she murmured. 'I never realised that they would dig up the work I did at Orian Foods. I knew it would look bad if I advised you about my qualifications and where I had previously worked, and I just hoped it would go away. I've been a fool not to tell you.'

Matthew was on the verge of telling her that he agreed completely with her last statement when Lena placed a warning hand on his arm.

'Is there anything else that you would like to clarify?' Lena asked quietly. 'Do you still say that you have never seen the bottle at your house?'

'Never. You have to believe me.'

Her voice had taken on a shrill tone, and for a moment Matthew thought she might be on the verge of an emotional collapse. Lena walked over and placed her arm around Jessica's shoulder, speaking to her so quietly that Matthew could not make out the words.

'They've changed the label since I worked there,' Jessica said between sobs, 'I've never seen this new design before.'

'I don't think we need to worry about label designs, my dear,' Oscar replied, somewhat sharply, 'what we need to concern ourselves with is how on earth we can change the minds of the jury. Del Assandro's cross-examination has all but destroyed our case, and I just don't know what to say to them.'

After a further uncomfortable silence, Lena took the initiative as she helped their client to her feet. 'Jessica needs to rest,' she announced. 'Nothing more can be achieved here today, so if you will ring the hire-car driver, Matthew, we can all recharge our batteries for tomorrow.'

Matthew escorted their client to the waiting hire-car, which was on call for each day's hearing, then returned to the interviewing room.

'I don't know about the two of you,' he announced, 'but I'm heading for the pub to drown my sorrows.'

'I'll second that,' Lena replied as she stood and gathered her papers and briefcase.

'Show me the way,' Oscar said. 'Just give me a few minutes to change in the robing room.'

Matthew ordered the first round of drinks as the trio sat dejectedly in a quiet corner of the grand old hotel that they usually frequented. Matthew was the first to break the ice.

'We're absolutely stuffed. Not one chance in a million of an acquittal.'

'Eloquently put, as usual,' Oscar replied.

'But accurate, nevertheless,' Lena added.

'I have the greatest admiration for your talent for subtly assessing the true motives of our clients, Lena,' Matthew said, 'and I admit that this woman has got me completely baffled. What's going on?'

Lena swirled her drink slowly as she made a small grimace. 'Something is. What about it, Oscar?'

'Don't ask me,' Oscar replied as he held up his hands in surrender. 'She has a science degree, so this is not some empty-headed society matron we're dealing with. She knew there'd be a good chance that her qualifications and prior employment would come out, but she refused to forewarn us. Why do you deliberately sabotage your own lawyers?'

'Did you observe that during cross-examination,' Lena added thoughtfully, 'she was completely in control of her emotions? Bearing in mind the issues the prosecution hammered her with all day, it's remarkable that she never wavered. It's almost as though she knew what Del Assandro would ask.'

'What about her performance in the interview room? Was it acting or was it the real Jessica?' Matthew said.

'I think it was genuine,' Oscar announced. 'I think she truly regrets not telling us.'

Matthew and Lena exchanged a glance.

'When she told us that we've never dealt with anyone like her before,' Matthew said, 'she was telling the truth. She truly is unique.'

Chapter Forty-one

Matthew lay in bed tossing restlessly and grumbling irritably to himself as he tried to gain some respite from the trial disaster and sink into a restful sleep. After failing for over an hour, he swung out of the bed, walked sluggishly into the tiny kitchen, and filled the kettle. He plugged it in and turned it on, then commenced his usual ritual of emptying out the old tealeaves before replacing them in the teapot. The mechanics of this ritual always had a calming effect – something that he knew was common during Asian tea ceremonies. He walked over to the record player and pulled out an LP of *The Marriage of Figaro* from its plastic sleeve and cardboard cover. Placing it on the turntable, he flicked the start switch. Mozart's glorious music flooded his tiny flat and soon the kettle emitted its strangled scream to alert him to its completed task.

As he sat in his favourite padded swivel chair, watching the darkened beach through the study window, something kept coming in and out of his consciousness – but try as he may, he could not identify what it was. Then – as soon as he refused to worry about the trial and deliberately concentrate on the opera music – it came to him.

They've changed the label since I worked there, Jessica had said. What did it mean? Was it of any significance? It was common for companies to regularly change labels on products, so that consumers felt they were buying a new product – so what?

Matthew remained in the chair for over an hour, arguing with himself, taking different roles to put forward different viewpoints. As he clambered back into bed, exhaustion slowly took hold of him.

'It's worth looking into it,' he mumbled to himself. 'What have we got to lose?'

The next moment he was startled into consciousness by the strident alarm clock. It can't be 6 am, he thought irritably. But it was, and the murder trial awaited.

Chapter Forty-two

That morning, Matthew, Oscar and Lena arrived at court early, as was their normal behaviour during the trial. Even with an hour to go before the trial resumed, the foyer was a little like a crowded train station to Matthew, with defendants, witnesses, lawyers and onlookers scurrying in all directions, impatient for the day's proceedings to commence. As the minutes ticked by and there was no sign of their client, the trio went downstairs to wait in the court foyer.

'Perhaps her solution was to flee the jurisdiction?' Oscar said with an anxious glance towards the entrance door.

'It's possible,' Matthew replied, 'but I don't think so. My bet is she'll turn up with a large hat.'

'Are you feeling all right, my boy?' Oscar said, unable to conceal his irritated tone.

'You should know by now to wait for the punch line, Oscar,' Lena remarked dryly.

'A large hat containing a rabbit,' Matthew added. 'For production therefrom.'

As Lena gave him a gentle punch on the arm, a black hire-car arrived at the kerb with a squeal of tyres. Jessica Vandermeer alighted with a bright smile for the reporters and cameras, and then held the door open for a bald, middle-aged, string-bean of a man who jumped out after her. Matthew bolted through the glass entrance doors and forced his way through the crowd to take hold of his client by the arm. Cameras flashed and microphones were thrust into the path of the trio, with a dozen or more questions being yelled simultaneously. Their usual practice of saying 'no comment' to the press was continued, and introductions were postponed until the defence team, their client and the stranger were alone in the lift as it propelled them towards the trial floor.

'Oscar, Matthew and Lena, I'd like to introduce Pieter Siwecki,' Jessica said with a smile. 'He's the manager of production at Orian Foods. We worked together for a few months some two years ago. But you already know that, don't you, Matthew?'

When court resumed, but in the absence of the jury, Oscar rose to make a submission.

'Your Honour, I seek your indulgence in a critical matter which has only just now been brought to my attention. I ask leave to recall Detective Sergeant Paul Brooks so that I may place before the court this new essential evidence.'

Judge Benoit looked enquiringly at the prosecutor. 'What do you say, Mr Del Assandro?'

'My friend spoke to me a few minutes ago, and I have to agree that this would appear to be crucial evidence. I am obliged to take the broad view, and say that if this court did not hear the evidence, then an appeal court may well order a re-trial. Bearing that in mind, and in accord with my general belief that the jury should hear all admissible evidence in a criminal trial, I have no objection to the detective being recalled.'

'Very well, then,' Benoit replied. 'Recall Detective Brooks.'

When the jury was recalled and the witness was re-sworn and had given his name, rank and station, Oscar was on his feet before Del Assandro had sat down.

'I'm sorry to have to ask a few more questions, Detective Brooks, but I'm sure that you have a complete explanation for a certain fact that has come into my possession only a few minutes ago.'

The witness looked warily at the aged barrister.

'Did you think it was suspicious when a bottle containing shrimp paste was located in my client's home, Sergeant?'

'You mean hidden in the garage. I would classify it as extremely suspicious, particularly when I discovered that your client had analysed the paste at the very factory where it was manufactured.'

'Would it be fair to say that this evidence convinced you that my client had murdered her husband?'

'That is a fair assessment.'

'But what if this bottle had never been discovered at all? Where would that have put the police investigation?'

'But it was discovered.'

'Humour me, Sergeant.'

Brooks raised his eyebrows whilst glancing towards the jury.

'We would have had suspicions, but as they say in the B-grade movies, no smoking gun.'

'No smoking gun. Let me just take a note of that, would you?' Oscar made an elaborate production of writing down some words on the brief laying before him.

Matthew glanced at the brief. Oscar had written: *Got the bastard.*

'You do remember, Sergeant, that I asked you whether you had planted this bottle in my client's garage?'

'I recall something fanciful along those lines.'

'Fanciful, you say. Could the exhibit be handed to the witness please?'

The sergeant's eyes narrowed in Oscar's direction and then fixed upon the bottle the Sheriff's Officer placed before him on the flat edge of the witness box.

'Would you be so kind as to inspect the exhibit please?'

Brooks picked up the bottle and gave it a passing glance.

'Could you read in a loud voice the words that appear on the label?'

'Very well.'

The witness read aloud the words, and a silence fell over the courtroom until Oscar finally resumed the questioning.

'The next witness to be called by the defence, Sergeant, will give evidence that the label on that bottle is different from the previous label. Furthermore, there is a code etched on the glass which confirms the production date.'

'So?'

'What this tells us is when this shrimp paste was manufactured.'

The witness seemed to immediately realise the significance of Oscar's words. He glanced nervously towards the prosecutor, the bench and then the jury box. Oscar stood silently, staring at the witness. After several moments, Judge Benoit broke the silence.

'Very well, Mr O'Shannessy, if you would be so kind as to continue.'

'Guess when this bottle of shrimp paste was produced?' Oscar asked.

'I've no doubt you are about to tell me.'

'Two months after the death of my client's husband. Now Sergeant, does that surprise you?'

Brooks' jaw sagged and he stared open-mouth at the barrister. The effect on the jury was immediate, and they stared in disbelief at the witness.

'I am at a complete loss to explain it,' Brooks said quietly.

'My earlier question as to whether the bottle was planted now takes on a new importance, does it not?'

'I don't see how.'

'Well, now, Sergeant,' Oscar said with a querulous glance towards the jury, 'are you suggesting that my client purchased this paste several months after her husband's death, and then hid it in the garage in order to incriminate herself? Perhaps she is a masochist? I'll have to ask her.'

Matthew noted several members of the jury smile broadly, with some of them shaking their heads in confusion. Even Brooks was now shaking his head.

'It doesn't make any sense,' Brooks eventually answered.

'That is precisely the prosecution case in a nutshell, Sergeant,' Oscar said. 'It makes no sense at all.'

With that, Oscar enclosed himself within his gown and resumed his seat with a flourish.

Chapter Forty-three

The evidence of Pieter Siwecki was exactly as Oscar predicted. He produced the original company records of the manufacturing process in relation to the shrimp paste, and was unshakeable in his assertion that the code etched on the bottle proved the date of manufacture.

'I can even tell the court to whom and on what date that particular batch of our product was dispatched from our premises,' Siwecki announced.

'Is there any way that the records could be misleading or defective?' Del Assandro asked plaintively when it came his turn to cross-examine.

'Never. I personally control the entire process and make numerous spot checks every day to make sure that there is no error. The records speak for themselves,' the witness announced as he tapped the folder that lay in front of him.

Whilst Siwecki was a generally unimposing figure, his bookish manner and pedantic adherence to his evidence cast him as completely honest. After the judge excused the witness,

Del Assandro rose, asking that his application be dealt with in the absence of the jury.

'This evidence places me in a very difficult situation, Your Honour,' the prosecutor said after the jury had filed from the courtroom. 'On the face of it, the bottle of shrimp paste would appear to have nothing to do with the doctor's death, but I really need some time to enquire into the manufacturing process at Orian Foods.'

Judge Benoit turned towards Oscar with an enquiring glance. 'Perhaps both parties and the jury could visit the company tomorrow for a demonstration, so that the jury can satisfy themselves of the truth of the evidence?' Oscar said. 'The court could resume the following day and I'm sure that no one would object to a day-excursion. Mr Siwecki tells me he doesn't even require a search warrant, and he will make sure that everything will be available for inspection. Your Honour may even gain some valuable knowledge into the production of shrimp paste.'

'Your generosity knows no bounds, Mr O'Shannessy,' the judge replied with a brief smile. The judge had a discretion whether to allow this to occur, but it was not uncommon to grant the application. Del Assandro shrugged his consent, and Judge Benoit recalled the jury before giving them the necessary instructions for the following day.

The next morning, Matthew quickly realised that Pieter Siwecki was the ringmaster of the factory floor, someone to whom all the staff responded immediately when given a direction. He was completely in charge of all aspects of the production line. The judge did not allow any questions during the demonstration at the factory – indicating that he would deal with any issues in the confines of the courtroom the following day. Siwecki gave a running commentary on the production process, explaining how each machine worked and giving samples of the various products at different stages, which were inspected by the group.

After the judge, jury, defence and prosecution had departed back to the Supreme Court, Detective Brooks remained to quiz Siwecki on any issues that he wanted clarified. The following day, Del Assandro announced that the prosecution would not be calling any further evidence. Oscar made a similar disclosure, and the trial had thus arrived at that time where the eloquence of the barristers could sway a jury one way then another: final submissions.

Chapter Forty-four

Matthew's attention to the closing addresses was also a type of final preparation for his upcoming admission to the bar. It was one thing to be clever in cross-examination or to be continuously alert throughout the trial, always ready to object and press their client's case, but it was another thing altogether to make an impassioned speech to the jury. Matthew acknowledged that this was Oscar's area of expertise, and he looked forward to the performance of the aged barrister.

The address by Del Assandro came first, and was impartial in the extreme. A prosecutor technically has an obligation to present the Crown evidence calmly, test the defence case fairly, and then leave the issue to the jury with no interest in the outcome. In reality, the majority of prosecutors get caught up in the chess game of a criminal trial, and often give a passionate plea to the jury demanding a conviction in their final submissions. To Matthew's surprise, the closing address of the prosecutor could almost have been for the defence. Del Assandro admitted that the crucial evidence about the shrimp paste's date of manufacture had cast doubt on the prosecution case. He also conceded that the insurance policy, which showed Angelina Smythe-Baker as a beneficiary, was also a mystery, and admitted that its existence should have been disclosed by Detective Brooks in evidence in chief.

When it came time for Oscar to display his talents in front of the jury, he adopted a kindly persona, expressing sympathy towards the prosecutor for the shamble of a case, whilst briefly castigating the evidence of Detective Brooks and Angela Smythe-Baker. He smiled benignly, made a few lame jokes, then quoted the officer in charge of the prosecution – Detective Sergeant Paul Brooks – 'It doesn't make any sense'.

Whilst Judge Benoit went through the entire case painstakingly, the thrust of his instructions was clear to all – with so many unexplained issues, a reasonable doubt may well exist. Whilst Matthew had hoped that he would direct the jury to acquit, knowing that this was within his judicial power, he also knew it was a rarely used discretion. In any event, his instructions to the jury left no one in doubt as to his opinion.

The jury returned less than half an hour later. The foreman of the jury formally announced a verdict of not guilty, and the courtroom burst into a spontaneous round of applause, shared by all except the prosecution and their witnesses.

Chapter Forty-five

A familiar figure was waiting for Matthew in the court foyer, and he could tell by her approach that she meant business.

'Time to pay the piper, Matt,' Emma Saunders announced in her usual deep growl.

'In one hour at the usual place,' Matthew replied.

Oscar was still basking in the limelight as a dozen reporters fired questions to their client. Matthew stood to one side, leaning against a nearby wall. He had to admire the poise and skill Jessica exhibited in answering every question, either with a studied seriousness or some appropriate light-hearted reply. It was only then that he appreciated how talented she really was. Angelina Smythe-Baker was simply not in the same class as an actress.

Two days prior, Matthew had rung Jessica early in the morning and asked her to contact someone in charge of production at Orian Foods, to check when the new label on the shrimp paste had become available. She had rung him back within the hour to confirm his suspicions, and that a code etched on the bottle would confirm this to the court. Jessica had even arranged for Pieter Siwecki, whom she had worked closely with two years prior at the firm, to come to court with her to give evidence.

Matthew could not put into words what caused his sense of unease, but Jessica's transformation from hysterical wreck to today's vision of poise and elegance was simply too smooth, too polished, and all too convenient. He saw Pieter Siwecki standing off to the side, and he walked over to him and thanked him for coming to court without any prior notice. He was stunned when the manager had replied, 'That's all right, I always knew I'd be called as a witness.'

It was at that moment that he knew for certain that Jessica had poisoned her husband.

It was now clear that Jessica Vandermeer had Siwecki waiting on a phone call to come and give evidence. If Matthew had not picked up on her hint about the changed label, she would have pretended to discover it herself.

Jessica Vandermeer's words came back to Matthew as he stood, looking at the media grouped around her and Oscar.

You have never met anyone like me ... I am truly unique.

Matthew smiled and gave a wave as he approached Emma Saunders who was engaged in the serious business of emptying another schooner of beer. Whilst some people underestimated her, Matthew well knew that her intelligence was razor sharp. Surprisingly, for a member of the fourth estate, she was also completely trustworthy. When they had met a decade earlier, her information in his assault charge had proved invaluable. His personal interview with her had been the required quid pro quo, and she had been able to progress from a reporter of fashion and gossip to her main obsession – crime reporting.

'Another triumph?' she enquired as she waved to the barmaid for another beer.

Matthew replied, with a shake of his head, then held up one finger to indicate his usual order. One of the benefits of this old-fashioned hotel, certainly in the quiet times, was that the staff was willing to provide table service.

'Well, well,' Emma replied with a grin, 'a modest lawyer. Rarer than a Tasmanian tiger.'

'It's a little delicate. I can't say what I want to. Not at present. You'll just have to trust me.'

She gave him a shrewd look. 'I can get by with what's in the public domain, provided that you come clean in the foreseeable future.'

Matthew nodded his assent. 'OK. But I'm more concerned with Angelo at present. Any news?'

'Not much, I'm afraid. You no doubt know D'Ascenzio is a heavy gambler. Apparently Blackjack is his poison.'

'So I've heard.'

'He's also a car fanatic. Antique MGs are his particular obsession. What do they say about men with their toys being a phallic symbol?'

Matthew feigned a serious face. 'That's a very sexist comment from a sensitive lass such as yourself.'

'You mean it's not true?'

'I didn't say that.'

They lapsed into silence, apart from a muttered 'thanks' as the barmaid delivered their beers. For several moments, they concentrated on their drinks before Emma broke the silence.

'That's all I've got, I'm afraid.'

Matthew gave a quiet sigh. He had been hoping against hope that Emma would come through for him once again with some information, but even the reporter with the best contacts in Sydney was of little help.

'To be honest, things look bleak,' he murmured.

'Sorry.'

'Keep trying?' he queried.

'Sure. Something will turn up.'

'Bound to.'

Neither of them believed a word of their platitudes.

Chapter Forty-six

'Another victory snatched from the jaws of defeat,' Fenella said, eyeing him closely. 'It's getting to be a habit with you and Oscar.'

'Not my finest moment, to be truthful,' Matthew replied.

'No? Why's that?'

'I think we may have been manipulated from the very beginning.'

'How shocking,' she said with feigned surprise. 'A defence lawyer with a conscience? We'll have to mount you in bronze somewhere.'

Matthew gave a chuckle.

'I often think of what you once said to me when we first spoke alone in the foyer during the MacGregor trial.' He ran the back of his hand gently across her cheek. 'When you asked me to join the good guys.'

'You mean when I asked how you could sleep at night?'

'Something like that. But look at how wrong you were then.'

She shook her head. 'I don't know that. We still believe he's guilty. The verdict proves nothing.'

'Whilst I didn't know this at the time, I can tell you now that it wasn't Tom MacGregor and it wasn't murder.'

'Details, details. Come on.'

'You'll just have to take my word for it. Lawyer-client confidence. Ever heard of it?'

She looked at him through half-closed eyes. 'It's all academic now. In any event, what's the answer to my invitation from a decade ago?'

'I'm still thinking about it.'

'Don't let me rush you now.' She rolled over onto her stomach. 'I'll forgive you if you give me a back massage.'

'Sounds fair.' He gently rubbed her shoulders and lower back with one hand as he lay beside her. He still believed she was the most stunning woman he had ever seen, who grew even more beautiful as she aged.

After twenty minutes or so, he stretched his arm and rubbed it with his other hand.

'Cramp has intervened, I'm afraid.'

'Why the change of heart?' she murmured sleepily. 'Why the phone call to come over after going all Catholic on me earlier?'

He slowly traced his finger around the contours of her back. 'Perhaps it's a malaise called Fenella,' he eventually replied. 'What would be the medical term for that? Ella-virus perhaps?'

'A romantic would call it love.'

'A realist would call it lust.'

She gave an involuntary guffaw. 'Well no one would ever mistake you for a romantic. If it's lust, then let's make the most of it. We might even be able to soothe that guilty conscience of yours.'

Chapter Forty-seven

Matthew's swearing-in as a barrister took place a few weeks later on a bitterly cold Friday morning, with rain pounding down throughout the city. He had reluctantly attended the customary legal outfitters a week prior for the required garb of the bar: black gown, barrister's jacket and jabot with a wing collar, topped off with the traditional horsehair wig.

Oscar moved his admission and the oath was solemnly chanted by a dozen or so applicants before the full bench of the Supreme Court. The atmospheric old sandstone court building in King Street gave some semblance of tradition to the gathering. The Chief Justice gave a lengthy and earnest speech to the new appointees, but Matthew, whose mind was on the upcoming trial, was relieved when the ceremony finished.

Matthew was an only child and he had invited his parents to the ceremony. Their unbridled happiness at having him admitted to the bar provided his only real pleasure in the ceremony. Both his mother and father were products of the Depression, and, like most of their community, had never had the opportunity of attending university. They clearly saw the swearing-in ceremony as a milestone in their own lives, which was illustrated by their animated banter with Oscar both before and after the event. This continued throughout lunch at The Summit, a revolving restaurant in the city atop Australia Square Tower, the tallest building in the city.

Matthew was careful not to spoil their pleasure by expressing his true feelings, and when they caught the afternoon country train back to their Blue Mountains home, he breathed a sigh of relief.

'Thanks, Oscar, you've excelled yourself today.'

'It was my pleasure, Matt. Your parents are the salt of the earth and you should be proud of them.' He made a sideways dip of his head, signifying some reproof.

Matthew held up his hands, part in explanation, part in excuse.

'I am, I am. It's just that they see the ceremony as some momentous occasion, whereas I just see it as legal mumbo jumbo with the wigs and gowns being some servile gesture to English tradition. We're not Pommies, Oscar, we're Australian, and this nonsense should be abolished.'

'Tradition, my boy. Tradition is the foundation of the legal profession and the bedrock of our legal system.'

'I'm a little confused. Perhaps you can clarify tradition for me. Is that the tradition of the star chamber, the rack or the hangman's noose that you're so sentimental about?'

'Well ... I have to admit that not each and every tradition is acceptable today.'

'But prancing around with silly wigs is perfectly acceptable?'

'When you put it like that ... perhaps you have a point.'

'Have you ever come across a Hans Christian Andersen tale called *The Emperor's New Clothes*? The moral of the story is that, when even children start laughing at you, perhaps it's time to have a look at yourself. Whilst I don't admire everything about the American justice system, I might remind you that they don't see the need for lawyers to dress up in silly costumes.'

'Well, it's all academic to me. I'll be here to give advice when asked, but I'm happy to ease into retirement gracefully.'

Oscar had arranged for Matthew to be given a room at his chambers floor for a trial period, and, as Oscar still intended to attend chambers, he would be nearby if Matthew called upon him.

'My only concern is leaving you with Angelo,' Oscar had confided as they sipped their schooners of Guinness at their usual bar near chambers. 'I can recommend several brilliant QCs who will jump at the chance to take over.'

Matthew shook his head.

'I've explained it all to Angelo and Rose several times, but they're adamant they want us to appear. Deep down, I think Angelo doesn't trust anyone at the bar, apart from you of course. He says that over the years he's seen too many shifty barristers distort the truth and skirt the rules, and he lacks any respect or confidence in them.'

'Well I have to admit that some barristers in criminal trials are ruthless and unprofessional, but it's unfair to paint everyone with the same brush. The silks that I recommend are not only brilliant lawyers, but also straight as a die.'

Matthew sipped his Guinness slowly.

'I don't think it matters who appears for him. Unless I can think of something clever, he's going down. For something he did not do. It will ruin him and destroy his family.'

'A barrister can't become personally involved. I've told you this before.'

Matthew gave a bitter laugh. 'I know the theory Oscar. It's the practice that's eating away at me.'

Oscar shook his head in admonishment. 'I'll ignore my doctor's orders for this one last trial with you, but we're not miracle workers, Matthew. We can only do our best.'

Chapter Forty-eight

Franz Mannheim drove his late model BMW to one of several flats that he owned, parking one block away and carefully pausing several times to check for anyone following him. He was confident that no one replaced the tail that he had disposed of several weeks ago, but it was in his nature to be cautious. That was what had kept him alive in his native Germany during the war, and he saw no reason to break old habits.

Letting himself in the front door, he waited patiently in a dimly lit lounge room for his visitor to arrive. When he heard a light tapping, Mannheim sprang up, crossed to the front door, then opened it. 'Good to see you, Phillip,' Mannheim said, guiding the detective into the house and pouring a glass of Chivas Regal for each of them.

D'Ascenzio glanced around nervously. 'You're sure this place is not under surveillance?'

'One hundred percent certain. You're not my only contact in the force, you know.'

D'Ascenzio did not know if Mannheim was being truthful or merely boasting, but he let the comment pass.

'Well I'm here. What's the change of heart about us being seen together?'

'No change in that regard. No one knows about this place and we weren't followed. At least I wasn't.' Mannheim sipped his scotch and gave the detective an unblinking stare.

'Don't worry about me, I can spot a tail a mile off. What's tonight about then? What's the urgency?'

'You're about to do us all a favour. Assist the police with their enquiries, as it were.'

The detective shifted on the lounge chair. It had suddenly become uncomfortable. 'Go on.'

'First, let me tell you a little story. Background information, you might call it.' Mannheim paused to savour another sip of the scotch. 'It's always important to know who you're dealing with. To know how committed they are to a certain result. Now, Rufus Tomlinson thought he was an accomplished professional, but he was really an amateur. Never completely committed, you might say.'

D'Ascenzio froze, his glass halfway to his lips.

'In fact, he was exceedingly polite, and even opened the window of his car and apologised for being lost. Wanted to know the shortest way back to the shopping centre.' Mannheim gave a chuckle. 'There we were, the two of us in a deserted new housing estate, and that was the best he could come up with. Sad, really.'

'Who's Rufus Tomlinson?' D'Ascenzio asked in an attempt at a normal voice. Unfortunately the tone betrayed his anxiety.

'You well know who he is. What I'm telling you tonight will bind us like brothers. Blood brothers in fact.' Mannheim's features remained calm, but his eyes narrowed to pinpricks that burned through D'Ascenzio. 'A millisecond after the bullet pierced his outer skull, the back of his head exploded, with fragments of brain and bone splattering the interior roof of his car in a crimson spread.'

Mannheim took his time to let the words have their effect as he sipped from his glass.

'It's good to keep your hand in, I always say. What do you think Phillip?'

D'Ascenzio took a large gulp of scotch but made no reply.

'Certainly, in my experience, you can't just rely on a conventional bullet. You know, one time I shot one of my closest friends in the left eye. I was amazed later to hear that he'd survived. The bullet had circled around the inside of his skull, making a groove as it went.' He gave another mirthless chuckle. 'Do you know what? I had to do the job again a few weeks later. So now I have my ammunition specially made by a little man who is a wizard with such matters. The bullet explodes inside the skull. No second chances there, Phillip.'

D'Ascenzio now realised the true nature of the person with whom he had aligned himself. He stared at Mannheim with revulsion and a growing sense of dread.

'You did a great job with the drugs in Cattani's car boot, but now I want you to add a little corroboration to the story. You do remember the little problem that I solved for you a few months back, don't you, Phillip?'

The little problem had been almost a year's salary owed to Mannheim for losses at the casino. Mannheim cancelled the debt, saying to D'Ascenzio at the time, 'What are friends for?' The detective now knew the answer to that question.

'I thought we were even after I planted the drugs?'

'Even? No, Phillip. We'll never be even. We're now bound together for life.'

Chapter Forty-nine

Oscar held the conference in his chambers, as Matthew's nearby room was not only much smaller but lacking in basic comforts, like carpet, comfortable chairs, or even a small window to let outside light enter the tiny room.

Oscar's room was no great improvement, but it at least had an old-world, lived-in atmosphere – much like an old pair of shorts or a worn tee-shirt – that somehow relaxed Matthew's spirit. Oscar was busily reading the three-page statement for the fourth time, totally immersed in his task. Angelo sat slumped in a chair, his eyes closed and his body completely still. Lena sat beside him, also skimming a copy of the statement, although she knew the wording almost by heart.

The fresh statement by Constable Phillip D'Ascenzio had been served on Lena only the day before the conference. It alleged that Angelo had confided to him during a late-night drinking session, spreading over some six hours, that he had been systematically dealing heroin for the past year, with Reginald Smithers as his supplier. The statement went on to allege that Angelo had paid Matthew and Lena $25,000 in cash to defend him against the current charges, and that both lawyers knew of Angelo's drug activities and where the cash had come from. If the Law Society or the Bar Council found that Lena or Matthew had known that this was the true source of the money – that would constitute professional misconduct. It could also lead to the end of their legal careers.

Matthew waited for Oscar to raise his head before he opened the discussion.

'It's got to be Mannheim, his fingerprints are all over it.'

'Not in the physical sense,' Oscar replied, 'but in every other way. You do of course realise that the trial will not be the end of this?'

'If Mannheim has his way,' Matthew said, 'it will only be the start. With Angelo convicted and serving a long sentence, the drug conspirators will be released, their charges withdrawn, and complaints regarding Lena and myself made to the various disciplinary bodies. Probably disbarment for me and cancellation of Lena's practicing certificate. Anything I've missed?'

Oscar reached for his pipe and commenced his ritual of packing then stoking the rich tobacco mixture. Previously, this had irritated Matthew immensely, but now it was a triviality and almost completely ignored.

'That about covers it, my boy,' Oscar replied. 'Any contributions, Angelo?'

The detective shook his head slowly, but did not answer.

'Lena?' Oscar nodded in her direction.

Lena paused for a moment to collect her thoughts before replying. 'I warned Matthew ten years ago how dangerous Mannheim was, and if anything he's become more powerful and destructive. He's clearly out for revenge. This isn't something he dreamt up last week.'

'I presume it's the carrot and stick method with D'Ascenzio,' Matthew added quietly. 'A new sports car perhaps, with unlimited access to his stable of high-class call-girls and casino tables. Alternatively, it's a bullet to the back of his head. Not much of a choice really.'

'When you look at possession of the drugs and the evidence of Reggie the Rat, this new evidence makes the Crown case rather imposing,' Oscar muttered, almost to himself.

'That's one way to phrase it,' Angelo replied.

Matthew reflected that knowing Mannheim's influence in the corridors of power, an arrest of them both for receiving the proceeds of drug dealing was also not out of the question. Matthew massaged his temple absently with the middle finger of his left hand. He could feel the tightness that preceded a blinding headache, yet he knew that he had to take control of the conference and inject some confidence into the group.

'What have you heard on the grapevine about D'Ascenzio?' Matthew asked, looking at Angelo.

'He's not a womaniser and he's not into drugs. The only thing I've heard is that he loves going to late night sessions at an illegal casino up at the Cross,' Angelo replied.

'He was boasting to me six months or so ago that he'd learned to count cards and could make a living as a professional gambler,' Angelo continued. 'He believed that he could beat the house at Blackjack. Said it was only a matter of memorising the cards already dealt.'

'I've been hearing stories like that for the past twenty years,' Lena said with a chuckle. 'Then the so-called expert goes quiet and starts selling his shares or a car or a house. The boasting doesn't last long.'

'It's an interesting topic,' Oscar said between puffs of his pipe. 'I knew a young lawyer just after the war, '46 or '47 it was, and he was brilliant at numbers with a memory to match. He was into card counting and he did beat the house, but when the casino bosses realised what he was doing, he was tossed out and barred for life.'

'What happened to him?' Matthew asked.

'No one knows,' Oscar replied. 'He went over to the States after telling me that he was going to take on the Las Vegas casinos. Suddenly he disappeared, and even his close relatives never heard from him again.'

'I think we can guess,' Angelo said. 'The Mafia doesn't take kindly to card counters. I think the remedy was usually a new pair of shoes.'

Oscar gave him a questioning look.

'Concrete ones,' Angelo added.

'Isn't Las Vegas in the middle of a desert?' Lena asked.

'The concrete shoes are a metaphor,' Matthew said. 'Whether he ended up in the ocean or the sand hills, the end is the same. Let's just say he would have had limited rights of appeal.'

'With no legal representation,' Oscar added.

'Getting back to D'Ascenzio,' Matthew said, 'we know he is hand in glove with Mannheim, probably due to gambling debts. To weaken his credibility in court, we need some solid evidence of that relationship. Lena has been advised of a new mention date, and it's probable that Judge Benoit has spoken to Judge Latimer regarding Oscar's rise from the sick bed. I suspect that we'll be facing a trial in a few weeks at most. What we all have to do is concentrate on D'Ascenzio. I'm open to any and all suggestions.'

The other three shifted in their seats. After a few minutes, Matthew stood and suggested they adjourn for lunch at their usual café.

'These people are not masterminds,' Matthew said quietly as they waited for the ancient lift to finish clanking up to their floor. 'I know there are mistakes that we can discover. We just have to apply ourselves to the task.'

'They're not masterminds,' Angelo replied in a dispirited tone, 'but neither are we.'

'No, Matthew is right,' Lena responded sharply. 'If there's a flaw to be exposed, one of us will discover it. Trust me; giving in to these bastards is not an option.'

Chapter Fifty

Matthew regularly jogged on the grass footpath that commenced near his unit, averaging some three to five kilometres each run – the distance being dependent on his energy levels that day. He used these solitary runs to reflect on any problems that were troubling him, but since joining the bar his main concern had been Angelo's upcoming trial. Despite Lena's encouragement at the conference, they all knew that they were facing probable defeat. Worse still, it would be a conviction engineered by Franz Mannheim, whom Matthew regarded as the most malevolent individual he had ever encountered. The trial date now was only a few weeks away, and an overwhelming sadness had enveloped him.

Several of his old football mates had been constantly ringing, demanding he join them in what they called a *fun run* of some fourteen kilometres. Instead of some gentle grass track, they ran on a baking hot bitumen path with several steep grades, both ascending and descending, and alongside some ten thousand fellow masochists. It was the sixth running of the event based on the San Francisco *Bay to Breakers* run, and was called the *City to Surf*. In a moment of weakness, Matthew had agreed to join them, and on an overcast Sunday in August, spitting with rain and accompanied by a gusting southerly wind, he and six other retired footballers tried to relive their past, when everything seemed possible and no barrier was too large to overcome.

Not that any of them intended to compete with the five-foot-tall, fifty-kilogram race favourites; whose main profession Matthew thought must be as a jockey. Apart from Matthew's knee reconstruction, the other six had a litany of operations, accompanied by the insertion of screws and metal plates that now held them together. They wore their old football guernseys, and starting at the rear of the pack, Matthew's intention was to jog without stopping, enjoy the camaraderie of the crowd and take time to admire Sydney Harbour and the Opera House once they had conquered the infamous *Heartbreak Hill* – a steep two-kilometre climb that tested even the most ardent runners.

The familiar smell of the football change room flooded back to him at the starting area as the pungent smell of liniment liberally applied to thousands of hamstrings, calves and quadriceps wafted over the runners. As the good-natured babble of voices chattered endlessly throughout the crowd, the Sydney Lord Mayor counted down to the start and the gun signalled a frantic surge of runners. After a few metres, however, everything came to a halt as several falls, caused by plastic bags and spilt water on the smooth bitumen road, created a bottleneck.

Indeed, the first kilometre of the run proved to be a stop-start affair, as Matthew concentrated on avoiding runners as they overtook then cut in front of him. Mostly these were young children or one of several obese older specimens, some morbidly so – who believed their excess baggage would not inhibit their natural running ability. As Matthew entered the Kings Cross tunnel, a haze of perspiration and heat from the prior nine thousand runners enveloped him, and his tee-shirt was soaked even though he had only been jogging for about five minutes. As he emerged into the daylight, he recognised several of the enthusiastic overtakers stretched out on the side of the road, much like beached whales, with ambulance officers already attending them. So much for misplaced enthusiasm, Matthew thought with a wry grin.

The course wound slowly out of the city and down to Rose Bay as the overcast sky parted temporarily, allowing a pale sun to shine where a low seawall framed a harbour dotted with yachts bobbing peacefully at anchor. Matthew grabbed a plastic cup of water at the first drink station, swallowed it in one gulp and then tossed the cup amongst a sea of others in the gutter. He once again eased back into a slow jog, then focused on his six companions as they passed the five-kilometre sign. Their blood-red faces, sweat-drenched clothes and wild hair told him all he needed to know about their state of fitness. An enthusiastic jazz band gradually came within their hearing range, and, as he jogged past the musical trio, Matthew gave a half-hearted wave of appreciation. As they approached the six-kilometre mark, the road began to rise sharply, and he knew they had started to climb the psychological part of the run. The aptly named Heartbreak Hill was a mountainous stretch where Matthew saw that most of the runners were now walking, half bent over to gain some oxygen whilst trying to relieve the various cramps and acute pains that had overcome them. The seven aging footballers, however, still shuffled forward without a break to the crest of the hill, where not only a welcome drink station but also several eager ambulance officers awaited. Matthew's plans to enjoy the panoramic view from the Kincoppal – Rose Bay Convent had completely slipped his mind, his field of concentration now being exclusive to the few metres of bitumen in front of his aching feet as he gulped more cold water from a plastic cup. Strange, Matthew thought, how something as basic as water could taste as magnificent as the most expensive French champagne when your body was screaming for refreshment. At that moment, he saw a sign that made his spirits nose-dive. They had only reached halfway and still had seven kilometres to run.

For some reason, Matthew had imagined that the second half of the run was downhill, but like every other first-timer he soon realised that he was yet to face the hardest part of the event. A succession of short downhill stretches was complemented by equally sharp rises that seemed to repeat themselves endlessly, breaking the spirit of many of the runners as they slowed to a crawl. He was vaguely aware of a cold spray occasionally hitting his body as onlookers hosed the runners from their front gardens, but all conversation between the seven footballers had ceased many kilometres ago, and now only the pounding of jogging shoes and the laboured breathing of the runners rose from around Matthew.

A tantalising glimpse of the ocean came near the eleven-kilometre sign, but it disappeared just as quickly, and it was only in the last few kilometres that the runners descended from the heights to Bondi Beach. A last piece of cruelty awaited as he passed the winning post, which was located on an adjoining road. Matthew had to continue the struggle for several hundred metres before making a U-turn and staggering down a seemingly unending stretch of road back to the finishing banner. To add to his exhaustion, a large timing counter flashed above the runners to record seventy-five minutes since the gun had sounded. Matthew's disjointed recollection was of thousands of cups of green liquid, apparently some type of sports drink, lined up on temporary trestles, followed by an icy blast of saltwater as he half-dived, half-fell into the surf. He had no memory of covering the hundred or so metres of grass and sand between the finish line and the water, but was vaguely aware that all of his companions had collapsed into the water at approximately the same time.

Never in his life had he endured such sustained fatigue for so long, and he was secretly amazed that he had not let the pain from his knee force him to stop. Rugby league called for intense bursts of energy for ten or twenty seconds a time and, as the game wore on, the cumulative effect resulted in exhaustion. This run was completely different. He now realised that rugby league was a game played largely on emotion, fueled by a competitive spirit and a need to support your teammates to overcome the opposition. This type of event however was one where you competed against yourself, and you only completed the event by forcing your brain to ignore the constant pain. How competitive runners in a half or full marathon endured the physical attrition on their bodies was beyond his comprehension.

Some half an hour later, after collecting their plastic bags containing a change of clothes and a towel, they changed from their running shorts and tee-shirts into jeans and dry shirts. No one seemed to mind that they all stripped to their underpants to perform the change, as similar exercises were taking place amongst thousands of other exhausted runners, both male and female. They made their way to a collection of shops and restaurants opposite the beach, grabbed an empty table outside a local café, and slumped into a welcoming seat.

As the group relaxed with their first beer, talk was about how hard the run had been.

'It's not until you actually run the bugger that you realise the true nature of the beast,' Greg, a heavily built ex-front rower, murmured between mouthfuls of beer from the stubbie he grasped with a determined grip.

'You mean, *walk a mile in my shoes*,' Matthew replied with a chuckle.

'Or run fourteen clicks in mine,' an ex-winger named Geoff chipped in.

After several more stubbies of beer, the group ordered hamburgers and chips, and several hours passed in blissful ease as they re-lived their past football triumphs. The stories were a complete exaggeration of the truth, but no one disputed the remembered events. The group had planned a pub-crawl from Bondi Beach back up the steep incline to Bondi Junction train station, but Matthew, who had been lost in thought, held up his hands.

'Sorry boys. I know what we agreed, but believe it or not I've got to catch the bus and head back to work.'

'Bullshit,' the other six called out in unison.

'I'm a lawyer. Would I ever deceive you?' Matthew replied with a grin.

'Always,' was the immediate combined reply.

'Who's the lucky lass?' one of the group demanded.

'No, no. It's work, not pleasure,' Matthew insisted. 'But I tell you what. After I've finished a trial I've got coming up, I'll get us all together and tell you the story over a barbeque and a few beers.'

After numerous complaints, Matthew managed to break away from the group. He then lined up in a queue that was at least seventy runners deep to wait for the next bus.

It was a long shot but Matthew was desperate.

'*Walk a mile in my shoes*,' he said to himself. 'Perhaps I can.'

Chapter Fifty-one

Inspector Mike Gordon's stony-faced glare, together with his silence, did not set a favourable tone as Matthew sat opposite him at a small Greek coffee shop that the head of Internal Affairs had selected. Matthew had phoned his private number late at lunchtime to arrange the meeting that afternoon.

'I'm all out of favours,' Gordon announced, 'and I've stuck my neck out too far already.'

Matthew gave a soulful look but did not reply.

'I'm sorry for Angelo,' he continued, 'but ruining my career won't help him. Word's come from on high that we should keep our hands off the case. To let justice run its course, as it were.'

'Justice?' Matthew queried.

'Yes, I know, I know. Don't preach to me.'

'You know this latest statement from D'Ascenzio is a load of crap. Pure fantasy – no doubt created by Mannheim and his mates.'

'Entirely possible. But it's out of my hands.'

Matthew hesitated.

The Ancient Craft

'There is one last thing you could do for Angelo. In the interests of justice, of course.'

'Go on.'

'Yesterday I had an epiphany of sorts. I ran in the City to Surf …'

'You're wasting my time.' Gordon half-rose to leave before Matthew grabbed his arm.

'You've got to at least hear me out.'

The inspector slowly sank back to his seat. 'Make it short, then.'

'I decided to recreate the actions of whomever it was that put the drugs into Angelo's boot. *Walk a mile in his shoes*, as it were. I've made an educated guess that the likely time would have been when his wife parked the car outside the building where she has her weekly yoga session. The car's unattended for ninety minutes or so. That's ample time to pick the boot lock, remove the spare wheel and take it somewhere convenient. The tyre is levered off, the drugs planted, and then the tyre is refitted and re-inflated.'

Gordon gave Matthew a suspicious glance. 'What about eye-witnesses?'

Matthew replied with a slow smile. 'Exactly. That was the problem that he faced. The yoga is in a church hall. Where the cars park at the back of the building, passersby could easily see them from the street. So, I asked myself, *where would you go to plant the drugs?* Too dangerous at a nearby service station. Too many customers. I suppose you could have arranged a lock-up garage, complete with tyre levers and an air compressor. But that's too much trouble, surely?'

'Go on.'

'So yesterday I checked the yellow pages and drove around the area near the church hall. Within about a ten-minute drive radius. I could find no tyre fitters, but I located three car mechanics. Two of them were large businesses with at least half a dozen employees, and with people coming and going all day. Only one was a small outfit, with one mechanic and one apprentice. Five minutes from the church. So I had a quiet word with Joe the owner this morning.'

'Where's this going? The drugs were found months ago.'

'Stay with me on this. The drugs would never have stayed in the boot for more than a day or so. Too dangerous to risk a flat tyre causing someone to discover the drugs in the spare. Probably planted when Rose was at yoga. She was there the day prior to the police raid.'

'That would make it,' Gordon paused as he checked his pocket diary, 'the eighteenth.'

'Just so. It was an outside chance I suppose, but I asked the owner if on that date, someone had come to his garage and borrowed some tyre levers and used his air compressor.'

Gordon leaned forward in his chair. 'You couldn't rely on anything he told you that had occurred months ago.'

Matthew raised his eyebrows. 'Unless something happened that was unusual. Out of the ordinary. Something that would stick in his mind.'

'And?'

'He said that around that time, he can't recall the exact date, that someone did exactly that.'

'I asked him how he could remember the incident. He said that he doesn't lend his tools to anyone. Old school, you see. He told this bloke to bugger off and stop wasting his time. That's when it happened.'

'What?'

'This character produced his ID. His police ID. The copper said he was a plain-clothes detective and was on the job searching for drugs in the tyre. Joe, that's the owner's name, wasn't sure whether to believe him, and took no notice of the name on the ID, but being a law-abiding citizen and wanting to keep the copper happy, he said OK.'

Gordon nodded. 'That's interesting, but not much more than that.'

'There's more. Joe loaned him his own tools. Said that it was their only use in the past twelve months. He reckoned that it was a bugger to take tyres off the rim with levers, and it was easier for him to run the car down to the nearest tyre fitters and let them do the tyre repairs and any balancing and alignment. He said the tools haven't been touched since the copper used them.'

Gordon leaned forward and lowered his voice. 'So you'd like me to …'

'What I'd like you to do is to find some fingerprints. I checked with Joe and he said that this character didn't use gloves. He had to use the office washbasin to clean his hands afterwards. If you do locate any prints, that will ID the copper. Joe can then be asked to take part in a line-up.'

'That's what I'd call a very long shot.'

'Better a long shot than being shot dead. If Angelo's convicted, he may as well be. His career, his reputation, his finances and possibly his family – all destroyed.'

Gordon ran his hand through his thinning hair, his face tense as he looked warily at the barrister. 'You're a pain in the bloody neck, Jameson.'

'I think I've heard that before. It's so nice to be appreciated.'

Chapter Fifty-two

Matthew's knee had grown progressively stiff and painful following his ill-advised fun run, but several days after the event it became so difficult to walk that he rang the orthopaedic surgeon who had reconstructed the knee over a decade ago. Not that he actually spoke to the doctor, as the receptionist performed her guard dog duties with the usual stubbornness.

'If you wish to speak to the doctor personally, you will have to obtain a referral from your GP and then make an appointment through me,' the elderly voice announced.

'Might I ask how long I will have to wait for an appointment?' Matthew asked through gritted teeth.

'First the referral, then the appointment, I believe I said.'

'Let's pretend I have a referral. When is his next free date?'

There was a frosty silence before the reply came with deliberate articulation. 'Six months. Give or take a few days.'

Matthew recognised that the woman fell into that category of people who, when given a small amount of control claimed absolute authority. It doesn't matter whether they were old, young, male, or female – legions of these frustrated dictators abound everywhere. Changing his tone, Matthew asked if it would be too much trouble to ask the doctor to recommend a physiotherapist who might be able to give him some assistance.

'No trouble at all, Mr Jameson,' was the immediate reply. 'We have an excellent young woman who treats all of our patients, post-operation.'

What *young* meant to the woman on the phone was something that Matthew felt was best not to pursue.

Samantha Wright turned out to be early thirtyish, with jet-black hair and a face of porcelain skin. She displayed a crinkling of the skin around her eyes, accompanied by a sharp, inquisitive voice – as though she was trying to place him into a category but was unable to do so. Matthew felt that if she had let her hair fall rather than tie it severely with what looked like a stout rubber band, her face would soften considerably.

'May I ask what it was that made you believe you were still twenty-five and superbly fit?' she enquired with a sideways glance as she busily made notes. 'You're the fifth person in the last week that has told me the same story. City to Surfers, one and all.'

'I suppose you could call it male pride,' Matthew replied with a grin.

'I would actually use another expression myself, but let's see how much damage you've inflicted.'

For the next half hour, the physiotherapist bent his leg this way and that, stretching it at acute angles and causing him to grimace with pain every few minutes. When she finished, she gave him a rueful look, shook her head and scribbled in her notepad.

Matthew eventually broke the silence. 'How bad is it?'

'What I just cannot understand, Mr Jameson ...'

'Please ... Matthew.'

'Very well then, Matthew. I cannot understand how you could have been so foolish. Your specialist used all his knowledge and experience to repair your knee a decade or so ago, only for you to ruin his work with this crazy fun run.'

'I think that the usual reply is that it seemed like a good idea at the time.'

She gazed at him for a few seconds, until a faint smile appeared. 'I think I may have heard that once or twice before.'

After giving him a series of exercises to perform three times per day, demonstrated in a pamphlet by little stick-figure diagrams, she wrapped his knee in a tight elasticised bandage. She gave him instructions on replacing the bandage, closed her notebook and adopted what he assumed was her lecturing face.

'It's a little like AA – the instructions are excellent, but if the alcoholic doesn't want to help himself, then there's no point at all.'

'Do I have a twelve-step programme then?'

She regarded him for a few moments before softening her tone. 'It's just that I see so many ex-footballers who live their lives in the past. Still believing that they are young and strong and fit, with everyone pandering to them. When the adulation stops, they find it difficult to adjust to a normal life. They just drift along with no plans for the future and little discipline to start a new life.'

Matthew gave a bemused grin. He realised that he did not look like a typical lawyer – he had come to the appointment in old jeans, a faded tee-shirt and scruffy joggers. He had intended to go for a very slow run on the grass expanse of Hyde Park, to test his knee before the visit to the physiotherapist, but the pain he experienced had reduced that to a slow walk. He did not have time to change before the appointed time, and had forgotten about his casual appearance.

'Your sign outside is too modest. It should also mention counsellor and motivator.'

Samantha turned her head to one side and gave him a questioning gaze. 'I realise that it's none of my business, but do you mind if I ask what your achievements are since the knee reconstruction ended your dream of playing for Australia?'

'I was never at that level. A promising club footballer was as high as I reached.'

'Even so. The injury destroyed whatever dreams you may have had at that time.'

'I suppose you could say I have reached some modest level of achievement in my life.'

'As in?'

Matthew paused momentarily before replying. 'It's fair to say that I use my training and experience to help the innocent and disadvantaged against the might of an oppressive state.'

'Do you have a costume or a cape?' Samantha replied, eyes wide with amusement.

'I do wear a wig sometimes.'

Samantha struggled to contain a giggle. 'Whatever makes you happy. I have a few clients who admit to cross-dressing, so you're not the first for me.'

'That's absolutely fascinating. What would you say is the most common injury that you treat cross-dressers for?'

'Sprained ankles,' she replied with a straight face. 'They keep falling off the high heels. Not used to them you see.' She rose and walked to the door. 'Well I must say it's been a very interesting session, Matthew, but all good things must come to an end.'

'How about dinner one evening? You could give me advice on fulfilling my destiny,' he said as he heaved himself awkwardly out of his seat. The earlier manipulation of his knee had done nothing to improve his flexibility.

'Thank you, Matthew, but no thanks. Just remember to do the exercises. I will know if you don't follow my instructions.'

'I always do as instructed. Obedience is my middle name.'

Matthew had no idea whether Samantha was serious or simply pulling his leg, but he appreciated the sharp exchanges and her quick wit. Another visit might prove to be very interesting.

Chapter Fifty-three

Rose Cattani had rejected her husband's request and stayed in Sydney awaiting the trial, and she now grasped his arm tightly as they pushed through the throng of reporters, onlookers and various court staff as they entered the District Court building for the first day of the case.

How quickly life can change, she reflected. Just a few months ago, Angelo had a promising career, but today he faced humiliation and a probable gaol sentence. She could not think of a word or even an expression that would encompass her level of bitterness. All caused by a lie – and she well knew that even the smartest people can fall for the biggest lies. Although she trusted Matthew like a brother, she knew he was inexperienced as a barrister, and Oscar surely was well beyond his best. She had tried to convince her husband to instruct a Queens Counsel to defend him. But he would not listen. Now it was too late. The cards had been dealt and she already knew the result.

When Matthew caught sight of Angelo and his wife amongst the crowd, the detective seemed to lack energy or confidence, and his stooped shoulders and ashen face indicated his resignation.

'Straighten up, mate,' Matthew murmured as he took Angelo's arm, guiding him towards the lift. 'Remember what I told you at the committal court. Don't go around looking like a condemned prisoner awaiting the gallows. Smile for the press if you can manage it.'

'You're not my PR agent, Matt. Who cares what the unwashed rabble of the press think?'

'You never know when the odd prospective juror might stroll by. Or even a Hollywood agent. They might sign you up for a film about your illegal persecution.' Matthew's attempt at humour fell flat.

'Or my incarceration, more likely.'

Matthew was trying to inject some enthusiasm into his friend, because he knew that the critical moment would soon arrive when he would be cross-examined by the Crown prosecutor. It was essential that Angelo display a combination of outrage and honesty, rather than one of despair, but even as he encouraged him, Matthew felt something of a fraud.

Inspector Mike Gordon had phoned Matthew a few days previously to give him an update on the enquiries they had discussed at the café. He told him that the search for fingerprints had come up empty, and that the photo ID arranged for the garage owner had proved inconclusive. 'Could be him,' was as much as Joe Simpson would commit himself.

Matthew had spent the few days leading up to the trial in silent apprehension, waking at 4 am each morning from a dream that terrified him, but of which he could never remember any details. As further sleep was no longer an option, he would instead go for long walks on the beach, but no further inspiration had burst upon him.

Changing into his barrister's regalia prior to Angelo's arrival, Matthew felt no excitement but rather a listless despondency.

Now that the trial was about to commence, the crushing weight of responsibility seemed to force the air from his lungs, and he kept taking deep gulps of air to steady his nerves. When he had accompanied Angelo and his wife in the lift to the designated floor, he saw Rose looking closely at him and he knew that she sensed his true feelings.

'Just do your best, Matthew,' she had said quietly to him as they walked over to the conference room where Oscar and Lena were waiting.

It was as if she were already consoling him by saying, *Don't blame yourself.*

Matthew looked away from her, unable to reply.

Matthew's encouragement did not lift Angelo's spirit. Although the detective had not spoken of it directly to anyone, he had resigned himself to a conviction. His spirit had revived for a brief time when Matthew told him of his latest meeting with Mike Gordon at the café, but when the results proved fruitless that was the final straw. Strangely enough, he was not bitter. He knew from experience that unfairness came in many guises – innocent car crash victims, children with inoperable cancer, women battered to death by drunk or insane husbands – none of them deserved their fate. He knew that only a simple-minded person would believe that fairness and honesty always prevail.

Being truthful to himself, he admitted that he had lost the will to fight.

Chapter Fifty-four

Judge Hugh Latimer, QC, cast a baleful eye over the defence team and shook his head. *How on earth did the accused detective think it would be a good idea to instruct a geriatric barrister to lead an inexperienced junior barrister to defend him?* he mused to himself. *Did he think that the trial was some sort of game?*

There was nothing he enjoyed more than to joust verbally with a brilliant Queen's Counsel in a high-profile trial. He regarded it as a type of legal chess, and in cases where the stakes were a sentence of perhaps fifteen or twenty years, then so much the better. Latimer's life at the criminal bar had been a glittering affair, but his subsequent appointment to the District Court bench, the second tier of state judicial life, had been a bitter disappointment. He could not understand why he had not been appointed to the top tier – the Supreme Court bench – and this perceived slight at his ability was a cancer eating away at him every day that he presided.

He privately believed that a brilliant exhibition of his legal talent at trials such as this would convince the right people that he should be elevated to his rightful legal position – the Supreme Court, then possibly Chief Justice. As such he did not intend to allow any judicial leeway towards an incompetent defence team.

As the parties announced their appearances, Latimer drummed his fingers on the bench and displayed a slight scowl. 'The defence is ready to proceed, Mr O'Shannessy?' Latimer queried. 'No last-minute request for an adjournment to instruct senior counsel?'

'Thank you for your enquiry, Your Honour,' Oscar replied. 'I may have my failings, but owing to my age, seniority is not one of them.'

'I wasn't referring to age.'

Oscar gave a disarming smile. 'Of course not, Your Honour. I'm sure that no offence was intended, and I certainly take none. We are ready to proceed.'

'Well said,' Lena murmured to Oscar as he sat down.

A barely disguised snort of amusement came from beside Matthew. He glanced over towards Fenella Montgomery, whose left hand was shielding her face. She was instructing the Crown prosecutor who sat alongside her, and whose face betrayed no emotion.

Tobias Blackmore, QC, was a towering giant in his mid-fifties, some six-foot-five inches in height, and feared by most criminal defence lawyers. His bushy eyebrows and extravagant moustache added a dash of élan to his otherwise severe appearance. Although considered fair, he had an uncanny knack of making every juror his friend. Matthew knew that human nature plays an essential role in any jury trial, and to acquit an accused against the wishes of an advocate they admired naturally ran counter to that premise.

Oscar had often repeated to Matthew, 'If you want to succeed at the bar, you must get your jury onside.' Matthew knew that his mentor was a master of self-deprecating jokes that took the jury into his confidence, and, by the end of each trial, the jury would invariably regard Oscar with some affection. In the present trial, however, a similar story was true for Tobias Blackmore, who boasted a conviction rate of ninety-three percent, with some three years having passed since the last acquittal.

Fenella gave Matthew a sideways grin as he sat beside her at the bar table. She leaned towards him and murmured, 'Nothing personal, Matt. I trust this won't affect our little arrangement?'

The arrangement she spoke of was a weekly tryst, usually Saturday night stretching into Sunday lunchtime when her husband was staying at his club. Matthew had sworn to himself repeatedly that he would cancel the meetings and defeat what clearly was an addiction to her – but like millions of smokers, alcoholics and other addicts, he had always found himself weakening. Not that he cast any blame on Fenella, but he knew that their affair would never result in happiness for either of them.

'I need to have a word about that,' he replied quietly. 'I'll see you after court.'

Matthew had a faint inkling that there may be some relationship in the future with Samantha Wright, and realised that now would be a sensible time to break his addiction. In reality, their affair was the least of his problems, and his full attention swung back to the trial.

The jury selection proceeded smoothly. As Oscar had predicted, Blackmore sat quietly, not challenging any of the persons called out by the judge's associate. The defence team had discussed this critical procedure on numerous occasions, and eventually the decision was that a male jury of some maturity was preferable. Older citizens generally relied on the police force to protect them as they aged, whereas anyone under thirty was likely to view them less favourably. Lena argued vehemently on the question of female jurors, but, as Oscar was the most experienced in jury trials, his opinion took precedence.

'Women hate drugs,' Oscar had argued, 'more so than men, because they see the devastation visited on their sons and daughters by an addiction. I'm not sure of any statistical data, but I think it's safe to assume that a higher percentage of the male of the species have experimented at some time, so may be less righteous.'

As it turned out, the associate called the names of two middle-aged women, but as the defence had exhausted its allowable peremptory challenges, Oscar could not challenge them. The other ten men were at least of middle age or older, so both Oscar and Matthew were satisfied they had chosen well.

The judge addressed the jury briefly on their role and the evidential issues they were to decide, and after an adjournment for morning tea, Tobias Blackmore rose to give his opening address.

Chapter Fifty-five

The address by the Crown prosecutor was brief, tinged with traces of legal instruction and homespun wisdom, and delivered with a pleasant smile. He professed sadness at the downfall of an officer thought to be an exemplary police detective, but he reminded the jury several times of their obligation to be impartial with their decisions. Pity was not a relevant emotion.

The defence elected not to make an opening address, a course they had followed in the Vandermeer trial. Oscar had once again counseled that it was unwise to reveal to the jury the defence case at the beginning of the trial. *Drip feed them – keep them interested*, was his belief.

Inspector Bill Etheridge was the first witness for the prosecution, and although he was really a non-contentious witness, Oscar felt he could make some headway with the jury regarding Angelo's behaviour. When the inspector had finished in chief, Oscar rose to cross-examine.

'What was the accused's demeanour when he first opened the door?' Oscar asked.

Etheridge paused momentarily. He could paint Angelo as embarrassed, afraid, surprised, guilt-ridden or any combination of such emotions. It was really a question about the inspector's opinion of his character, and in commencing the cross-examination in this way, Oscar was taking a calculated risk. The witness shifted uncomfortably in his chair before replying.

'He was, in my opinion, surprised, and then he became quite agitated.'

'Outraged, perhaps?'

'Perhaps.'

'In fact, the reaction you might expect from an innocent man who was being raided by the very organisation that he had served faithfully for more than a decade?'

'That's not for me to say.' Etheridge glanced involuntarily towards Angelo, as if to apologise for his reply.

Oscar looked towards the jury, sighed loudly to signal his disappointment, then picked up his brief and ruffled through the bundle. He selected one of the pages, held it up to eye level, and then adjusted his glasses to the end of his nose.

'I see from your statement that you have forgotten to tell the court what the accused said to you when you asked for his car keys. Perhaps that was an oversight?'

'I haven't included everything spoken during the search. It would have taken up dozens of pages and simply would not be relevant.'

'So, you decide what is relevant? Or do you perhaps decide to include only material that helps the prosecution?'

'Of course not.'

'Then let me jog your memory. Did the accused immediately allege the search was a set-up? That it was based on someone claiming there were drugs in his car, and your search of his house was a sham?'

'He may have.'

'Come now, Inspector. Didn't the accused immediately say that if any drugs were found in his car, they would have been planted by a drug syndicate? By criminals who were desperate to avoid my client giving evidence in a huge drug importation case which is pending?'

'I do recall something along those lines.'

'That, of course, is the case, is it not?'

'That the drugs were planted?'

'Let me spell it out for you. If my client is convicted of this charge, the case against the drug syndicate members would collapse, would it not?'

'That's not for me to say.'

'Of course not. You can only say things that will assist the prosecution. I momentarily forgot your function here today.'

Blackmore rose to object. 'Your Honour?'

Latimer took the hint. 'Mr O'Shannessy, that comment is improper, and is to be ignored by members of the jury.'

'Certainly, Your Honour,' Oscar replied. A faint smile appeared on his face as he glanced towards the jury. Several of the panel grinned in reply.

'Now, turning to the forensics of the search,' Oscar continued, 'were any fingerprints found on the spare wheel or the tyre where these drugs were eventually discovered?'

'No.'

'Surely, then, you were amazed at this discovery?'

'What?'

'Do you not understand the question?'

'No. I mean, why would I be amazed?"

'According to the prosecution, the drugs were secreted inside the spare tyre by my client?'

'That's correct.'

'But why would he place drugs in his spare wheel, then carefully wipe off his fingerprints when those same prints were all over the car? Surely there's no issue that the car belonged to him, and that he had unfettered access to the car's boot?'

'I can't read his mind.'

'But we can all read the mind of someone who plants drugs on behalf of a drug syndicate. He or she would be quite anxious to remove all fingerprints from the wheel and tyre, surely?'

'I just don't believe it.'

'Why not?'

'How could anyone remove then replace the inflated tyre with the car parked and open to the gaze of the public? Surely you would have to perform the task in the security of a garage?'

'I'm glad you asked. Perhaps if you wait until the defence witnesses give evidence, you might just discover how it was done.'

Oscar sat down with a flourish of his gown, slamming the brief he had been holding onto the bar table.

Chapter Fifty-six

With the tension of the trial, Matthew had almost forgotten that his next appointment with Samantha Wright was at 7 am the next morning. He was inclined to cancel the visit, but decided that a break from the case would do him some good.

Wearing the same old jeans, tee-shirt and joggers that he had worn on his initial visit, Matthew made his way to the offices where Samantha had treated him some weeks prior. She motioned for him to come into her treatment room, and avoided his smile with a look of disinterest. After manipulating his damaged knee for several minutes, albeit not as severely as on his initial visit, she scribbled some brief notes in her notebook.

'What's the verdict?' Matthew asked.

'Some slight improvement. Keep up the exercises and I'll see you in a month.'

She rose and walked to the door, then paused with one hand resting on the chrome handle.

'No movement on the dinner offer, I suppose?' Matthew queried with a hangdog look.

Samantha folded her arms across her chest and gave him a long stare before replying.

'The last time I saw you I didn't know if you were a cross-dressing caped-crusader or an escaped mental patient. Then last night I saw you on the TV news, and the truth was even worse than that. You're some sort of tricky lawyer trying to protect a crooked copper.'

Matthew took a step back in feigned surprise. 'I don't think I'd like you on our jury.'

'They said on the news that the copper you were representing had been caught with a large amount of heroin hidden in the spare wheel of his car. Don't tell me – the fairies came and hid it there.'

'Now I *know* I don't want you on our jury.'

'If I may be honest, Matthew, I think that lawyers are the lowest rung of professional life. They spend all their talents getting murderers and child molesters off scot-free, and parade around boasting that "it's better to have a thousand guilty people set free than to have one innocent person convicted". That's when they're not acting for some corporate criminals to avoid the consequences of ripping off the public.'

'You will excuse me, Sam, if I have a different opinion of my profession.'

'There's a surprise.'

'Without the constraints of law, and lawyers to ensure that those laws are adhered to, society would collapse. Criminals would run riot and companies would act without any consequences from their misbehavior.'

'You mean lawyers are a necessity, like rat-catchers or sewerage workers?'

'I wouldn't have put it quite like that.'

'I think you'd better go,' she said.

Matthew held his hands up in surrender. 'Fine. But before I go, can you answer one question for me?'

She nodded her assent.

'I take it that you don't give career advice to all your clients?'

She shook her head slowly.

'In fact, it's quite rare, is it not?'

'You're the first, and as far as I'm concerned, you'll be the last.'

Matthew gave what he hoped was his most appealing smile – a mixture of openness and honesty – at least that was his intention.

'You must have seen something in me. As for being a tricky lawyer, I'm actually a struggling, inexperienced barrister. As far as Angelo goes – that's our client by the way – he's a close friend of mine and I regard him as the most honest detective I've ever met. What I'm trying desperately to do is to have Angelo acquitted of a criminal conspiracy against him. If I don't succeed, then his life and that of his lovely wife and two small children will be destroyed.'

He paused to let his words sink in before continuing in a softer tone.

'He's facing a frame-up by a bunch of drug importers who are desperate to avoid gaol themselves. If they could kill Angelo and get away with it, they wouldn't hesitate.'

'Isn't that what all druggies say – it's not mine, someone planted it?' she replied defensively.

'That may be so, but here we are dealing with the most dangerous criminals there are in Sydney. Did you by any chance see a report in the paper recently where a private detective was shot dead in a deserted housing estate that was under construction?'

'What's that got to do with your case?'

'That private detective was Rufus Tomlinson. We employed him to carry out surveillance on someone connected with this case. He left a wife and three children. He had the back of his head blown off.'

She looked at him with her head at an angle, as if appraising his honesty. After a few moments, she replied in a conciliatory tone.

'Perhaps I've been unfair to you – and your client. It's easy to fall into the trap of believing that everything you see and hear on the TV news is true. I appreciate that it's only one side of the story.'

Matthew gave her a stony-faced look. 'I'm sorry but I'm afraid I can't forgive you for your outburst.'

Her head flinched backwards as if slapped.

'Unless you accept my dinner invitation,' Matthew added with a slight grin.

She gave a small shrug and the beginning of a smile. 'I suppose that I owe you that much.'

'Do you know what one of the great things about our justice system is?' Matthew continued. 'It's open to the public. Why not call in and watch the proceedings from the public gallery tomorrow and see for yourself?'

Chapter Fifty-seven

After court resumed at 10 am there was a succession of purely technical witnesses that were necessary to prove the safe keeping of the drug, as it was conveyed from police headquarters to the analytical laboratories. Then, as Reginald Smithers took the stand, a ripple of conversation ran through the courtroom. After guiding him through his evidence in chief, the prosecutor went on the offensive to counteract the predicted attack on his credibility.

'You are not pretending, are you Mr Smithers, that you are a person of exemplary character?'

'What?'

'Let me rephrase that. You are not suggesting that you have always been honest and law abiding in the past, are you?'

'I'm as honest as the next bloke.'

'That may be,' Blackmore replied with a forced smile. 'Though I suppose it depends on who that next bloke might be. To be frank with the jury, you admit to several prior convictions for various drug offences, is that not so?'

'My lawyer told me to plead guilty. Said I'd get out sooner. But I'm not admitting to nothing. I'm as good as anyone in this courtroom, that's for sure.'

Tobias Blackmore knew that the defence had subpoenaed Smithers' prior criminal record, and that they would attack him with it as soon as they got the chance. His attempt, however, to place some level of credibility on his witness was floundering. He tried another approach.

'You admit to several spells in various establishments of Her Majesty in the past?'

'What?'

'Gaol, Mr Smithers, gaol.'

'Oh, yeah.'

Matthew knew that Oscar could have objected to these leading questions, but they had agreed that in issues that they did not dispute, it was better not to get the jury offside by interrupting constantly.

'Am I correct in saying that Detective Cattani was the officer in charge in several of those cases?'

'Yeah.'

'Could you tell the court what happened after you were last released from prison on parole?'

'Well, Cattani came to see me. Said that if I didn't supply him with various drugs, he'd fit me up again and I'd go away for a long stretch this time.'

'What type of drugs?'

'Whatever I could get. Hash. Smack. Coke. He didn't mind. But it had to be worth his while. No small stuff.'

'Did he say what he was going to do with these drugs?'

'Nope. Didn't ask him. Didn't want to know.'

'What happened then?'

'The bastard just took them. Didn't pay me any money – just said that he'd sling me something when they were sold. I knew that'd never happen.'

'Would you take a look at exhibit number five, please?'

Blackmore nodded to the sheriff's officer who placed the drugs contained in a plastic zip lock bag onto the witness box ledge.

'Sure looks like the stuff.'

'What type of drug did you supply?'

'Smack. Very pure it was.'

'So, after you gave him the heroin ... I mean the smack ... what convinced you to go to the police?'

'Because he ripped me off. Fair's fair. I'm a businessman you see. I've got my expenses too, you know.'

'Quite so. Very understandable.'

Blackmore sank to his seat with a somewhat sheepish grin showing briefly on his face.

Oscar stood and stared at the witness for several moments without speaking.

'Mr O'Shannessy,' Latimer growled, 'we have not got all day.'

'Oh, I'm sorry, Your Honour. It's just that I've never seen a performance this impressive for many a long day.'

'If you are not able to behave properly, I will have to ask your junior to take over, Mr O'Shannessy.'

'My humble apologies, Your Honour,' Oscar replied with a glimmer of a smile.

Latimer's eyes narrowed, and a faint blush crept up his neck to his cheeks, but he restricted himself to a repeated shaking of his head.

'Any idea why you're called *Reggie the Rat*?' Oscar asked.

The witness gave a broad smile. This caused a display of the largest front teeth that Matthew had ever seen. The entire courtroom burst into laughter, and even the witness joined in the merriment.

Latimer's booming voice silenced the courtroom. 'I'll clear the courtroom if this foolishness continues,' he barked.

The Ancient Craft

'There's no need to answer that question,' Oscar said, 'but I am interested in your belief in the fellowship of man.'

'My what?'

'Your comment that you are as honest as the next man,' Oscar said. He carefully shuffled through several pages that he had removed from his brief. 'Does that mean that you think that everyone else is as honest as you are?'

'I'm as good as the next man.'

'I see. Perhaps you could look at this document. It's a record of your past criminal convictions, and I'm afraid it runs to over five pages. The total amounts to over one hundred convictions and eight separate gaol sentences.'

The Sheriff's Officer carried the document to the witness box, and silence ensued as the witness painstakingly read each page. When he had finished, he placed the pages down onto the ledge of the witness box, then raised his eyes towards Oscar.

'Well?' Oscar asked.

'Well what?'

'I take it that the document reflects your criminal history?'

'You take what?'

'Is the document true and correct?'

'I dunno. It's got nothing to do with me.'

Oscar shook his head in amazement. 'That is your fingerprint record is it not?'

'No, no. That's the old Reggie Smithers. He was a real bastard. Drug addict. Drunk. A real no-hoper. I'm not him.' The witness leaned towards the jury as if to take them into his confidence. 'I've seen the light. The Bible has shown me the way. I've got nothing to do with that deadbeat.'

'I'm so sorry. I didn't realise that we're all seeing the new Reggie today,' Oscar replied poker-faced.

'That's all right. We all make mistakes.'

'Can you tell me when this conversion took place? Was it recently?'

'Oh, just a while ago.'

'Was it before or after you had a conversation with some drug associate about lying to the police about my client?'

'Not me, mate.'

'Perhaps it was the old Reggie. The one with eight trips to the slammer? Would he lie to the coppers?'

'You're just trying to trick me now.'

'Well we can't have that now, can we? Let's make it simple. My client never demanded drugs from you, did he?'

'He bloody well did.'

'He never received any drugs from you, did he?'

'I've just told you he did.'

'What did Franz Mannheim tell you about my client?'

'Well, he said that … I mean … who is he? What did you say? Frank someone?'

'Whoops. Sorry about that. The old Reggie the Rat seems to have popped his head up for a few seconds.'

Oscar let the witness stew for a few moments. Reggie's eyes darted between the lawyers' faces and those of the courtroom observers like a fat Christmas turkey searching for his executioner. A murmur of amusement rippled through the public gallery.

'Surely you remember Franz Mannheim? Drug dealer, brothel owner, illegal casino boss. Does the description ring a bell?'

'Oh, him. No, I don't know him.'

Oscar slapped his brief down on the bar table with a loud crack, then raised his voice.

'You've lied so often throughout your life, I put it to you that you can't tell the difference between truth and fiction?'

'I certainly can.'

'How, then?'

'It's not a lie until someone can prove it is.'

Oscar shook his head slowly towards the jury box.

'The sad thing is that I think that you believe that. Unfortunately for you Mr Smithers, it shows the jury how much confidence they can place on your evidence. None at all.'

Reggie was lost for words and Oscar resumed his seat. The prosecutor did not re-examine.

Chapter Fifty-eight

'That was brilliant work, Oscar,' Rose Cattani said brightly. 'Things are looking up.'

The court had adjourned for a break and the three lawyers, together with Angelo and his wife, were crammed into the small interview room.

'It was very well done, Oscar,' Lena added. 'You've earned your keep today.'

Oscar held up one hand to acknowledge the comment.

Matthew cleared his throat for the tenth time that morning. 'Reggie was never much of a threat,' he said. 'Even Mannheim realised that. He knew they needed someone higher up the food chain to tip the scales. In this case, a nice juicy copper, and to top it off – Angelo's partner.'

'So we attack him,' Lena said. 'No holds barred.'

Oscar shook his head. 'It's a balancing act. Whilst we have to discredit him, it has to be with a scalpel, not a sledgehammer. We can't afford to put the jury offside, but at the same time we must put doubt into their minds.'

'How are we going to do that?' Angelo said. He was slumped in his chair and his voice had a lifeless tone.

'I had a long chat with Emma Saunders after the murder trial,' Matthew said.

'How long?' Oscar queried.

'Several schooners long. Boy, can that girl put them away. In any event, I'd asked her to see what she could come up with concerning D'Ascenzio. She has a nose like a bloodhound, and she always comes up with something.'

'And?' Angelo asked.

'Well, he's well known around all of the illegal casinos. It's a bit of a running joke really that he thinks he's a card sharp, but he loses nine times out of ten. A casino owner's dream, in fact.'

'What about something we don't know,' Angelo replied.

'He's a car nut,' Matthew said.

'That's nice,' Oscar added. 'We can ask for a report on the latest sports car. Very entertaining for the jury.'

'It's little things like that which can turn out to be momentous,' Matthew replied defensively. 'Anyway, it's a start. I'm going to attack him on the casino front, and we'll see how it goes from there. My theory is that juries don't like gambling cops, and casinos are still illegal. Before the end of the trial, they'll be asking themselves how he pays his gambling debts on a police constable's wages.'

'Don't the coppers get a kick-back from the house?' Lena asked dryly.

'Unfortunately,' Angelo replied, 'I can't dispute that. The higher up the ladder, the worse the rumours get.'

'As the saying goes,' Matthew added, 'the fish rots from the head.'

Chapter Fifty-nine

Matthew knew that after evidence in chief, Detective Constable Phillip D'Ascenzio would come across to the jury as an excellent witness – confident, polished and convincing.

Although Matthew had invited Samantha to attend the trial, he was now regretting it. Walking back into the courtroom, he glanced at the public gallery, and there she was, a bemused smile playing across her face as she gave a tiny wave. He gave a brief nod in reply.

At this critical moment in the trial, it would be bad enough for him to ruin the cross-examination, but it would be devastating to also make a fool of himself in front of Samantha. Matthew's throat felt as dry as blotting paper and his hand shook as he leaned over the bar table and filled the plastic beaker with water from the carafe. He remembered that they used to be made of glass until a disaffected accused decided to use one as a projectile in the direction of the bench. He gulped the tepid water, trying to ease his throat. All eyes were focused on him as he rose to cross-examine, and a sardonic grin played on the face of D'Ascenzio as he eyed the barrister.

'This alleged drunken admission by my client was, of course, in the absence of any witnesses, I take it?' Matthew asked. He had decided to confront the crux of the detective's evidence head on.

'Naturally.'

'Why do you use that term?'

'Because he didn't want witnesses, of course.'

'Did my client volunteer any gems of his private life to you, apart from admitting, as you allege, to being a drug dealer?'

'What do you mean?'

'Surely if he was that close to you, so confident of your trust, he would have told you about his family life? What, for example, are his children's names?'

D'Ascenzio was taken aback for a few seconds, pausing before he replied.

'His kids' names? I don't know.'

'His wife's name?'

'No.'

Matthew reasoned that it was a line of questioning that had little downside, for if the witness did know the names, no damage would have been likely.

'So my client doesn't tell you about his family, but blurts out a most incriminating admission about criminal activity.'

'Well ... he was drunk.'

'So you say.'

'You weren't there.'

'I put it to you that you weren't either. That no such foolish comment was ever made. That it's all a fiction.'

'Why foolish?'

'I ask the questions, Constable. It's called cross-examination.'

'OK,' D'Ascenzio replied with a sly smile towards the jury.

'Are you having a good time?'

'What are you talking about?'

'Surely if you were telling the truth in giving evidence that would send your partner to gaol, you would be devastated, not smirking at the jury?'

'Objection, Your Honour,' Blackmore said, springing to his feet.

'I saw no smirk, Mr Jameson,' Latimer announced without hearing arguments from either barrister. 'The jury is to disregard that offensive comment.'

Matthew gave a resigned glance towards the bench before continuing. 'Now, I understand that you are something of a card player, Constable?'

D'Ascenzio gave a smug smile. 'I dabble sometimes.'

'Dabble. Now there's an interesting word. Doesn't that mean *occasionally*? *In a casual manner*, perhaps?'

'So?'

'But in fact you are an inveterate gambler, playing cards until the early hours of the morning at a variety of illegal casinos, aren't you?'

'I wouldn't say that.'

'You don't deny frequenting illegal casinos on a regular basis, do you?'

'It's part of my duties to obtain information from certain criminal elements, and to do that I have to visit these places from time to time.'

'With your partner, Detective Cattani?'

'No, by myself.'

'With the imprimatur of the chief of detectives?'

'What?'

'With the express approval of your boss?'

'I have a free rein. I can do as I please.'

'Very convenient. Well, let me ask you this. Is Franz Mannheim one of your informants?'

'Of course not.'

'That's because he's the boss of some of these casinos, isn't he?'

'Not to my knowledge. He's a legitimate businessman, and we are just passing acquaintances, that's all.'

'So he's not a drug dealer and a crime boss, then?'

'Your Honour,' Blackmore objected, 'what has this person got to do with this trial? The question is surely irrelevant.'

The prosecutor spoke in an urgent tone, and Matthew sensed his unease at the mention of Mannheim.

'I can't see any relevance,' Latimer announced.

'Your Honour,' Matthew replied in a tone as even and calm as he could manage, 'the credit of this witness is being challenged. The people he associated with, his gambling habits and his presence at illegal casinos are all matters the jury is entitled to be aware of.'

'He said he's just gaining information from his sources,' Latimer replied. 'Perfectly understandable.'

'I know that's what he says, Your Honour, but the defence does not accept that. We wish to test him on that issue.'

'Well, don't labour the point. I'll allow a little leeway. Just don't waste this court's time, Mr Jameson.' Latimer gave his ruling with an edge to his voice. His narrowed eyes fixed Matthew with an unblinking stare.

'Your Honour pleases. Now, Constable, how often have you spoken with this Franz Mannheim in the past six months?'

'Oh, once or twice in passing. Just talking about the weather and that type of thing, you know.'

'No conversation about your gambling debts?'

'I don't have any.'

'Is that so? What about in the past?'

'No.'

'I put it to you that you have a reputation in the force as a heavy gambler, with large debts.'

'Who says?'

'My client will, of course.'

'Well he would, wouldn't he?'

'So there's no truth in the suggestion that you intend to move to Las Vegas and count cards for a living?'

'What on earth are you talking about?' Latimer interrupted, glaring at Matthew.

'It's a gambling ploy, Your Honour,' Matthew replied, 'used by card players to obtain an advantage over the house when playing Blackjack.'

'I have heard mention of it, Your Honour,' Blackmore said, half-rising. 'I believe that legal casinos such as Wrest Point in Tasmania frown on the practice. Not illegal but never welcome.'

Latimer gave a loud sigh and shook his head. 'I think that's enough card lessons for today. Let's get back to relevant issues.'

Matthew paused before resuming his cross-examination. 'The last question, Your Honour?'

'Is disallowed. It's irrelevant and time wasting,' Latimer announced.

Matthew battled to control his temper, but at least the prosecutor had been even-handed on the issue. Perhaps it was because Blackmore knew how dangerous it was to the prosecution case, and had sought to glide past the issue without debating it in front of the jury.

'I put it to you that it was you who planted the drugs in my client's spare tyre?' Matthew asked.

'Rubbish.'

'I see. What about the suggestion that you removed the spare wheel whilst my client's wife was at a yoga class in the church hall only three hundred metres from where she lived?'

'Sheer fantasy.'

'I further put to you that you then took that wheel to a nearby garage called Joe's Mechanical Repairs, where you borrowed some tools and then placed the drugs inside the tyre before re-inflating it.'

'Do I have to answer this nonsense, Your Honour?'

Latimer paused, and for a split second, Matthew feared that the judge would refuse to let him put the defence case to the witness.

'Yes, you do,' Latimer eventually said, 'although we all know the answer.'

'The answer is *absolutely not*.'

'Have you ever been to Joe's workshop?' Matthew asked.

'Don't know Joe. Don't know his garage. Don't know where it is. Don't know anything about him. That precise enough for you, sir?'

'Absolutely. Now I understand that you are something of a car enthusiast?'

'How is that relevant?' Latimer interrupted sharply.

'My friend has not raised any objection, Your Honour,' Matthew replied evenly. 'It all goes to his credit.'

Latimer clearly realised that he had been taking over conduct of the prosecution case, and for the benefit of the inevitable appeals court he must have felt it wise to step back a touch.

'Go on, then,' he announced, tossing his pen onto the bench. This was to advise the jury subtly what he thought of the issue, and several members of the panel nodded their heads imperceptibly.

'Well?' Matthew continued.

'We're onto my hobbies now, are we? Well, I'm prepared to say that, like millions of other red-blooded Australian males, I like nice cars. Not all types of course. We all have our little favourites, as well as our prejudices.'

'What's your poison then, Constable?'

'I'm only a humble copper. My pay doesn't run to the machines I admire. I've got a second-hand Holden sedan. The workhorse of a nation, you might say.'

Matthew did not continue, but stared at the detective. Surely he could not be stupid enough to lie about his current car, Matthew thought. But, then again, he believed he could beat the house counting cards in Las Vegas, so perhaps he was.

'Yes, Mr Jameson,' the judge said, tapping his fingers impatiently on the bench.

'Sorry, Your Honour,' Matthew responded. 'I was just reminiscing on the good old days when a Holden was considered a prized possession.'

Latimer scratched his scalp under the faded horsehair wig, and then gave a look of exasperation towards the jury box. 'Just get on with it.'

'Do you hate my client?' queried Matthew, as he resumed cross-examination.

'Of course not.'

'But surely you must. According to you he's brought the entire police force into disgrace in the eyes of the community by his behaviour.' Matthew hoped that this change of tack might throw D'Ascenzio off his stride.

'Oh, that. Yes, well I suppose you could say he has. Still, I just regard him as any sort of addict. With pity more than hate really.'

'Very touching. Do you also feel sorry for his wife and children?'

'I hadn't really thought of them.'

'Never thought of the destruction visited on all of them by your evidence, have you?'

The detective shifted in his seat. 'It's not my concern.'

'Such loyalty to your partner and his family. We're beginning to see the real Phillip D'Ascenzio, aren't we?'

The witness did not reply. Matthew continued in a similar vein for the rest of the day, going over the evidence of the witness in detail until he finally gave up, resuming his seat with an involuntary sigh.

'Hopeless. Didn't get anywhere,' he muttered quietly to Oscar. 'We're done for.'

Oscar patted Matthew's shoulder in silent support.

Fenella leaned over towards Matthew. 'Can't win them all, Matt,' she said in a whisper.

Chapter Sixty

As the defence team emerged from the courtroom into the foyer, Matthew saw Samantha standing by herself near the far wall. He excused himself and walked over to her.

'Lovely to see you, Sam.'

'It's true then. You really are a cross-dressing crusader in a wig. You actually look quite cute in that outfit.'

Matthew removed his wig and looked at it forlornly. 'Unfortunately I am more like *Don Quixote* today. Just tilting at windmills.'

'Well, I don't think you can be faulted for effort.'

'Thanks, but I'm afraid it had no effect on the jury. Things look pretty bleak, actually.'

Samantha took his arm in a friendly grip. 'Perhaps I can cheer you up. What about that dinner that you were on about?'

'Who's paying?'

'Fifty-fifty.'

'Just joking. I made the invitation, so I'll be paying.'

'In that event, what's the most expensive restaurant in town?'

'Harry's Café de Wheels, I believe.' This was a famous Sydney café whose main fare was take away pies and peas, sold from a converted caravan.

'The last of the big spenders, I see.'

'Nothing but the best will do.'

Matthew arranged to pick Samantha up from her flat the following Saturday night. Then she leaned over and gave him a chaste peck on the cheek.

'By the way,' she said as she turned to leave, 'I wouldn't believe a word that copper said. How could anyone trust him when he admits gambling at illegal casinos and mixing with a gangster? And I didn't like that judge at all.'

Matthew smiled in appreciation.

'I've changed my mind,' he said. 'I think I'll have you on our jury after all.'

Chapter Sixty-one

In an attempt to dispel the gloom that had spread over the defence team, Matthew suggested a return trip to Leichhardt for dinner at the same restaurant where they'd had lunch after the committal proceedings. He was hopeful that the rustic Italian food and homespun bonhomie of the proprietors might revive the spirits of their group, but even Oscar was unusually sombre throughout the meal. It was Rose Cattani who made small talk and encouraged the three lawyers in an attempt to brighten the mood. Everyone knew that the next day's hearing would decide the outcome, and Matthew was worried that the depressed demeanour of his client would send a terrible message to the jury. At the back of his mind, there was a fragment of an idea that flittered in and out of his consciousness, much like the name of a song, or a place, or a person that continuously defeated his memory. He knew that it was important, but the more he concentrated, the further away it seemed. The prosecution had closed its case before the adjournment, and Angelo was to give evidence upon resumption the next morning.

'Outrage is the perfect riposte,' Matthew said. 'You are an innocent man whose life is about to be crushed by a tidal wave of lies.'

'Waves don't crush you, Matt,' Lena said between mouthfuls of pasta, 'they drown you.'

'How about an avalanche, my boy,' Oscar added, 'that will certainly crush you.'

'Well ... whatever,' Matthew replied, 'but you do get the general idea, don't you Angelo? It's not enough to tell the truth, you have to sell it to the jury.'

'Now I'm a salesman,' Angelo replied. His food lay untouched before him.

'More an actor than a salesman,' Oscar said. 'The actor strives for that magical place where the audience believes in him, and wants him to succeed in his quest. To slay the dragon – to save the damsel in distress – to vanquish the villain, as it were.'

'That's a little theatrical, Oscar,' Lena said, 'but I think we get the general idea.'

'Think of Atticus Finch in *To Kill a Mockingbird*,' Matthew suggested. 'Outrage with dignity.'

Angelo raised his eyebrows and glanced towards Matthew. 'If I recall the film correctly, the wrongly convicted accused was shot dead by his gaolers whilst trying to escape. I trust that's not the message of this little lecture?'

'It's good to see you haven't lost your sense of humour, Angelo,' Lena said with a gentle smile as she patted him on the shoulder. 'We're just worried about you. Tomorrow's a big test. The biggest test of your life. You've got to go in fighting, and give as good as you get.'

'Except I think you really mean "go down fighting",' Angelo replied. 'Because we all know that will be the probable result. My middle name is Mario, not Pollyanna.'

Chapter Sixty-two

A freezing rain had been hammering down since just after daybreak, and it seemed to Matthew a perfect accompaniment to the mood of the defence team as they entered the courtroom. The only smiles came from Tobias Blackmore and Fenella. She did murmur 'good luck' to Angelo as they took their respective seats, but Matthew knew that her combative nature longed for a conviction, whether it was a just decision or not.

Angelo gave his evidence in chief in a calm and professional manner, but the test was to come in cross-examination. After the morning tea adjournment, Blackmore rose to begin his questioning.

'I believe that you are, in fact, admitted as a barrister, is that not so?' the prosecutor asked.

'Yes.'

'Congratulations.'

Angelo did not reply. The legal game of cat and mouse had commenced.

'I take it from your evidence that you were not surprised when the drugs were located in your family car?'

'I was furious. I knew when Etheridge asked for the car keys that someone had planted something there. It wasn't hard to figure out.'

'So you would have the jury believe it was your colleague, Detective D'Ascenzio, who planted the drugs?'

'I'm certain of it.'

Blackmore gave his best impression of amazement as he glanced towards the jury. 'You have proof of this?'

'If I had concrete proof, I wouldn't be here now.'

'So, no proof at all?'

'I didn't say that. You'll shortly hear from Joe Simpson who runs a motor repair garage about his observations.'

'That will certainly be fascinating, but as you say, nothing concrete. More like quicksand perhaps?'

Once again, Angelo did not reply. Matthew and Oscar had repeatedly lectured him about becoming involved in an argument with the prosecutor, and so far, he had restrained himself.

'Don't become embroiled in a debate with Blackmore,' Matthew had stressed. 'He doesn't get a vote. It's the jury you have to impress. Like a politician, you just keep hammering away at the point you want the jury to accept. Don't worry too much about the questions. Let Blackmore stress about them. Just keep on with your own message.'

'You have to attack Detective D'Ascenzio, don't you?' the prosecutor continued. 'Because he told the truth about your drunken confession, didn't he?'

'Perhaps you could explain why he is hand in glove with a gangster like Mannheim, then? I'll tell you what he's doing. He's doing Mannheim's bidding; that's what this is all about.'

'You have no proof of that either, do you?'

'The private detective who was tracking Mannheim was murdered. It's a little hard for him to give evidence today with half his head blown off.'

Angelo was well aware that the investigation into Tomlinson's murder had proved fruitless. Mannheim had refused to speak to the investigating police, and with no witnesses and no murder weapon, the police had reached a dead-end.

Blackmore raised his hands in a gesture indicating his confusion. 'Surely you're not suggesting that your colleague is a murderer as well?'

Angelo shook his head. 'No, I don't think he'd sink that low. It was obviously Mannheim or one of his henchmen who carried out the killing.'

'Why haven't you charged him then?'

Angelo remained silent.

'It wouldn't be because you have absolutely no evidence, would it? That these unfounded allegations are your last desperate attempt to avoid a conviction?'

'There were no witnesses to the killing. But who would profit from his death? Not only Mannheim, but if I'm convicted then a drug trial will be aborted. Three drug conspirators will be back on the streets, importing and distributing heroin that will certainly result in many deaths from overdoses in the future. As I said in evidence in chief, there is a good reason for planting the drugs and framing me.'

'Well, perhaps we can put aside the conjecture and the fantasy for a while and clarify one issue. You have no evidence whatsoever to justify these wild allegations, do you?' The tone of the prosecutor became more strident and he was now pointing his finger at Angelo in accusation.

'That's for the jury to decide, Mr Blackmore. They're not as simple-minded as you think.'

Blackmore smiled briefly and adroitly sidestepped the trap. 'That was never my belief, Detective. Perhaps it was yours.'

The cut and thrust of questioning raged on for several hours, continuing after the luncheon adjournment, well into the afternoon session. It was a small mercy to Matthew that, when Blackmore finally resumed his seat, Angelo had given as good as he had received, and had remained in control of his emotions throughout.

Chapter Sixty-three

What the jury would make of Joe Simpson's evidence was a complete mystery to Matthew, but it was the last roll of the dice for the defence. Like a gambler who had lost all but his last few dollars at the casino, Matthew felt that even a miniscule chance was better than none at all.

'You do realise you have sworn on oath to tell the truth?' Oscar asked Simpson after he was sworn in and had given his name and address.

'I do.'

This first question clearly showed that Oscar was concerned about what the witness was about to say.

'Then can you please tell the court about something that occurred earlier this year?'

'About the copper changing a tyre with my tools?'

'If you could go through the incident in detail for the members of the jury, please?'

Simpson went into some detail about the events of the day, with Oscar prompting him gently throughout. Oscar then placed his brief down on the bar table and paused before asking the vital question.

'When the police officer showed you a folder of twelve photographs, were you able to identify anyone who had changed the tyre?'

'Ah, I think so.'

'Did you sign your name on the back of the photograph after it was removed from the folder?'

'Yes I did.'

Evidence had been given earlier by the detective who conducted the photo ID, that the photo which had Simpson's signature on the back was that of Detective Constable Phillip D'Ascenzio. It had been tendered as an exhibit earlier in the day.

'Could the witness be shown exhibit eight, Your Honour?'

Judge Latimer nodded his consent and the photo was handed to the witness.

'Can you identify that signature on the back of the photo please?'

'It's mine.'

Oscar resumed his seat with a resigned sigh.

Tobias Blackmore rose and immediately went on the attack.

'You're not sure, are you?'

'Well, it could be him.'

'That is exactly what you said to the police when they showed you the twelve photos, isn't it? "It could be him"?'

'I don't remember.'

'Then we can look at your evidence today. "I think so" ... is that any more certain than "it could be"?'

'I don't know.'

'Perhaps if we approach it another way. Could it be Santa Claus?'

'Nonsense.'

'Could it be Elvis Presley?'

'Rubbish.'

'So you can be positive about who it is not, but you cannot be positive about who it is?'

The witness shook his head angrily. 'All right. I don't know. OK. I can't be sure.'

The worst moment came when Matthew glanced at the jury and caught amused grins on several of the panel during cross-examination. The dice had rolled for the last time.

Chapter Sixty-four

The courtroom was hushed the following morning as the various parties anticipated final addresses from both barristers and finally the judge. Fenella and Blackmore were chatting animatedly to each other, D'Ascenzio was grinning broadly. The defence team as well as Angelo and Rose were downcast and sombre.

'It grieves me, members of the jury,' Blackmore said in a gentle tone in his closing address, 'more than I can express to you, to ask you to convict a man who in times past has been a conscientious officer. But we all know too well the scourge of drugs, and how they can drag down even someone like the accused. So much money can be made by buying and selling drugs, even for the middle-man. He doesn't have to dirty his hands by selling the drugs to a desperate addict on the street and risk being arrested. He only needs to be a link in the chain. The temptation is enormous. We all know the salary of a detective sergeant is not large. Not with a young family and a mortgage. But where do those drugs end up? They end up destroying the lives of thousands of men and women.

That is why you have to render a verdict of guilty. Because the purchase and distribution of heroin is the greatest blight on society that I know of.'

Blackmore continued in this manner for over three hours, and Matthew's black mood intensified as, one by one, the jury nodded in silent agreement with the prosecutor's arguments. Worse still, as Blackmore resumed his seat, they gave him a warm smile. A silent round of applause. That old death rattle to the defence.

During the luncheon break, Angelo made the choice of who was to make the final address for the defence, and Matthew felt relieved when he said that Oscar might elicit more sympathy from the jury. Sympathy was, of course, their last chance, and Oscar was the perfect supplicant.

'Ladies and gentlemen of the jury,' Oscar commenced, 'what we are facing here is nothing less than a travesty of justice if this man is convicted today. Angelo Cattani has served this state with honesty and courage since he was appointed probationary constable as a young man. He has risked his life on several occasions, coming close to death more than once. Why has he done this? Was it for the enormous wages paid to detective sergeants? Was it for medals or glory? Of course not. He has dedicated his life to the service of the community out of a wish to protect the men, women and children who rely on him and other honest police officers like him.

'You have been asked to look at three critical issues. Firstly the evidence of Reggie the Rat – oh, I'm sorry, Reginald Smithers.'

Several of the jurors gave amused smiles.

'Have you ever heard a more unreliable person in your whole life? A career criminal and admitted liar who has given evidence today of his criminal behaviour in exchange for freedom and a new identity. I put to you that you would have difficulty believing him if he said it was day or night.

'Secondly, we have evidence of the drugs being found in the family vehicle of my client. Who in his right mind would hide the drugs in a vehicle that could be stolen, or destroyed in an accident, when other more secure places are on offer? It makes no sense. Why not bury them in the ground, hide them in a nearby drain, or simply leave them with an accomplice? What does make sense is that my client is a crucial witness in a large drug conspiracy trial, and that the defendants in that trial would have access to large amounts of drugs and a perfect motive to frame my client. If they succeed, their trial will not proceed and they will be released from custody.

'Lastly, we have the evidence of Detective Constable Phillip D'Ascenzio. It is no coincidence that he is the other critical witness in the drug conspiracy trial. If he has lied to this court, one might suspect he will have a sudden lapse of memory in relation to that case too. If he ever gives evidence.'

Oscar paused, suspecting that Blackmore might object to this latest suggestion, as it was really only speculation. Matthew saw the prosecutor turn towards Oscar for a few seconds before shaking his head subtly. No objection was made.

'Let us compare these two police officers,' Oscar continued. 'My client is a family man with a wife, who you have seen in court each day supporting him. He also has two young children. There has not been a skerrick of evidence of any impropriety or negligence against my client in the past. He comes before you with an impeccable record. On the other hand, we have Constable D'Ascenzio, an admitted gambler who frequents illegal casinos late at night, and who is on good terms with a convicted gangster, Franz Mannheim.'

Oscar continued in this vein for over an hour before concluding his submission.

'Ladies and gentlemen of the jury, which of these two police officers would you like your son or daughter to marry?' He paused.

'Who would you trust with your life?' He paused again.

'Who do you believe?'

Judge Hugh Latimer gave a sickly smile to the jury, as if to bring them into his confidence. He then briefly summarised the evidence of every witness, before coming to the end of his address.

'It has been said today that it is a question of whom you believe. But do not forget there are a number of facts which are not in dispute. Firstly, the drugs were found in the extended possession of the accused – that is, in his private motor vehicle. Secondly, the accused has admitted to arresting Reginald Smithers on several prior occasions, and whilst you have to be careful in assessing the truthfulness of this witness, his prior criminal record does not mean he must be disbelieved. Thirdly we have the evidence of the accused's colleague, Detective Constable Phillip D'Ascenzio. It is not in dispute that they worked closely together. They were workmates, not strangers.

'I can only imagine how difficult it must be to give evidence against your police superior, largely due to the well-known practice of police supporting each other's version of events. One might predict that Detective D'Ascenzio will not gain any favour or advancement in the police force by giving evidence today. Indeed, he may have destroyed his career. Why would he do this if his evidence is a lie? This is a matter for you to decide. It is your duty to decide on factual issues, and I will make decisions about legal matters.

'A verdict of guilty can only be given if you have no reasonable doubt as to the guilt of the accused. I am sure that you will have no difficulty in arriving at the correct decision.'

As Judge Latimer spoke those last words, he gave what Matthew felt was a sly grin to the jury. It was not necessary for the judge to stick the knife into the defence, but Matthew now believed it was inherent in his nature. His words spoken in summing up to the jury were innocuous, and any reading of the transcript by an appeals court would find no judicial error, but there was no doubt in everyone's mind that he believed Angelo was guilty.

Chapter Sixty-five

As Latimer's directions to the jury finished late that afternoon, he excused the jury until the following morning, indicating that he would sequester them at 10 am to retire and consider their verdict. From that moment, they could not communicate with the outside world until they either reached a decision or advised the judge that they were deadlocked.

'Take Rose out and buy her the most expensive bottle of champagne that you can afford,' Matthew suggested to Angelo when they were settled back in the interviewing room. 'Have a meal together that she will never forget.'

'The verdict's not in, yet,' Rose objected. 'Don't tell us you've given up?'

'We're not giving up,' Lena responded, 'and I won't let either of you give up either.'

'Matthew's right,' Oscar added. 'Take Rose out for a great meal and I'll pay the bill.'

'Thanks anyhow, Oscar,' Angelo said quietly. 'Whatever happens, I don't regret anything we've done. Your summing up to the jury was brilliant. I owe you my thanks. Tomorrow I may not be able to communicate them too clearly.'

'If the worst happens, there's still the appeal to come,' Matthew said. 'Latimer couldn't help himself jumping into the arena, so there's several appeal points that I've already jotted down.'

'The fat lady's not sung yet,' Oscar added, 'and there's plenty of dialogue still to come in this little soap opera.'

'Let's hope it's not a tragedy then,' Angelo replied.

Chapter Sixty-six

Oscar hoped that the jury would be out for several days, perhaps reaching a verdict sometime next week, but the message relayed by the Sheriff's Officer came after just two hours of deliberation.

The mood of the defence team at the bar table was the complete opposite of that displayed by the prosecution. Fenella and Blackmore could barely conceal their delight, whilst D'Ascenzio did not even bother to try. Even Judge Latimer seemed to join in with the prosecution's elation, but Matthew felt that it might merely be his imagination. It was as though the entire courtroom already knew the verdict. The jury shuffled back to the jury box, keeping their eyes fixed on the floor, their faces solemn. The announcement seemed almost superfluous to Matthew, with every juror's face seemingly displaying the verdict.

When asked by the judge if they had agreed upon their verdict, the answer from the foreman came in the affirmative.

'How say you, is the accused guilty or not guilty?' Latimer enquired.

'Guilty,' came the immediate loud reply.

'Your foreman has said that the accused is guilty, so says your foreman, so say you all,' the judge intoned, in what seemed to Matthew like a triumphant tone.

Latimer thanked the jury for their efforts, remanded Angelo in custody for sentencing two weeks hence, and then adjourned the court. It all happened in a blur, and Matthew barely registered the events before the courtroom started to empty. Matthew and Oscar sat silently, not moving, their eyes fixed on the bar table. Lena, also silent, shook her head slowly.

A light touch on Matthew's shoulder jolted him from his stupor.

'Commiserations, Matt,' Fenella whispered near his ear. 'Don't let this ruin our relationship.'

'Sure, Ella,' Matthew replied sharply. 'Nothing personal. That's what you mean, is it?'

The smile vanished and Fenella turned on her heel. He was determined to phone her in the coming days to end their 'relationship' once and for all.

'It's no surprise, mate,' Matthew said, his voice attempting some optimism. 'We'll put all our energy into the appeal. You just have to watch out for yourself in prison.'

They were speaking in the basement cell complex of the court building, separated by bars. Several other prisoners milled around in other small cells, perhaps awaiting a verdict from one of the several courts that were sitting, or possibly due to be sentenced either on a guilty plea or a guilty verdict.

'Don't worry about me,' Angelo replied. 'I can take care of myself. I'll be kept in protection, so there's not much actual danger. I just want you to promise me that you'll take care of

Rosie and the kids. When they're in Sydney, I mean. They'll all be staying in Queensland after sentencing until I'm released. Whenever that might be.' His words were positive, but his voice was not. A slight quaver betrayed him.

An uneasy pause settled over them, until Matthew spoke.

'I've let you down, mate. When it really mattered, I've stuffed up. I just don't know what to say. Whatever I can do for them, I promise I will.'

Chapter Sixty-seven

Two weeks later, Oscar's plea on sentencing faced the obvious problem that their client was still denying any wrongdoing. He was limited to a recital of Angelo's police service and his family situation. It was no surprise to Matthew that Latimer focused on Angelo's lack of remorse or contrition, together with a breach of trust as a serving police officer. One of his more colourful phrases spoke of 'an arrow to the heart of public confidence in the police force'.

Latimer announced a sentence of eight years' hard labour with five years non-parole.

Oscar and Matthew visited their client in the cell complex but, in truth, they had said everything previously. Later, at their usual hotel, Matthew, Oscar, Lena and Rose huddled around a table at the rear of the room, a round of drinks sitting before them untouched.

'I've failed you, Rose,' Matthew said, his eyes fixed on the drinks as he avoided eye contact. 'You, Angelo, and your children. The worst part is that I don't think it was a case of *doing my best*. Instead, it was a situation where I've been deluding myself that I could substitute enthusiasm for experience and real talent. I've got no excuses. I've been a fool.'

'That's enough of that,' Rose replied, her face flushed with annoyance. 'You and Oscar and Lena did all you could. It wasn't your fault that poor Tomlinson was shot dead. Just think for one minute of his family and their grief. And none of us could predict that a crooked copper would perjure himself. Stop trying to play God.'

'I'm sorry,' Matthew replied quietly.

'Well, stop being sorry,' Lena snapped, 'and start working on the appeal. Mannheim and D'Ascenzio are not geniuses. If we keep working away, they'll make a slip. I guarantee it.'

'I agree,' Oscar said, lighting his noxious pipe and then puffing smoke over the quartet. 'Give the three wise men something to get their teeth into.'

'The three wise men?' queried Rose.

'The Court of Criminal Appeal has three judges sitting on the bench,' Matthew replied. 'Whilst it's pretty hard to convince them that a sentence is too harsh, they do know what reasonable doubt is and whether a verdict is beyond the pale. If we can give them something concrete, we'll get a fair hearing, which can result in a new trial or even a dismissal of the charges.'

'I still say that another drug-dealing scumbag with even ten pages of prior convictions would have got less than half of Angelo's sentence.' Oscar added with a shake of his head, 'I know that's not our main concern, but I can almost guarantee that the sentence will be substantially reduced.'

'That's a relief,' Rose replied. 'Five years in gaol instead of eight ... What a marvellous justice system we have.'

'There's nothing marvellous about it, Rose,' Oscar said quietly, 'it's just the best that we can manage. The jury system is just as fallible as any other human endeavour, but it's all we've got.'

Chapter Sixty-eight

'Joe Simpson worries me,' Matthew said, half to himself, 'but I can't put my finger on it.'

One week had passed since Angelo's sentencing, and Matthew had joined Lena for their Friday night pizza and red wine ritual. They were in her new office on the twentieth floor of a city office tower, occupied by the large law firm that she had joined.

'What do you mean?' Lena said between mouthfuls of the pizza. 'You think that someone got to him?'

'He was a different man in court. Initially I thought that he was just overawed, had stage fright. But the more I think about it, the more he seemed hell-bent on helping the prosecution. I don't think he's the type to be bribed – frightened, perhaps, but not bribed. If he's got a wife and kids, the threat could be in that direction.'

'Perhaps he's worth another visit,' Lena replied. 'I could try if you'd like?'

Matthew ate in silence for a few moments, then took a gulp of cabernet sauvignon. 'I might do it myself,' he announced finally. 'It's just a question of approaching him the right way.'

'You mean in your usual diplomatic manner?'

'I can be persuasive when I put my mind to it.'

'You've got a plan?' Lena asked with a sideways glance.

'More a vague idea, really. Emma Saunders is always on the money. She was adamant that D'Ascenzio was a vintage car fanatic, but he denied it in cross-examination. Perhaps, more accurately, he downplayed the idea. Then his current car set me thinking. There's no way a character like him would enjoy driving a run-of-the-mill Holden sedan. It just doesn't fit.'

'How about a registration check on the cars he's owned in the past?' she asked.

'That's not so easy.'

'Unless you've got a contact in the RTA.'

The Roads and Traffic Authority kept the details for every vehicle registered in the state.

'So you're more than just a pretty face, then?'

'Behave yourself, Matthew.'

For the first time since the trial, a brief smile showed on his face.

'That's a good sign,' Lena murmured. 'I was getting worried about you.'

'Always the mother hen.'

'I value you, Matthew. Not just as a lawyer or as a legal partner. You know that without me having to say it.'

Matthew swirled the crimson wine in his glass and gave a long sigh. 'I've been thinking about chucking it in.'

'It?' Lena replied with a start.

'The law.'

She gazed at him with narrowed eyes.

'Angelo's verdict has gutted me. It's robbed me of my sense of worth. My purpose in life, if you will.'

'What about the Vandermeer trial? You and Oscar were brilliant, even if I do say so myself.'

'What a joke,' Matthew replied with a grimace. 'She played us for fools. I was merely the court jester to her queen.'

Lena shook her head in confusion. 'What are you going on about?'

'Haven't you worked it out?'

'Worked what out?'

'She stage-managed it from the start.'

'Tell me everything.' Lena curled her feet underneath her on the spacious leather chair, her face alert with curiosity.

Matthew finished off his wine and poured himself another glass.

'I can't say that I follow the fashion pages in the Sunday papers, but just before Angelo's trial, I was flipping through the paper when a photo of her caught my eye. It showed her at some premiere or another, posing for the cameras, arm in arm with an unnamed man. Except I recognised him. It was Hans Schrieber.'

Lena raised her eyebrows. 'That's a name that rings a bell. A TV star or actor, I think.'

Matthew shook his head.

'No? What then?'

'An insurance broker.'

The information did not register with Lena right away, but when she connected the name with her client, her eyes grew wide. 'The one who gave evidence.'

'The same one.'

'But surely that could be a coincidence?'

'Coincidences when added together become something else.'

'What else do you know that you're not telling me?'

Matthew walked over to a small table upon which he had seen a copy of that day's *Sydney Morning Herald*. Opening the paper to the business section, he folded the broadsheet into a manageable size, then dropped it onto Lena's desk. She scanned the opened page, and then focused on an item involving an announcement by a Swiss multinational company. The mention of Dr Cornelius Vandermeer grabbed her attention. The article announced that the company had reached an agreement with the estate of the deceased doctor involving a patent that he had held over a breast enhancement insert. It did not mention the amount of the settlement.

'Well, that's interesting, I suppose,' Lena said, 'but I don't see the … oh … Jessica told us he didn't leave a will. He died intestate.'

'In which case his widow receives the entire estate.'

'The missing motive that no one knew about.'

'Except our client, of course.'

'If she knew Schrieber prior to the doctor's demise,' Lena continued, 'then who better to also organise the insurance policy?'

'The prosecution said all along that the doctor's signature was forged on the insurance proposal.'

'But what about the last-minute evidence of Pieter Siwecki?'

'She always had him on tap, and just waited for the right moment to produce him. If I hadn't picked up on her "new label" clue when she feigned her hysterical outburst for us, she would have claimed to make the discovery herself. Siwecki himself told me he always knew he was going to be called as a witness.'

Lena gave a slow smile, as the realisation hit home. 'You think that she added the shrimp paste to his magic elixir?'

'Of course. I am also certain that she knew that he had not replenished his supply of epinephrine at his surgery. If you recall, she was very vague when I specifically asked her about it.'

'Presumably, neither the insurance policy nor Siwecki's evidence would ever see the light of day unless she was arrested,' Lena added.

'Quite so. But when you put all of the pieces of the puzzle in order, you can see that this was all planned several months before his death. You only have to look at the date of the insurance policy.'

'As well as the ingenious purchase of the shrimp paste that was manufactured after his death, and then planting it in the garage just in case her premises were searched.'

Matthew nodded. 'But it wasn't enough to use Schrieber to facilitate the insurance policy. After the trial, she had to parade him through the social pages to show everyone just how clever she was.'

'The reason she briefed us ...?' Lena asked.

'She believed that she'd be acquitted, but she chose us to put the prosecution to sleep. If they thought that the defence lawyers were incompetent, they wouldn't have to try too hard. Just another chess move in her board game of life and death.'

Lena remained silent for several moments before replying. 'You've told Oscar?'

Matthew shook his head. 'No. He still regards it as a brilliant victory. I don't have the heart to disabuse him.'

'So, she got away with murder?'

Matthew gave a resigned shrug. He glanced at Lena and noticed that the smile hadn't left her face.

'You think the adulterous doctor got his just desserts?' he asked.

'Never.'
'So you don't harbour some fleeting admiration for her?'
Lena did not reply, but her smile slowly grew wider.

Chapter Sixty-nine

Matthew arrived unannounced at the garage just as Joe was closing up for the day. He gave Matthew a hard stare before pulling down the garage roller door with a loud clatter and a final bang.

'How's it going?' Matthew asked.

'I've said all I'm going to,' the mechanic replied tersely.

Matthew remained silent for a few moments, waiting patiently for Joe to finish locking the small side door of the factory.

'Who was it?' Matthew said.

'What?'

'Who got to you?'

'I don't know what you mean. No one got to me.'

'My guess is that it wasn't money.'

The mechanic turned to face him, both fists clenched, the veins on his neck standing out, his face growing pink.

'You don't know what you're talking about. I'd advise you to get lost before I hurt you.'

'You've already done that to Angelo.'

Joe turned away then walked towards a battered old Falcon sedan parked opposite his garage. Matthew followed him, catching the edge of the car door as he tried to close it.

'I see you're married,' Matthew said as he nodded at the wedding ring on Joe's finger. 'How many kids?'

'None of your business.'

Matthew took out his wallet and pulled a small photo from it. He held it in front of Joe's face. 'That's my business.'

The mechanic glanced at the photo before turning away and starting the engine.

'Look,' Matthew said, 'just let me talk to you. There's a pub down on the corner, and I'll buy you a beer. No obligations, no promises either way. You owe them that at least.'

Joe put the gearstick into reverse, but left his foot on the clutch, the car vibrating as the eight-cylinder motor strained like a greyhound on a leash.

'Five minutes, that's all.'

Matthew bought a half-pint of Guinness for himself and a schooner of beer for Joe, then led the way to a quiet corner of the pub.

'Well, how many?' Matthew asked after they each had their first mouthful.

'What?'

'You know – kids.'

'Three.'

'My guess is it all comes down to them.'

Joe took another sip of the foaming beer but did not reply.

'Probably you just received a phone call. Not even in person.'

'My priority is my family. Without them, I'm nothing.' He cast a glance towards Matthew. 'I'll bet you're not even married?'

He shook his head, leaned closer to Joe, and spoke in a quiet tone even though no one was in earshot. 'Listen, anything you tell me won't go any further.'

'Trust the word of a lawyer,' he scoffed. 'That'd be a first.'

Matthew absently ran his hand through his hair, searching for the right words. 'How can I get you to trust me?'

'You can't.'

'Why did you come here then? Something must have convinced you.'

Joe did not reply.

Matthew decided to try another tack. 'What did you do before you opened the garage? Were you always a mechanic?'

'I was in the army for twenty years. That's where I learned my trade. Left in '66.'

Matthew appraised him afresh. The mechanic's florid face conveyed a fondness for alcohol, and his expanding girth gave him the promise of a man sliding into obesity and probably type 2 diabetes. His sad defiance reminded Matthew of several Vietnam vets that he had appeared for in court.

'Vietnam?'

He nodded.

'Twelve months, '65 to '66 with the first RAR. You put your life on the line for your country, and then come back to derision, even contempt. I'd had enough; I'd done my bit, so I got out and started the garage.'

'What was the army doing there in the first place?'

Joe banged his glass down onto the table where they sat, and half-yelled at the solicitor.

'I suppose you were a smart-arse university protester? Throw some red paint on the troops, did we?'

Matthew recalled that the regiment's commanding officer had red paint thrown on him during a welcome home march for the regiment. He held his hands up in surrender.

'Absolutely not. I hated that behaviour as much as you did. What I meant was that you were over there for a good reason. Regardless of what the politicians were spouting, I'm sure you felt that?'

Joe relaxed a little, and then took a large mouthful of his beer.

'We thought we were. I'm not so sure now.'

'But clearly you're a man of principle. To let Angelo rot in prison, with his wife and children trying to cope with the aftermath, is not in your nature. You know this.'

Joe sat silently, his face betraying an inner conflict. Eventually he replied in a softer tone.

'That's a photo of the copper's wife and kids?'

Matthew nodded.

'How would your family cope if you were Angelo? Do you think they'd survive?'

Simpson shrugged. 'Probably not.'

'We've checked the RTA records and it shows D'Ascenzio owned a vintage MG sports car. Racing green. He sold it just prior to the trial commencing. That's why he could claim to own an old Holden when I cross-examined him.'

'So what?'

'What I think happened is that he drove his MG to your workshop. He was off-duty that day and used his own car. As a car mechanic, I think you had a good look at the car and discussed it with D'Ascenzio. I'm not a car nut myself, but I know how obsessive they can become.'

'What if I did?'

'If you talked to him about his car, he was more than just a passing interest, he was someone you'd recognise again.'

Joe was silent.

'I'm also guessing that he spoke to you before the photo identification was carried out at police headquarters, and he told you not to mention the MG and not to ID him on any photo. He threatened your family, didn't he?'

There was a long silence, followed by a barely perceptible nod from the mechanic.

'I'll get you another one,' Matthew said, nodding towards his empty glass. 'It's time we had a good talk.'

Chapter Seventy

'I'm sorry about Angelo and his family but it's out of my hands. I've told you before that word has come from on high that it's a closed book. I'm to leave it alone.'

Inspector Mike Gordon had initially refused to meet with Matthew but, when reminded of Rose and the children, he had reluctantly agreed, albeit for only five minutes. They sat at the rear of the Greek coffee lounge where Matthew had met him previously to ask for the check on Joe's garage.

'I've got some news,' Matthew said. 'Who can you trust in Internal Affairs?'

Gordon narrowed his eyes. 'Why do you ask?'

'Someone told D'Ascenzio about the phone tap and also Joe's garage.'

Gordon paused until his coffee and Matthew's tea arrived, then waited until the old Greek yiayia had slowly shuffled away before he replied quietly. 'It's hard to know these days.'

'The fish rots from the head?'

'Something like that. We live in dangerous times.'

'I think they've been saying that since the days of the Rum Corps.'

Gordon gave a slight smile accompanied by a snorting sound. 'You're probably correct.'

The Rum Corps was Australia's first military force whose incompetence was only matched by their corruption.

'I'll tell you what Joe Simpson told me,' Matthew continued, 'and then I'll tell you what I want you to do. Needless to say, if even a whisper of this got out, D'Ascenzio would know all about it before day's end.'

Gordon listened reluctantly with a look of distrust on his face whilst Matthew recounted his story.

'I know if it goes wrong,' Matthew added, 'there will be repercussions for us all.'

'You mean for me – and that's putting it mildly. How does dismissal for deliberately disobeying a direct order sound? If you think Mannheim is ruthless, wait till you see my boss in action.'

'Don't you believe me?'

'I think you're telling me what Joe told you. But that doesn't mean it's true. If it is, he's committed perjury, or at least not told the whole truth to the court. There's an old police saying – *don't rely on a liar*. That's because you never know whether they're giving you fact or fiction.'

'I'd stake my life on what he told me, and I'm a good judge of people. That's also why I absolutely believe Angelo, and why I'm trusting you.'

Matthew paused for a few moments to let his message sink in. 'If you believe in Angelo, you have to help him. Your conscience can't allow you to do otherwise.'

Gordon eyed him closely. 'You don't know how the force operates. When the word comes down from on high – it becomes law. To do what you are suggesting may very well cost me my job. My conscience, as you put it, is primarily with my wife and our three kids, who by the way are teenagers – the most expensive house guests there are. I can't look after them if I'm unemployed.'

Matthew's shoulders slumped and he slowly shook his head. 'In that case I'll have to go it alone.'

'Just remember your PI,' Gordon replied quietly. 'These blokes don't play by the rules. They make them up as they go.'

Chapter Seventy-one

Matthew had never seen Oscar angry, putting aside his feigned outrages exhibited sometimes during cross-examination. He had cornered Matthew in the tiny shoebox-cum-chambers where he was languishing whilst on a trial period to see how he performed at the bar.

Oscar's scalp blazed into a deep red, and his face was a mottled pink as he stood only a metre or so from where Matthew was sitting and commenced the lecture.

'I can't believe you would be so stupid, so stubborn as to risk your life in this mad scheme.'

'I take it that Lena has had a word,' Matthew replied in a conciliatory tone.

'She's beside herself, and with good reason. Mannheim is a cold-blooded killer, and you're determined to play Russian roulette with him. All based on the word of a perjurer. Haven't I taught you anything over the years?'

'You're right again, Oscar. I'm a slow learner.'

'If you're to survive as a barrister doing criminal work, as I've told you before, you have to be like a surgeon. You give your very best, but never become personally involved.'

'That's a little difficult in this case.'

'Don't put yourself above the law, and don't pretend you're the judge, jury and executioner. It will destroy you.'

Matthew put his hands behind his head, leaned back in his chair and closed his eyes. After a few moments, he looked at Oscar. 'I'm afraid that my faith in the law has receded in recent times. Did Lena tell you about our little chat?'

'She said you were thinking of packing it in,' Oscar replied.

'Let me put it this way,' Matthew said as he removed his hands from his head and steepled his fingers, not in prayer, but to emphasise how serious he was. 'If I don't do anything to help Angelo, then I'm nothing but a fraud. A blowhard who espouses noble ideals, but is really just a legal windbag. If my plan works, then justice will truly have been done.'

'And if it goes pear-shaped?'

'Then my decision about the future may well be made for me.'

Chapter Seventy-two

It was perhaps the last thing that Matthew felt like doing, but he had promised to take Samantha out to dinner, and Saturday had arrived. He picked her up at her inner-city flat just on dark, and drove them in his VW to a small café that Sam picked out named VIBE, hidden away on a back street in Newtown.

'Very trendy,' she had promised him.

When they arrived, it was clear to Matthew that 'trendy' actually meant tiny and rather grubby on the outside. Inside, however, it was both clean and jam-packed with a clientele that Matthew thought was interesting. The day had been overcast with showers, and the evening was turning cool. There was an abundance of beards and duffle coats amongst the men, as well as florescent hair, startling lipsticks and bright-coloured clothing amongst the women.

'You've been here before?' asked Matthew.

'One of my favourites,' replied Sam.

'Students mainly?'

She nodded. 'From Sydney Uni just down the road.'

They ordered from the menu written in chalk on a blackboard, Matthew settling for a chicken pizza and Sam for a bowl of mixed seafood penne. After the drinks had arrived, Matthew sipped a green bottle of Heineken whilst Sam played with a glass of chardonnay. The heavy beat of the latest pop song pulsed through the tiny room. Matthew vaguely remembered it from somewhere, but could not recall the name.

'I have to apologise to you, Matt,' Sam said after a few minutes.

'I love apologies. I so rarely hear them.'

'My little speech about low-life lawyers.'

'Some of us are.'

She swirled the wine around the glass as she held it in both hands. 'Going to see you in court has opened up a new world to me. I've never been in a courtroom before, and I was struck by the intensity and commitment from the lawyers on both sides. I suppose I thought it would be some sort of slanging match that we see so often on American TV.'

'American television has a lot to answer for.'

'Then when you told me that Angelo was convicted and sentenced to eight years in gaol ... I was absolutely stunned.'

Matthew took another sip of his beer.

Sam reached over and squeezed his arm gently. 'I know how the verdict has upset you.'

'Devastated might be a better word.'

'I haven't met Angelo or his wife, but I was watching them in the foyer. They looked like the loveliest couple as they hugged each other, and that copper D'Ascenzio just looks like a creep. The judge wasn't much better.'

'Angelo is one of my best friends and I know that he is totally honest, but this conviction has destroyed him and his family.'

Sam watched him closely for a minute or so. 'What are you going to do?'

'I'm not going to let it lie. I couldn't live with myself if I did nothing.'

'But those drug conspirators are capable of murder. You yourself said they killed the PI.'

Matthew remained silent.

Sam eyed him with concern. 'Just remember, Matt, you won't help Angelo by losing your life.'

Chapter Seventy-three

It was a Wednesday night, around 8 pm. No one remained in the factory complex apart from Matthew Jameson and Joe Simpson, and a bitter wind swept in from the Southern Highlands, lowering the temperature to around nine degrees Celsius.

The concrete floor seemed to transmit this frigid air into Matthew's body, and he constantly rubbed his hands together and stamped his feet to keep his circulation moving. Since just after noon he had been hiding in a tiny storeroom behind the mechanic's office. There was no heating of any kind, and Matthew cursed himself for not bringing any warm clothing or food to keep him from his present miserable state. Even a book to keep his mind off the coming confrontation would have been clever – then again, not being at the workshop at all would have been even smarter. Matthew would have given a considerable sum for a pot of steaming hot tea and some warm food, but that was not possible. He had given Joe strict instructions not to open the storeroom door, and to ignore his presence completely. To ensure the safety of his mechanical apprentice, Joe had told him to take a half day off work, and he had left before Matthew arrived.

Joe had agreed to give evidence, identifying D'Ascenzio not only as the detective who borrowed his tools and changed the tyre from Angelo's car, but also as the man who'd threatened him about his children's lives. Whilst Matthew knew that he had the outline of a challenge to Angelo's conviction, it would not be sufficient for Joe to merely give new evidence. The Court of Criminal Appeal would almost certainly say they could not rely on the evidence of an admitted perjurer, and would discount his evidence totally. What Matthew needed was an admission from D'Ascenzio or Mannheim, and he had decided that this desperate plan was the only course available.

The prior day, Joe had followed Matthew's instructions carefully, ringing D'Ascenzio and telling him that he'd now had second thoughts about failing to positively identify him to the police at the photo line-up and also at the trial. He suggested a meeting with the detective at his workshop, hinting that money might be a salve to his conscience. Matthew had reasoned that both D'Ascenzio and Mannheim might be suspicious of a change of heart, but would rise to the bait of Joe being a common blackmailer.

Now that Matthew had placed himself in the firing line, he had gradually come to realise that all of his experience acting for criminals of various degrees could not assist him in the real world of a life and death situation. He had no idea whether D'Ascenzio would come by himself, or with Mannheim, or with one or more hitmen. As he sat in the cramped storeroom, a feeling of panic kept rising to the surface, which he battled by focusing on the destruction of Angelo's family and the necessity for this drastic action. He knew not only that he was placing his own life at risk, but also that a lone gunman could

The Ancient Craft

stride into the workshop and kill Joe with one bullet to the head. Almost certainly there would still be no connection to Mannheim, who would use a contract killer at arm's length from himself. Unless he was able to obtain some admission from either D'Ascenzio or Mannheim, Joe might die for no valid reason. What could he tell Joe's wife and children if that disaster did occur? Two innocent people dead, three families ruined and Angelo still a convicted drug dealer.

Matthew had been feeling more despondent since 7 pm, and an hour later had convinced himself that no one was coming. He did not hear the car arrive, but was startled to hear three car doors slam in quick succession. From the storeroom, he could not see the new arrivals, but by opening the door a fraction, he could hear the conversation clearly.

'Well, Joe,' a familiar voice echoed through the motor workshop, 'that phone call was a surprise. I thought that we'd had a clear understanding?'

'It's just a business transaction, Detective D'Ascenzio, nothing personal,' Joe replied, his voice higher than normal.

'Sounds like a blackmail transaction to me,' the detective replied, 'so I've brought along a couple of assistants to help me decide what to do.'

'You haven't heard my proposition yet.'

'Does it really matter?'

Joe's voice rose even higher. 'What do you mean by that?'

'It's a problem that I've got with someone who says, *Trust me, it's only the one time*, but who can come back again and again for a little more each time.'

'We both know it was you who changed that tyre,' Joe said in an attempt at a defiant tone.

Matthew held his breath for the reply to the rehearsed question. It only took one admission to prize open the mind of the appeals court bench, but those few words remained unanswered.

'Let's put that aside for now while we concentrate on more pressing matters,' the detective replied in a casual voice. 'You've had your day in court and given your evidence on oath. You know there's a gaol sentence for perjury, of course?'

Matthew felt that the detective was making one last attempt to convince Joe to remain quiet with the threat of a prison sentence. If that did not work, then D'Ascenzio would ramp up the stakes.

'But there's now an appeal,' Joe persisted. 'I can still be called as a witness and my memory may have improved since the last occasion.'

D'Ascenzio remained silent for several moments before replying in a flat, menacing tone. 'Who told you that?'

'Jameson. The copper's barrister.'

'Did he now? What else did he say?'

'He wants me to tell the court about your phone call before the photo ID.'

'How would he know about that?' D'Ascenzio had now dropped all pretense of civility. 'Could it be that someone's been whispering in his ear.'

'I don't have to give evidence again, if we could come to some arrangement.'

Matthew could hear the edge of fear in his voice.

'You won't be going back to court, Joe. Not now, not ever. Your whispering days are over. We're taking you to see a friend of ours. At a convenient location, of course.'

'Don't worry about the money then,' Joe replied quickly. 'Let's forget all about it.'

'It's a little late for that, I'm afraid.'

Matthew was listening intently in the hope of an admission, but realised that he could not delay any longer. He opened the door of the storeroom and strode through the small office into the workshop area.

'Hello there, Sergeant,' Matthew said with more confidence than he felt. 'I hope you're not leaving us yet?'

Immediately, and without any indication from D'Ascenzio, both of his companions pulled handguns from their belts and pointed them, one at Joe and one at Matthew.

D'Ascenzio was not lost for words for long, and he slowly shook his head at Matthew as he spoke in what seemed a disbelieving tone. 'You stupid bastard, what the hell are you doing here?' Without waiting for a reply, he continued in a voice that became loud with anger.

'You've made a very serious mistake, Jameson. It may even be fatal.'

'We're all going to see Mannheim, then?' Matthew replied. 'That's nice.'

D'Ascenzio gave a crooked grin. 'It would be nice for him, but I doubt it would be for you.'

'This is crazy,' Matthew replied in an attempt at an indignant tone. 'You can't be serious about kidnapping a vital witness as well as the barrister for the accused copper?'

'You're quite right, of course. Kidnapping would be stupid,' the detective replied. 'You don't need to worry about that any more.'

'You don't frighten me, mate,' Matthew growled at him. 'Your threats may influence Joe here, but not me.'

D'Ascenzio ignored the taunt, and instead looked around the workshop before muttering to the two gunmen.

'We'll have to torch the place. There's probably a bug here somewhere recording our little talk. We might find it but I don't think so. In any event, there's enough fuel in here to turn this place into an inferno. Nothing will survive it.'

'And us?' Matthew said, attempting a calm voice.

The detective gave them an appraising look. 'As kidnapping would be too dangerous, it might be better to leave you both inside.'

'You rotten bastards,' Joe yelled furiously. 'You're not burning me alive.'

He lunged at the gunman closest to him, but the man effortlessly stepped to one side and hit the mechanic a glancing blow to the side of his head with the pistol. Joe fell to the concrete and lay there, semi-conscious and with blood spurting from above his left eye.

D'Ascenzio eyed him dispassionately before speaking in a conversational tone to the gunmen. 'If we tie them up with rope, there'll be nothing left to indicate any foul play. Just a pile of charred bones. No bruises, no ropes, no fingerprints and, most importantly, no recordings.'

'The only thing remaining,' Matthew said, 'is the remnants of your conscience.'

'When you play with the big boys,' D'Ascenzio replied, not even bothering to look at him, 'words like *conscience* don't apply.'

Matthew sighed heavily and adopted a resigned manner, lowering his voice to a submissive tone. 'So it was you after all that planted the drugs in Angelo's car?'

'No reason to deny it. Neither of you will be telling anyone. For what it's worth, Angelo is not a bad guy. He just got in the way of an unstoppable force of nature, that's all.'

'You mean Mannheim?'

'He's got more power than you could ever imagine. He knows something about nearly everyone in a position of power, and is smart enough to use it wisely.'

'What about our PI, Rufus Tomlinson?'

'Mannheim did him personally. To keep in practice, he said. That's the thing, Jameson, once you owe him, he doesn't let go. It's nothing personal with Joe or you. It's just business. I've no choice you see, otherwise I might well end up like the PI.'

'That's what the SS and the concentration camp guards said after the war. *I was just following orders.*'

'I'm glad you understand,' D'Ascenzio said as he nodded towards the two gunmen. 'Let's get this over with. We'll tie them up, and then spread petrol all over the place.'

The detective gave Matthew a curious glance. 'We can tap you on the head first, if you like. I'm not here to torture either of you. You won't feel a thing. You just won't wake up.'

'Thanks for the offer, but I'd prefer to go home, grab a beer and a pizza and watch the Amco Cup football on TV. If it's all the same to you, of course?'

'That's what I like. A good sense of humour.'

'Indeed. It's going to be a valuable asset to you during your many long years in prison.'

D'Ascenzio looked at him with a puzzled expression.

'I think it's about time, Inspector,' Matthew announced in a loud voice as he kept his eyes on the detective.

A brief look of astonishment spread over the faces of D'Ascenzio and the two gunmen before the detective replied in a somewhat strangled tone. 'Rubbish. There's no one there. That's the oldest trick in the book. It's just pathetic.'

A few seconds later, the roller door started to clank open. As it did so, the faces of the three would-be killers stared in unison at the door. A thunderous voice blared through a loud-hailer, cutting the frigid atmosphere.

'This is Inspector Mike Gordon. Put down your weapons. When we come in, we won't hesitate to fire in self-defence.'

Chapter Seventy-four

Matthew had often been told by people who had faced extreme danger that events seemed to move in slow motion. He now understood what they meant, as the two gunmen extended their arms and pointed their pistols towards the four plain-clothes police as they ducked under the opening roller door and walked into the workshop. Everyone then stood perfectly still, and Matthew knew that any stupid move by D'Ascenzio or his henchmen would result in a catastrophic shoot-out.

The seconds ticked away until Gordon broke the silence by growling a final warning. 'Drop those guns. We will not miss if you are stupid enough to open fire. This is not a game, this is life and death.'

D'Ascenzio nodded subtly to his accomplices, and Matthew released a huge sigh as the handguns clattered to the concrete floor. Within seconds, D'Ascenzio and the two gunmen were face down on the concrete, their hands cuffed behind them.

'Thank heavens you arrived,' D'Ascenzio gasped. 'They were trying to blackmail us with a pack of lies.'

'You slimy bastard,' Gordon roared in anger. 'We've got the lot on tape. Legally, with a warrant. You and your mates are going down for decades. Sometimes I'm ashamed to be in the force when I see a scumbag like you. Take them out,' he said, nodding to his offsiders.

The three younger officers unceremoniously yanked the arrested men to their feet and pushed them out of the workshop. Matthew bent over Joe and checked his wound.

'Sorry about that. I couldn't tell you about the inspector because you may have alerted D'Ascenzio to our plan. When you charged towards that hoodlum, for a split-second I thought he was going to shoot you.'

'It's only my pride that's hurt,' Joe replied groggily as he grabbed Matthew's arm to help him rise from the floor. 'You might have told me.'

Matthew took out his handkerchief and pressed it against Joe's face where the blood was still oozing from the wound.

'Hold that there until we get to hospital,' Matthew replied. 'I just couldn't take the risk that you'd be devious enough. It's a backhanded compliment if you like.'

'Thanks for the compliment, then,' Joe replied as he stumbled towards a chair, and then sat down heavily. 'Takes me back to my days in Nam – except that in those days I would've had my SLR with me and those cowboys wouldn't have had a chance.'

Inspector Mike Gordon had been listening to the conversation before he uncharacteristically placed his hand on Matthew's shoulder. 'That was well done. Both of you. It just makes me sick to the stomach to realise what D'Ascenzio has done to Angelo and his family. Without this little pantomime here tonight, he would have got away with it.'

'We're both glad to see you,' Matthew said as he held out his hand. 'You weren't mucking around with those shotguns.'

Gordon took Matthew's hand. 'A .38 revolver won't stop anyone unless you hit a vital spot. A shotgun will stop an express train.'

Matthew gave him an enquiring look. 'Your phone call yesterday saying that you'd help us was the best news I've had in a decade. But why the plain-clothes cops? Where are the specialist squads with body armour and automatic weapons?'

'Your faith in the police force is rather touching,' Gordon replied with an ironic grin. 'Don't you recall what we spoke about earlier? I only picked men that I'd trust with my life.'

'Oh, that's right. The leak. Sorry about that. I've had a few things on my mind lately.'

'Just don't tell my wife about tonight if you ever happen to meet her. She'd never forgive me. I'm a desk jockey these days. My days of shoot-outs are supposed to be long gone.'

'From memory, that's what Angelo said when he transferred to the drug squad.'

'What's that saying? *Be careful what you wish for?*'

'Something like that.'

When they walked outside and locked up the workshop, the other police officers and their prisoners had already left. Matthew helped Joe into the passenger side of his old V8 Falcon, and then went around to the driver's door.

'I'll drive him to the local hospital. He might need a few stitches in that cut, and if there's any concussion they might keep him in overnight.'

Gordon nodded his approval. 'By the way, what were you going to do if I didn't come on board tonight?'

Matthew waved his hand dismissively. 'I had a plan to bring along some footy mates armed with cricket bats and star picket fence posts, but I'm very happy you changed your mind. Shotguns are a very persuasive accessory.'

'You really are pig-headed. It could have been a scene that resembled the Saint Valentine's Day Massacre. It only takes one person doing something stupid and the shooting starts.'

'But I knew that you wouldn't let Angelo and his family down. As I said earlier, I'm good at assessing character.'

Chapter Seventy-five

Franz Mannheim slowly sipped his Chivas Regal and admired the magnificent view from his penthouse apartment, as he contemplated just how good life is for those who take control and act decisively.

He was awaiting word from D'Ascenzio and his two hired thugs, who by now would have dealt with that idiot garage owner. When D'Ascenzio had told him about the attempted blackmail, he had contacted a close associate, and before the day was over two contract killers were on a flight from Hong Kong.

He knew that some others might have attempted to buy Joe off with a few grand, but that was not his style. *Finish it once and for all*, was his decision. Shortly, his final plans to destroy the lives of Cattani's legal team would be implemented. With Joe disposed of, there was no way that an appeals court would overturn Cattani's conviction, and his final revenge would be the most fulfilling of his life.

A knock on the door to the penthouse signalled the return of his hit squad, and as the door was opened by his burly security guard, Mannheim moved forward to congratulate them.

The Ancient Craft

The guard was suddenly pushed sideways, and Mannheim was dumbfounded to confront Inspector Mike Gordon and two plain-clothes detectives.

'So good to meet up with you again after all these years,' Gordon said in a booming voice. He had been the arresting officer ten years ago when Mannheim was charged with conspiracy to pervert the course of justice and perjury.

'What the hell are you doing bursting in here like this?' Mannheim said. 'One phone call from me to the police hierarchy and your career is over. Don't you know that your bosses answer to me, not to the police minister?'

Gordon was not going to dispute this. because he half suspected there was more than a grain of truth in the threat. Instead, he merely nodded to one of the other detectives. 'Cuff the bastard and don't take any notice of the threat,' Gordon ordered. 'It's so sad to be the bearer of bad news, Franz, but your mate D'Ascenzio has spilled the beans. A full confession on video that sends you all down the river. You just never know who to trust these days, do you, Franz?'

Mannheim was shocked into silence, and seemed to visibly deflate when the handcuffs were roughly clamped onto his wrists. After a few moments, Mannheim suddenly regained his venom.

'I'll have the best criminal QC in Sydney briefed before the day is out, and he will hang your guts out to dry, copper,' Mannheim snarled. 'Don't think that I won't be coming for you as soon as these bullshit charges are thrown out.' He glared at the other two detectives. 'That includes both of you as well.'

Gordon glanced at his watch.

'He'll have to be quick, then. It's ten to midnight already.'

The detectives grinned as they frog-marched Mannheim from the penthouse suite, leaving the open-mouthed security guard shaking his head in astonishment.

Chapter Seventy-six

Matthew had heard numerous anecdotes about the Court of Criminal Appeal, but this was the first time that he had entered that much-feared courtroom. The three senior judges that constituted the bench were of a similar age, perhaps mid-sixties, he assessed. Their faces were impassive, their demeanour was cold, and Matthew knew theirs was not a courtroom that countenanced any frivolity.

The barristers announced their appearances and the judge seated in the middle nodded towards Matthew. He rose to his feet and commenced in a slightly nervous voice.

'My client is requesting that the trial verdict be annulled, and that a verdict of not guilty be entered on all charges, Your Honour.'

Three pairs of eyebrows rose in unison.

'Indeed, Mr Jameson. I trust that you have some exceptional grounds of appeal to present to this court?' the senior judge replied.

'I am hopeful that my friend will join in this application,' Matthew continued, 'but perhaps I might let him tell the court what the Crown is prepared to concede.'

Tobias Blackmore, QC, rose to his feet in a manner that suggested his reluctance. 'A remarkable set of circumstances has arisen, Your Honour,' he announced, 'and, after careful consideration, the Crown will be joining in my friend's application.'

Three sets of eyes opened even more widely. Matthew carefully set out the events of the prior week, and then handed to Blackmore one set of documents, and three more sets to the Sheriff's Officer for the bench. Some ten minutes passed as the judges perused the documents, and then the court adjourned to discuss the merits of the appeal in private. As the judges left the bench, Matthew felt a sharp jab from behind strike him in the ribcage.

'Matthew, you bastard,' Fenella hissed. 'You're harder to pin down than a barrel full of monkeys.'

'What was that, Ella?' he replied with a grin. 'Did you say that you were delighted to be here to see justice at last being done?'

'How did you do it? What on earth did you do to change Joe's mind?'

'It was just a crisis of conscience, that's all.'

'Does Angelo know?'

'I talked to him yesterday at Long Bay Gaol. I kept it low-key, saying that there was some new evidence but not to get his hopes up. If it turns out as I hope, then I'll drive Rose out to the gaol.'

'But we're throwing in the towel,' she replied with a frown. 'You've won.'

'I hope you're right, but the three wise men aren't rubber stamps. They might ask witnesses to give evidence, they may want more enquiries; who knows what they might require.'

'What have you told Rose?'

'I left that to Lena. Once again, I said not to get her hopes up, so she's pretty much in the dark.'

Angelo's wife had been waiting in the foyer when Matthew, Lena and Oscar had arrived at court. Matthew could see at a glance the toll that the conviction had taken. When Matthew hugged her, she felt all skin and bones, and instinctively he had relaxed his grip to avoid injuring her. Her manner was detached and somewhat mechanical, as if any further outpouring of emotion might completely deflate her.

Fenella whispered that she had to console her Crown prosecutor, and Matthew eased back into his chair at the bar table. Oscar had earlier agreed to let Matthew address the appeal court, and before the court resumed, he wrapped his arm around the junior barrister at the bar table.

'You've done it Matt, despite my misgivings and my pessimism, you've actually done it.'

'Not yet, I haven't.'

'Don't worry. The three wise men are merely going through the formalities. Who'd have thought Inspector Gordon would help you bring down D'Ascenzio.'

'Restores your faith in the force, doesn't it, Oscar.'

'At least you took my advice not to carry out your plan without armed police backup.'

'I always take your sage counsel, Oscar, you know that.'

The court resumed after an hour, and the decision came swiftly.

'In all our years, both on the bench and at the bar, we have never seen a case such as this,' the senior judge announced. His tone had softened considerably, and he displayed a somewhat apologetic demeanour. 'It is clear to this court that a grave abuse of the trial process has occurred, largely through the perjured evidence of Detective D'Ascenzio. The court extends its apology to the appellant and his family for this miscarriage of justice, and formally makes an order that the conviction is annulled and a verdict of not guilty is entered in respect of all charges.'

A soft murmur grew to an avalanche of voices as the press, the packed public gallery, and even the court staff talked excitedly amongst themselves. For once, the judges let the noise continue unabated.

Rose Cattani sat in the first row of the public seating, her body shaking with emotion, a quiet sob occasionally bursting from her frail frame. Lena went over and enveloped her in a protective hug, and then led her out to the foyer. The court adjourned, the crowd thinned, and Matthew sat at the bar table in a daze. Tobias Blackmore mumbled some brief congratulations, and Fenella brushed Matthew's face with a fleeting hand as the prosecution departed the scene. Matthew sat at the bar table, like a prizefighter having won a brutal contest, unwilling to leave the scene of the victory.

'The most amazing day of my life,' Oscar said quietly, as he stood to gather his papers. 'As well as the most fulfilling. You see, Matthew, the law always comes to the right decision. Sometimes it just takes a little time.'

Matthew smiled at the aged barrister. 'If you say so, Oscar.' He rose, then patted Oscar on his shoulder. 'Time to go and speak to Rose.'

Matthew had barely passed through the doors into the court foyer before Rose raced over and embraced him.

'Matthew, Matthew,' she cried, clinging fiercely to him.

'Hush now. It's all been put right. All of you are safe. It's a new world from today. A new beginning.'

Lena joined in the hug, whilst Oscar stood proudly beside the trio, beaming from ear to ear like a proud parent over his children.

Chapter Seventy-seven

'Life's a mystery to me. The more I know, the more I realise I don't know.'

Matthew was slouched in a client's swivel chair in Lena's office. The building was quiet, except for the occasional obsessive lawyer who thought that working late on a Friday night was a clever way to conduct his life.

'Sounds like a troubled love life,' Lena answered.

They each held a glass of expensive Bordeaux, another mini-celebration of Angelo's appeal verdict. A month had passed since his release from prison, and that time had passed in a series of celebrations involving various well-wishers and professional colleagues. Matthew's permanent acceptance at his chamber's floor had swiftly followed the sensational newspaper and television coverage of Angelo's acquittal and the arrest of D'Ascenzio and Mannheim. As Oscar had succinctly put it – 'They can hardly refuse you when you have had four of the most prominent criminal victories of the past decade.'

Matthew toyed with his glass of wine and gave a small shrug of his shoulders in answer.

'Come on. Out with it,' Lena demanded.

'Well ... remember I told you that I had dinner with a friend after the trial?'

'The young woman I saw you talking to in the court foyer during the trial?'

'Yes, the physio.'

'The one that I saw kissing you goodbye.'

'She's an affectionate physio.'

'So it seemed.'

'Things were going so well. We had a great dinner in Newtown, but then, out of the blue, she left a message on the answering machine at home.'

'That doesn't sound good.'

'Paraphrasing her words, she said it was all over. Not to contact her again.'

'How about quoting her?

'She said, "You really are a bastard. A typical lawyer. Don't ever speak to me again." '

'And?'

'Of course I tried to, but she slammed the phone down when I rang.'

'You went to see her?'

'I thought it best to let things cool down.'

'There's something you're not telling me, Matthew. What have you done?'

Matthew took another gulp of the wine, glancing at Lena over the rim of the wine glass.

'She's a lovely girl. Raised in the country on a farm, but is somewhat – old-fashioned, you could say.'

'What did you do to her?'

Matthew hesitated briefly, then gave Lena a sheepish look. 'You remember that storm we had last week – lightning, gale force winds and torrential rain?'

'This is beginning to sound like the first episode of some soap opera.'

'Well ... it was around 9 pm, and there was a pounding on my flat door. When I opened it, you wouldn't believe who was there.'

'I could make an educated guess.'

'It was Fenella.'

Lena shook her head in a despairing gesture. 'Now there's a surprise.'

'She'd had a screaming match with dear old Horrie and he'd thrown her out. She just needed somewhere to stay for the night.'

'Then she landed right in your bed. That's what I call fortuitous.'

'She slept in my bed and I took the lounge. Nothing happened.'

'Matthew ... why did you let her stay?'

'It wasn't planned. I couldn't turn her out into the cold.'

Lena rolled her eyes. 'She couldn't afford a hotel room? Why did she need to visit you late at night? I'll bet that Fenella knew about you and Samantha.'

Matthew nodded. 'We bumped into Ella and the judge one day when I met Sam for coffee in the city. You know the place – that Italian restaurant down by Circular Quay. Sam and Ella were chatting about where each of them worked.'

Lena gave a knowing smile.

Matthew's shoulders sagged and he let out a huge sigh. 'Bloody hell.'

'When will you learn, Matthew? If you haven't worked out how devious Fenella can be by now, there's no hope for you.'

Matthew slowly sipped the wine. Several minutes passed in silence, but they both knew that any tension would not last between them.

'At least I've got some good news,' Lena announced finally. 'I'm engaged.'

'No.'

'You don't think I'm a good catch then?'

'Of course you are,' Matthew replied quickly. 'I just find it hard to picture someone deserving of you.'

'Very diplomatic. But it's not your choice, and let me make it clear that when you meet him, Matthew, you're going to greet him like a long-lost friend. No appraisals or criticisms allowed.'

Matthew raised his eyebrows. 'Then you're serious about him?'

'Would I become engaged otherwise?'

Matthew could not suppress an amused grin.

'If you mention the word *desperation*, I'm going to throw this bottle at you,' she added.

'No, not the Bordeaux,' said Matthew, feigning alarm. 'It cost me an arm and a leg.'

'Just behave yourself then.'

'Yes, dear. Who's the lucky fellow?'

'A non-lawyer, which is a blessing in itself. I'm happy that I don't have to talk legal gossip all day, and can have a sensible conversation with a well-rounded adult.'

'Unlike me, you mean?'

Lena shook her head firmly. 'Sorry. He's a principal of a troubled high school in the inner-city, and, like me, he escaped from Germany before the war. His parents and close relatives were also killed by the Nazis.'

Matthew held up his glass. 'To a long and happy marriage, then. No one deserves it more than you.'

Lena gave him a hard stare, to indicate that she was serious. 'I really want you to like him. It's important to me, Matthew.'

'You know me. The soul of discretion.'

'That's the trouble, I know you only too well. You can be a little critical at times.'

'Would I ever let you down?'

'Not intentionally. But, as you've just admitted, your personal relationships are about as stable as the Titanic.'

'Before or after it hit the iceberg?'

'You're hopeless.'

Matthew raised himself from the chair, went over to Lena, and gave her a hug and a kiss on the cheek.

'But a good friend,' he added, 'and as friends go, no one is more important to me than you. I rest my case.'

Chapter Seventy-eight

Spring 1976

The barbeque at Angelo's small fibro family home was held just over six weeks after his release from Long Bay Gaol. Matthew had advised him to settle down with his family before getting everyone together; a suggestion that Angelo had agreed was sensible. His wife and aged mother had cooked at least ten different Italian dishes of antipasto, pasta and pizzas to accompany the steaks. The house was crammed with the legal team, as well as several police who had surfaced as supporters only after the appeal decision.

'Can't blame them,' Angelo said to Matthew in an aside. 'If they'd spoken out for me prior to my release, they'd be regarded as suspect. Probably would have been charged with one disciplinary offence or another and eventually sacked.'

'What about Mike Gordon?' Matthew said, nodding towards the inspector, who was sharing an anecdote near the barbeque with Oscar and Lena.

'He really put his head on the chopping block. I don't think you realise how close he came to losing his job.'

'He did say something to me about how understanding his boss was.'

'Let's not go there,' Angelo interrupted. 'Whilst I was not surprised that you hatched a crazy plan, I was amazed that Gordon went along with you. He tells me that you manipulated him with stories about Rosie and the kids, and he couldn't live with himself if he stood aside and did nothing.'

'Manipulated – never. Gentle encouragement – that's all it was.'

Angelo glanced around, seemingly embarrassed. 'Listen, Matt … I don't know how to put this. You saved us all. Without you, I'd still be in gaol. I just don't know what to say.'

'We're even. You saved me ten years ago. Without you, I'd probably have gone to gaol myself. Friends look after each other. That's all that counts.'

Angelo embraced him in a bear hug. 'You know that Rosie thinks you're the cleverest person she's ever met?'

'No way. But I do appreciate the thought.'

'Let's go grab some food and get drunk.'

As the night wore on, and war stories from the increasingly intoxicated guests became even more extravagant, Mike Gordon shouted for a little quiet.

'As everyone here knows, Matthew Jameson is the bane of my professional life,' the inspector boomed, 'and every time I speak to him, I know it's more trouble for the force.' His impassive face cracked into a rarely sighted grin. 'But sometimes he does get it right.'

A round of applause broke out amid cries of, 'Lock him up … throw away the key.'

'Now that is very tempting, I can tell you,' Gordon continued, 'but in this instance he has precipitated a course of events that has seen our good friend and colleague, Angelo Cattani, released, reinstated and now rehabilitated.'

'Alliterations at this time of the night,' Lena whispered to Matthew. 'Wonders will never cease.'

'Of course, the police hierarchy had egg all over their faces,' Gordon said, 'and when faced with public humiliation, they've taken the only course available.'

He glanced in Angelo's direction with a stony face, and said nothing for a moment. Rose Cattani grabbed her husband's arm in alarm, and the room fell completely silent.

'Promotion,' Gordon yelled in triumph as he raised his beer glass above his head. 'I'd ask everyone to raise their glass to Inspector Angelo Cattani.'

The resultant explosion of noise reminded Matthew of the cacophony that followed a try when he had played rugby league – an unstoppable tidal wave of emotion that enveloped Angelo in well-wisher's hugs and backslaps.

When the noise eventually died down, Gordon's voice roared out again. 'I might also add that Angelo is now the youngest appointment to that rank in the history of the force.'

A renewed wave of cheering echoed throughout the house, and it wasn't for another twenty minutes that Matthew, Lena and Oscar were able to make their way to the new appointee.

'Who said that promotion by merit never applied to the good guys?' Matthew said, giving Angelo a bear hug.

'But if the truth were known,' Angelo replied, 'I don't think its promotion by merit – it's more a case of promotion by embarrassment.'

'I don't want to hear any more of that nonsense,' Lena said as she enveloped Angelo in her arms. 'Just take a look at Rose.'

All four of them turned in unison to see his beaming wife, each arm around one of her children, chatting animatedly to three detective's wives who had come to celebrate the appeal result.

'That's what it's all about, my boy,' Oscar said. 'It can't make up for the terrible past six months, but you can see how Rose has changed. This promotion is for her and the children. Embrace it – enjoy it – revel in it. God knows, events like this don't come along every day.'

'Amen to that,' Matthew added. 'Oscar, as always, knows what he's talking about.'

Chapter Seventy-nine

Around 2 am, the party started to quieten down. The children were long in bed, various guests were drifting home, and Matthew sat outside near the barbeque. A small table was beside him, with a bottle of Shiraz constantly being used to replenish his glass. Angelo sat opposite, rolling a glass of beer between his hands, idly watching the amber liquid slosh out of the bottle.

'That's a waste of good beer,' Matthew murmured, 'but in the circumstances, Rose will no doubt forgive you.'

'I think she might.'

Matthew took a long drink of the wine, expelling a satisfied sigh after he finished the glass. 'That's a good drop, mate.'

'I thought I might stretch the budget for tonight.'

Matthew again refilled his glass. 'I'm sleeping in this chair tonight. I'm not going to move a muscle until dawn.'

Angelo shook his head. 'It's too cold out here. I've got a spare bed for you in the lounge room. You're the honoured guest for tonight.'

'It will be a pleasure ... Inspector Cattani.'

They sat for ten minutes or so, listening to frogs croaking in unison, no doubt performing some ritual of their mating routine.

'Can I ask a personal question, mate?' Matthew asked eventually.

'Of course.'

'What do you now feel about D'Ascenzio?' Matthew let the question hang in silence for a moment or two before continuing. 'Not still thinking about some murderous revenge?'

Angelo gave a sigh, and then shook his head. 'He's not worth it.'

'But you did contemplate it?'

'As anyone would. But there's a world of difference between contemplation and action. In any event, someone may have removed the temptation.'

'What do you mean?'

'You know that he got bail?'

Matthew nodded. 'One of the top silks talked some new appointment to the bench into granting bail for both he and Mannheim,' Angelo continued. 'No one bothered to make any application for the two hired gunmen.'

'Even though the charges were attempted murder, kidnapping and perjury, as well as the murder of Rufus Tomlinson against Mannheim?'

'As I said, the judge was a recent appointment. He'd been an expert in company law at the bar, but had never sat on a criminal case before.'

'Who put up the bond money?'

'Mannheim's *associates*, putting it politely. His criminal mates, if you put it accurately. Money, as we all know, is no problem.'

'That bastard has nine lives,' Matthew said as he took another sip of wine. 'What did you mean when you said, "may have removed the temptation"?'

'Both are on daily reporting conditions.'

'So?'

'D'Ascenzio has not reported at all.'

Matthew let the information sink in before answering.

'So he's off overseas to a new life and a new identity?'

'Perhaps.'

'Which means …?'

'Perhaps he's been given a new pair of shoes.'

Matthew gave an involuntary snort of derision. 'I know I'm well past drunk, so you'll have to excuse me if I'm a bit slow. Why would Mannheim give him new shoes? He never impressed me as being the generous type.'

'The main evidence against Mannheim is that given by D'Ascenzio. It's only natural that he might begin to suspect that the detective could give Queen's Evidence. Perhaps the shoes were concrete ones.'

Chapter Eighty

Lunch was at a beachside restaurant of Emma Saunders' choosing – up-market and extremely expensive.

'This is on the boss,' she promised on the phone the prior day, 'so let's make the most of it.'

The window table overlooked Bondi Beach, and the rumbling crash of waves resonated throughout the room, periodically drowning out the murmur of chamber music that accompanied their meal.

'Let's start with French champagne,' she suggested, 'then we'll move onto some superb Aussie reds.'

'Sounds like you've got an ulterior motive.'

'Goes without saying. This is an official interview with the rising star of the bar. Four sensational cases and four victories, albeit spread over ten years. You didn't think this was a social event, did you?'

'Never.'

If he were truthful, Matthew would have preferred a pizza and a simple bottle of red, perhaps one from the Hunter Valley or from Coonawarra. He never mentioned this to the reporter, however, who revelled in her role of selecting the various courses, none of which Matthew had tasted before, and none of which he was likely to order in the future. As the meal continued and the superb Cabernet Sauvignon loosened their remaining inhibitions, Emma became more insistent.

'Now, what's the inside story on Jessica Vandermeer? We both know there's more to the case than you've told me.'

Matthew gave an apologetic shrug.

'Sorry. Some of it's confidential between lawyer and client. Some of it's gossip. Some of it's guess work.'

Emma leaned over the table, glanced at the other patrons, and then dropped her voice to a murmur. 'No one will know.'

'I will.'

'Remember – quid pro quo.'

Matthew gave a sigh but did not reply, seeking refuge in taking a sudden interest in the wine label. The reporter gave him a shrewd stare, then tried a different line of attack.

'Well ... just tell me what's in the public domain.'

Matthew gave a knowing smile. 'You would be aware of a recent article in your paper regarding the settlement of a patent. It involves the payment of a small fortune to the estate of Dr Cornelius Vandermeer?'

'I did see the article of course, but it didn't mean much to me at the time.'

'It came out at the trial that the good doctor died intestate. As she was his wife at the time of his demise, Jessica Vandermeer receives the lot.'

Emma's eyes widened. 'The missing motive.'

'That's an outrageous suggestion,' Matthew replied with a grin.

'What else?' the reporter asked, not looking at Matthew but scribbling furiously in her reporter's spiral notebook.

'You used to be the girls and gossip reporter some years ago?'

'The fashion editor, if you don't mind.'

'Sorry. The fashion editor. Do I take it that you no longer have any interest in the glamorous world of the glitterati?'

She hung her head to one side in an accusing manner. 'I trust that's not a criticism of my personal appearance.'

'Never.' Matthew said. 'Just for the record, Emma, I think you're one of the smartest women I've ever met.'

'So I can't have everything, is that what you're saying?'

Matthew did not reply.

'Well, let's just say that I've had my fill of that weird world with those plastic smiles and brain-dead conversations,' Emma added.

'I thought as much. Just after Jessica's trial finished, there was a photo of her with her latest conquest at some opening night or premiere event. You may not have seen it as it was in your opposition paper's gossip pages.'

'Go on.'

'The lucky fellow was Hans Schrieber.'

'Well, well. Dear old Hans. He of the insurance company. What a funny world we live in. I wonder what the prosecution made of the photo?'

Matthew sat back and sipped another mouthful of wine without replying.

'Where do you think the infamous bottle of shrimp paste came from?' she enquired with a narrowing of her eyes. 'Do you suspect that she planted it?'

'Once again, I couldn't possibly comment on such an outrageous suggestion.'

'She can't be tried twice for murder,' Emma continued, 'so she probably feels free to rub everyone's noses in how clever she's been.'

'Of course, if you published an article setting out your suspicions,' Matthew said quietly, 'she'd sue the paper for defamation, and probably succeed. We have a marvellous legal system, don't you agree?'

'It depends what it's done to you.'

'Anyway, regarding Angelo's trial and the appeal decision, not only can I give you his inside story, but he's prepared to talk to you exclusively. We've not forgotten your information about D'Ascenzio's obsession with antique cars.'

Emma nodded her head vigorously in agreement, as she attacked a mouthful of the main course that Matthew, try as he might, could not identify.

'You're also invited to lunch at Caesar's next Tuesday,' Matthew continued. 'I'm shouting Joe Simpson and his family, and I'm sure that he'll be only too willing to give you his story. It's not every day that a car mechanic risks his life for a detective sergeant who is a complete stranger to him.' The restaurant was the top Italian eatery in the city.

'That sounds great. I'll be there, notebook in hand. I've also heard some gossip from some informants about Angelina Smythe-Baker. Seems like the insurance company made it clear to her lawyers that they'll fight tooth and nail if she tries to claim the insurance policy money. As the test in a civil case is on the balance of probabilities, they'll use what came out at the trial to point the finger at her as the murderer.'

Matthew carefully refilled both of their glasses with the wine that Emma had ordered.

'If she lost the case,' Matthew replied, 'the costs would bankrupt her.'

'Also, as the case would be on the front page of the paper day after day, her reputation would be trashed. It doesn't matter if it's true, only if it's sensational.'

'What a cruel world we live in.'

'Certainly if you're the victim.'

The conversation moved onto legal gossip covering the usual suspects – politicians, business movers and shakers, and the police hierarchy. After an hour or so had passed, Matthew returned to their original topic.

'When you think about it, I wouldn't envy Hans Schrieber.'

'Certainly not if Jessica prepares his breakfast.'

Matthew stared at the foaming waves as they broke on the beach below the restaurant, with the regular boom that followed a split-second later mesmerising him.

'But put yourself in her shoes,' Matthew said eventually, half to himself. 'She'd never know if someone were to turn the tables on her, and slip a little something into her drink one boozy night. A little voice would always be there, saying, *Is that drink safe?* I don't think she'd ever be at peace with herself. There'd always be that little voice.'

'That's you and me, Matthew. Poisoners don't think that way.'

'Perhaps you're right, but I wouldn't trade places with either of them. I need a good night's sleep and I love the occasional drink. Let's just leave them to their own demons.'

'Well said,' Emma replied, raising her glass. 'To the sleep of the just.'

'And, of course, to the integrity of the press.'

'When we occasionally see it,' she replied with a grin.

Chapter Eighty-one

Summer 1976

The long days of winter had eased into spring, then burst into summer with its baking sun, ever increasing daylight hours, and glorious twilight evenings. Barbeques had been dusted off and cleaned, gas cylinders filled, and parties had sprung into life all over Sydney – accompanied by ample supplies of beer and wine, and the ever-present chorus of cicadas hammering out their insistent song. Lena had been briefing Matthew with a steady supply of civil cases since Angelo's trial; she had intuitively known that Matthew had lost any desire to spend the rest of his life acting only for criminal accused, and had even suggested that he perhaps was more suited to prosecution work. A hint that Matthew should apply for acting Crown prosecutors' briefs was met with a lukewarm response, but as Lena reminded him, 'You have someone at the Clerk of the Peace office that could put plenty of work your way.'

Lena was of course referring to Fenella, but he doubted that any favours would be coming his way from that direction.

Thinking back on his failed relationships, Matthew had come to terms with the realisation that life at the bar might be incompatible with a settled married life. When a civil case involving millions of dollars was on the line, he could hardly clock off at 5 pm, telling some high-powered company chairman that his personal life was more important. Whilst criminal work was not as pressured in terms of hours, a barrister would inevitably invest more emotion in a criminal case than he would in a corporate trial for some giant multinational company. As he worked away, often late at night and on weekends, the settled life of a Crown prosecutor as suggested by Lena seemed ever more appealing.

A welcome break from the monotony of life at the bar came in the form of Lena's engagement party, held at her fiancé's inner-city semi-detached house. In the tiny rear garden, sausages and steaks sizzled on the barbeque, the packed throng of guests chattered incessantly, and the various insects provided their musical accompaniment. Lena's fiancé had greeted Matthew with a huge grin and a crushing handshake.

'Ben's the name. Good to meet you,' he said as he introduced himself. 'So, you're the barrister that Lena never stops talking about. I'm going to have to keep a close eye on you.'

'She's my older sister figure,' Matthew replied with a chuckle. 'You've got nothing to worry about.'

Ben was around Lena's age, Matthew thought, tall and slim, but also fit and strong. Matthew took an instant liking to him, but that was not surprising, as he trusted Lena's judgment implicitly. Whilst Matthew knew about their similar backgrounds as Jewish children escaping from Nazi Germany, he deliberately kept the conversation to the topic of the school where Ben was the principal. He felt that keeping clear of serious issues was more appropriate at a celebration of the engagement of one of his closest friends. After ten minutes or so, Lena swooped in and grabbed Ben's arm, then propelled him across the room to meet some of her other guests.

Oscar, Angelo and Rose were also invited, and Matthew spent much of the night chatting to them with legal topics that are available when lawyers gossip with police.

'I've gone from having to be nice to clients when I was a solicitor, to having to be nice to solicitors now that I'm a barrister,' Matthew complained. 'One day, if I'm ever appointed a judge, I won't have to be nice to anyone.'

'But you will be,' Rose said. 'I know you. You don't have a mean bone in your body.'

'I did warn you, Matthew,' Angelo replied with a chuckle. 'You're now her golden boy.'

Matthew held up his arms in mock denial. 'That's not an opinion widely shared, Rose. I'm not anyone's golden boy, and I definitely am not nice to everyone. Franz Mannheim for one.'

'I forgive you in that case,' Rose replied, patting his arm. 'Just the mention of his name makes my blood boil.'

'You heard about the trial?' Angelo asked Oscar.

'I know the bastard wormed his way free again,' Oscar replied, 'but I don't know the details.'

'Well, as you know, Mike Gordon was the officer in charge of the case, and he gave evidence, as did Matthew and Joe Simpson.' Angelo said. 'I'm surprised that Matt didn't give you a complete rundown.'

'I told Oscar the result briefly on the phone, but I haven't seen him in person since the trial,' Matthew said. 'To be honest, I was so furious that I was trying to put it behind me. If I focus on the injustice of the whole thing, it's just too depressing.'

Oscar had kept his promise to hang up his wig and gown a few weeks after Angelo's appeal result, and Matthew had taken over his old chambers so that they now only met occasionally for lunch. Oscar certainly seemed to be more relaxed since his retirement, but Matthew knew that the pipe-smoking addiction had not lessened.

'I gave evidence, and Mike Gordon later gave me a blow-by-blow description of what happened when I was waiting outside to be called,' Angelo continued. 'It was the same judge that granted Mannheim bail. I'm told that it was his first criminal trial. Anyway, he used his discretion to disallow a great deal of the prosecution case, including admissions made by D'Ascenzio, which the prosecution argued were by a co-accused in pursuance of the conspiracy and thus admissible. D'Ascenzio hasn't been seen since the day he was released on bail, and the defence argued it would be unfair to allow the admissions as he could not be cross-examined about them. The judge then delivered the coup de grace by directing the jury to deliver a verdict of not guilty.'

'I know that it's within his power to do so, but it still leaves a bitter taste in my mouth, knowing what I do about Mannheim,' Oscar said. 'But what about the evidence of the two gunmen? I was told that both had agreed to give Queen's Evidence for the prosecution.'

'The judge said that it would be unsafe and unsatisfactory to convict on the uncorroborated evidence of the co-accused,' Matthew added. 'He apparently believed that the jury would place too much weight on their evidence, even after he gave them a warning.'

'So the gunmen get new identities and relocation to distant places,' Oscar replied, 'and everyone goes scot-free.'

'I don't think Phillip D'Ascenzio got off scot-free,' Angelo said. 'I believe he's gone to another jurisdiction. A higher court, you might say. In any event, you now know how the police feel when a clever barrister talks an inexperienced judge into taking the case from the jury. Dispirited, frustrated and angry.'

The three men were well aware that a seemingly innocuous decision by the judge on admission of evidence could destroy a prosecution case in the blink of an eye. Indeed, it was not unusual to hear of newly appointed judges sometimes being overawed by senior Queen's Counsel, and making decisions that they would never contemplate with more experience.

'Why wasn't Reggie the Rat arrested and charged with perjury?' Oscar asked.

'Reggie has also vanished,' Angelo replied. 'His protective custody obviously wasn't protective enough.'

'On the bright side,' Matthew interjected, 'I was glad to hear that your drug conspiracy trial was a great success. Everyone convicted and sentenced to gaol.'

'Not enough gaol time, though,' Angelo replied.

'Now why did I think that'd be your response?' Matthew said.

Angelo grinned.

'Did you mention anything about our drinks evening with the judges, Matt?' Oscar asked.

Matthew shook his head.

'Come on, out with it,' Angelo said.

'You tell it better than I do, Oscar,' Matthew said.

Oscar took another healthy mouthful of his Shiraz before replying.

'The bar hierarchy occasionally arranges a drinks night with some tasty hors d'oeuvres so that barristers can mingle with members of the bench from the District and Supreme Courts.'

'You mean like a work's barbeque?' Angelo said, referring to the trade union tradition.

'Something like that. A get-to-know-you with new barristers, or a catch-up with old members of the bar. So, just before I hung up my wig, I frog-marched Matthew to one of these little soirees, telling him that good relations with the bench were essential for a successful life at the bar.'

'Don't tell me,' Angelo said with a growing smile. 'You ran into Judge Latimer.'

'The very man,' Oscar replied. 'He immediately regaled us with his recollections of the trial, and said that he always believed that you were innocent, and that he knew that D'Ascenzio was a liar and was clearly at the beck and call of the drug criminals.'

'I think that is what you would call a convenient memory,' Angelo said. 'But I'm curious to hear what Matthew's reply was to the judge.'

'His reply was stony-faced silence, whereupon Latimer quickly departed our company,' Oscar replied.

'Well, I'm glad to see that you didn't display some of your trademark honesty,' Angelo replied with a laugh.

'I'm slowly learning,' Matthew replied, 'that sometimes the better part of valour is discretion.'

Chapter Eighty-two

About an hour after the party had moved into full swing, the front doorbell sounded and Lena grabbed Matthew by the arm.

'I've taken the liberty of inviting someone else,' she murmured. 'You're to make a proper apology and be on your best behavior, then perhaps there'll be some hope for your future after all.'

Matthew had no idea what she was talking about, but Lena put her finger to her lips, demanding silence. As the new arrival slowly made her way through the throng of guests, Matthew came face to face with Samantha Wright.

'Samantha,' Lena announced with a mischievous grin, 'let me introduce my colleague, Matthew, who by the way is also one of my closest friends.'

'We've met,' Samantha replied warily.

Matthew was momentarily lost for words.

'I'll just leave you two to do some catching up,' Lena added. 'Matthew has something he'd like to say.'

With that, Lena darted away and Matthew finally found his voice. 'Lena says that I have to apologise to you.'

'And what do you say?'

'In light of my prior relationship with Fenella, perhaps it was unwise to let her stay the night.'

'Is that some sort of lawyer's double talk? "I'm very sorry but it wasn't my fault?" It's the worst apology I've ever heard.'

'But nothing happened.'

'Fenella rang me the next day and said it was only fair to let me know of your past romance, and added that she stayed last night in your bed.'

'Perhaps she forgot to add that I slept on the lounge.'

'Has she exhibited this poor memory before?'

'Her memory isn't poor, it's just selective.'

'Are all lawyers this devious?'

'I'm not.'

Samantha gazed at him momentarily whilst subconsciously chewing her bottom lip before replying. 'Lena asked me to have a cup of coffee with her, and we had a long talk. She claims that you are the most honest person she knows. At the expense of diplomacy, very often.'

'Guilty as charged.'

'She also told me what you did to save Angelo and his family.'

'As I said to you earlier, I couldn't just look on and do nothing.'

'Lena said you could have been killed.'

'Mike Gordon was there with his mates to protect me.'

Samantha shook her head slowly then softened her tone, 'I also have to apologise.'

'That sounds promising.'

'I never let you explain. I just jumped to the wrong conclusion. I am sorry, Matthew. No ifs or buts. I was wrong.'

Matthew held his arms open and Samantha took a step forward then completed the hug.

'I'm also sorry,' Matthew said quietly. 'Can we start again?'
'Totally exclusive to each other?'
'Absolutely.'
'Can I have that in writing?'
Matthew took a step back, not sure how to interpret the words.
'I wasn't serious,' she said with a grin. 'Can't you lawyers take a joke?'

Chapter Eighty-three

After Lena and her fiancé made their farewells to the few remaining guests in the early hours of the morning, Lena walked Matthew to the front footpath where his battered VW stood waiting on the opposite kerb, her arm wrapped tightly around him. Samantha had caught a taxi home after a few hours at the party, telling Matthew that she wanted him to give Lena his undivided support at her engagement. They made plans for dinner the following night at her place.

'Now, Matthew. I want your honest opinion. No glad-handling. Only the truth.'

Matthew hesitated for a few moments before replying, aware how important his opinion was to Lena. 'I'm a good judge of character, as I'm always telling anyone that will listen.' Matthew gave her a mock-serious stare. 'My considered opinion is that … he's the one.'

Lena's face broke into a broad smile as she gave Matthew a fierce hug.

'Thank you,' she murmured.

'But if it doesn't work out, I'll appear for you pro bono in the divorce proceedings.'

'Bastard,' she growled, punching him on the arm.

They stood together under the light from a nearby street lamp. A small dog barked nervously as a distant car screeched its tyres, and then all was silent.

'You'd better get back to Ben or he'll start getting suspicious,' Matthew said eventually. 'Thanks for inviting Sam.'

'That's OK. How are things?'

'We're starting afresh.'

'That's good. She seems like a lovely young woman. You won't go far wrong there.'

'And Fenella is banished for good.'

Lena gave him a pointed stare. 'I certainly hope so.' She gave him a farewell hug then spoke quietly.

'It's strange how things have worked out. Justice comes to some people and completely deserts others. I'm really happy for Angelo and Rose and their children, but I still grieve for the family of Rufus Tomlinson. I suppose you could feel some sympathy for Phillip D'Ascenzio too, who it appears has paid with his life. Meanwhile, Franz Mannheim – in my mind – is the personification of evil, and he walks free.'

'As does Jessica Vandermeer.'

Lena gave Matthew a gentle smile. 'It's no use obsessing about matters that are out of our hands, Matthew. Justice is a fickle mistress and sometimes treats people terribly.'

'I think I may have heard that advice before, from an aged Irish practitioner of our own ancient craft.'

Author's Note

Some of the NSW laws described in this book have been amended since 1976 by subsequent legislation.

For example, the right to make a dock statement has recently been abolished, majority verdicts are now allowed in criminal trials, and records of interview are now videotaped by the police. Furthermore, the right to silence has been limited for serious offences, permitting unfavourable inferences to be drawn where the accused relies upon a fact not mentioned at the time of questioning.

Some things, however, have not yet seen the winds of change, such as the wearing of wigs and robes by barristers and judges, and the selection of judicial officers by the Attorney-General, not by an independent panel.

The author has run in the City to Surf fun runs for over two decades, and spent a similar period running in Sydney Half-Marathons, although *run* might be a slight exaggeration. Over 80,000 entrants started last year in the City to Surf fun run.

The author admits to a severe shellfish allergy, and is always very hesitant before consuming any 'elixir of life'.

For those readers who are interested in corruption both in the police hierarchy and their political masters, *The Woodward Royal Commission into Drug Trafficking (1977–1979)* and *The Wood Royal Commission into the New South Wales Police Service (1995–1997)* make interesting reading.

For any other legal or historical mistakes that sharp-eyed readers may discover, I apologise unreservedly and seek to raise the time-honoured defence of *poetic license*.

The plot and characters in this novel are completely fictitious and do not relate to any person, alive or deceased.

Acknowledgements

I would like to take this opportunity to thank Joel Naoum of Critical Mass for his professional advice and assistance, which has proved invaluable.

I also wish to thank my editor, Rebecca Hamilton, who has cast her eye over every word of the manuscript, and whose excellent grammatical corrections and brilliant structural suggestions have enabled me to present a story which I trust readers will find worthy of their time spent in the courtroom of my imagination.

CPSIA information can be obtained
at www.ICGtesting.com
Printed in the USA
LVHW041455020120
642350LV00001B/106/P